The Boneyard

by

Loretta C. Rogers

A Doc Holliday Mystery, Book 2

The Boneyard

COPYRIGHT © 2022 by Loretta C. Rogers

Cover Art by *Diana Carlile*

The Wild Rose Press, Inc.
PO Box 708
Adams Basin, NY 14410-0708
Visit us at www.thewildrosepress.com

Publishing History
First Edition, 2022
Trade Paperback ISBN 978-1-5092-4062-3
Digital ISBN 978-1-5092-4063-0

A Doc Holliday Mystery, Book 2
Published in the United States of America

"This place gives me the creeps." Grandmother's voice sounded strained. "Tullah, you're white as a sheet."

Dad adjusted the .45 on his hip as if expecting trouble. I felt as if someone was walking on my grave without me being in it. Part of me wanted to turn around, get on my horse, and race away from this place. The other part was held by a voice inside my head saying, *I'm here. We're all here. Find us. Please find us.*

I could feel that the voice was in a deep dark place. I felt it in me, and it clawed its way up my spine. I knew it would come out my mouth like a regurgitation of emotion if I let it.

I called out, "River…where are you, boy? Come…come here."

He answered with a series of yips. I called again, "Come, boy. Come to me."

He answered again, this time with loud and demanding barks.

Dad's voice was filled with concern. "What is it, Punkin…you've got a strange look on your face."

I inhaled. I would never get used to these surprise visits of the mind that iced my blood and burdened my heart. I never had them when my mother was alive. Had she somehow in death gifted me with this curse?

I stood there, listening to the hum of mosquitoes and my dog's whines, and staring into the dark marsh until I became aware of the welling of tears in my eyes.

Praise for Loretta C. Rogers' Mysteries

"An ingenious plot and a sufficient flow of suspense and occasional terror to keep the reader engrossed."

~Anonymous

~*~

"Fast moving, tightly written, with enough suspects and tricky solutions to keep the suspense high."

~Anonymous

~*~

"I love books with lots of suspense, great characters, and some romance tossed in for great measure. *Murder in the Mist* has all that…"

~Matilda, Coffee Time Romance and More

Also by Loretta C. Rogers at The Wild Rose Press

Contemporary Romance
Forbidden Son
Christmas at Hope Ranch

Historical Romance
Bannon's Brides
The Witching Moon
Lady Adel's Captain
Cloud Woman's Spirit
Taming the Lyon
When Comes Forever
Bitter Autumn
A Little Kringle Magic (novella)
Isabelle and the Outlaw (novella)
McKenna's Woman (novella)
Fate Comes Softly (Anthology)

Mystery and Suspense
Murder in the Mist
Shadowed Reunion
Fatal Passion
The Bone Yard

Audio Books
Murder in the Mist
Shadowed Reunion
Isabelle and the Outlaw
Taming the Lyon
McKenna's Woman

Acknowledgments

I'd like to express my sincere thanks to:

Dr. Lee Boney, Doctor of Dental Medicine, Tifton, GA, for his invaluable information on how forensic dentistry is used to identify a deceased individual when all that remains are the teeth and skeletal structure.

Stuart Taylor, Editor, *The Tifton Gazette*, *Tifton Scene*, Tifton, GA, for answering my questions about archived news articles and what happens to news articles when a newspaper goes out of business.

Sharp-eyed readers will notice that I have tweaked Kentucky's geography a bit. It's only to protect the innocent. Thank you to the people who read acknowledgments. I appreciate you.

"I was born with this devil in me. I could not help the fact that I was a murderer, no more than the poet can help the inspiration to sing. I was born with the evil one standing as my sponsor beside the bed where I was ushered into the world, and he has been with me ever since."

~H. H. Holmes, 1896
(the first documented serial killer)

Prologue

Indianapolis, Indiana
March 3, 2004

The missing person report read:

Female, age twenty-four, height five foot four, weight approximately one hundred two pounds, last seen February 28th. She has brown eyes and bleached blonde hair with pink highlights. Her vehicle was found parked behind the Cherry Pop Gentlemen's Club. She has a tattoo of a heart on her right ankle. Circumstances of disappearance: she was last seen after her pole dance performance.

Detective Thurston grimaced as he swallowed the last of his cold, bitter coffee. He opened the desk drawer and removed a bottle of antacid tablets. He popped two in his mouth to settle his heartburn. He gritted his teeth against the nagging pain from a bulging disc in his spine. He felt eons older than his fifty-five years.

"Here's another one, Detective Thurston."

Thurston reached out and accepted the file. He lifted a stack of manila folders in the wire stackable basket on his desk and stuck the new file on the bottom. "Twenty-five open cases." He harrumphed. "What's one more to solve before I'm outta here."

"How much longer before you wave bye-bye?"

"Fifteen days and some poor schmuck gets to take over all of this backlog of cases." He waved his hand over the file basket. "In the meantime, I'm only working the easy ones…you know, disgruntled sixteen-year-old girls who think they know more than their parents and run off with the pimply-faced boyfriend, only to spend the night in a bus station 'cause their piggy bank cash flow dried up. Yeah, thirty years of beatin' the bushes and I've got the achin' feet and bad back to prove I deserve a cabin on a lake, no phones, no internet, and plenty of beer." He ambled over to fill his cup with fresh coffee. "Tell you what—give the case to Rooks."

"Can't, sir. He was transferred to a different precinct."

"Oh, yeah. Forgot. What a schmo." The detective heaved a disgruntled sigh. He rescued the file from the bottom of the stack and opened it. "Has it been seventy-two hours since the alleged victim went missing?"

"No, sir."

The detective stuck the file back to the bottom of the stack. "Enough said. Now get outta here. I've got work to do."

Chapter One

The early Greeks and Romans believed the sultry dog days of August was a time of evil and bad luck because of unexpected thunderstorms and lethargy. Maybe I believe this. Maybe not.

My name is Tullah Crow Holliday. I am a doctor of veterinary medicine with secondary degrees in both human and animal forensics. I am licensed to practice in the state of Kentucky, operating an animal clinic in the small rural town of Enigma, where I have lived my entire twenty-nine years, not counting the years I attended the University of Georgia. And before you ask—yes, I do get kidded a lot about being someone's huckleberry, and yes, the infamous outlaw, Doc Holliday, is my ancestor on my father's side. By the way, it just so happens that my father, John Henry Holliday, is the sheriff of Enigma.

I don't consider myself an amateur sleuth. Rather, trouble seems to find me. My grandmother, Tanti Crow, who is full-blooded Cherokee, says it's because of my empathic abilities that lost souls seek me out to find their killers and bring them to justice.

On one of those sultry August days, the scorching air felt like it was sucking the breath right out of my body. There wasn't a hint of a breeze. I was glad I'd had the foresight to install fans in the barn. My horses preferred to stand in their stalls instead of grazing in the pasture on such a day.

In spite of the heat, Grandmother and I sat in the porch swing, sipping iced tea and watching the sun slide below the horizon. Occasionally we swatted a horsefly seeking to feast on our blood. It would be dark soon. Lightning bugs blinked across the pasture like tiny bobbing lanterns. We inhaled the sweet scent of night-blooming jasmine.

Grandmother lifted her face to catch the ceiling fan's cool air. "How much longer does Cindi have before she graduates with her degree in veterinary medicine?"

Too long, I thought. Not only did I miss my friend, but it was tough trying to run a busy animal clinic without a good assistant. "Two more very long years."

We resumed our swinging, and then grandmother asked, "Now that she's reconnected with her mother, do you suppose Cindi will return to Enigma?"

I sipped the last of my tea. "With Earl in prison, there's no reason for Cindi and Annie to stay away. Here's the thing, Grandmother. Annie has a good job at a bank in Lexington. I've offered Cindi a partnership in the clinic. She would run the small animal side while I take care of the large animals."

"That's sounds like a deal not to be passed up. What did she say?"

I sighed and gazed out at the fireflies blinking their lights. "She appreciated the offer, but this early in her education she'd rather not commit." I shifted to look at my grandmother. "Honestly, my gut instinct is telling me Cindi will never return to Enigma."

Grandmother made a *pffft* sound. "After all you've done for that girl. Took her in when no one else would give her the time of day because of who her daddy is, gave her a good paying job, even supplied her with a house and paid her first semester's tuition…why…"

I held up my hand. "Stop. You're getting yourself all worked up over nothing. Whatever decision Cindi makes will be because it's right for her."

Grandmother lifted my hand to her cheek. "You are just like my Josie, may she rest in peace—you have a good soul."

The mention of my mother sent a painful twang through my heart. I reminded myself that someday… someday when the time was right…I would find the monster that murdered my mother and left her like a heap of trash in a New York back alley.

We rocked back and forth in the swing in silence.

Grandmother shifted. "It's about time I gather up my dishes and head home. I have a busy day tomorrow."

"What new project are you presenting to the council this time?"

As the newly elected and overly enthusiastic mayor of Enigma, Kentucky, my grandmother's ideas weren't always met with exuberance from the city council.

She clapped her hands together. "I've contacted Premier Entertainment Productions, and they are interested. What better place to make a movie than our beautiful countryside?" Tanti Crow spread her hands to indicate all of our rural community. "And not to speak of the tourism dollars PEP would bring."

"That's a worthy idea, Grandmother. The council is foolish if they vote against it. "

An unexpected shiver slithered over me, prickling the hairs on my arms. I used my bare toes to abruptly halt the swing's back-and-forth motion. A vibration started in my chest, and I had the feeling something unexpected was about to happen. Grandmother calls this my inner sense. She says only special people are blessed with this secret sagacity. She also says it's because of my Cherokee heritage. Whatever *it* is, most of the time I consider it a curse.

"You're as pale as a ghost. Have you taken ill…Tullah…speak to me…what ails you?"

I clutched my wrist. The pain was almost unbearable. Tears flooded my eyes. The knot in my gut twisted tighter with the tingling premonition that something unusual was about to happen.

"I'm not sure." My heartbeat quickened, and I took a deep breath to calm the nerves that wanted to come.

Grandmother scooted closer and wrapped her arms around me. She said, "You are trembling like the weather just turned cold."

It was true. Shivers slithered up and down my spine. I looked at her and said, "My instinct is telling me to be watchful. For what, I don't know."

I gazed out at the open pasture, searching. Something about the evening and grandmother's mention of death had awakened my inner sense.

Grandmother rubbed her hand up and down my arm as if trying to warm me. She said, "For those who are blessed with the secret sense, it is the wisest part of them. It knows when the stars are out of kilter and steers us clear of what's bad for us. It also guides us toward what is right, and sometimes it's difficult to tell which is which."

"Whatever *it* is, I wish someone other than me had inherited *it*."

As quickly as it came, the feeling of unease fluttered away, leaving me to sigh a breath of relief. Grandmother and I sat in solitude, allowing the songs of the night creatures blending with the creaking of the swing to serenade us.

In the waning light, River, my black Labrador Retriever, danced up the porch steps and happily laid his trophy at my feet. Grandmother gasped. "Oh, my lands, is that…is that a…hand?"

River sat with his long pink tongue hanging from his mouth. He actually looked as if he was smiling. I reached forward and rewarded him with a pat. "Good boy, River." And then I leaned down and carefully lifted the boney skeleton of a hand.

Whatever *it* is—the inner sense—had opened the door to a mystery that I felt compelled to solve.

Grandmother's eyes were wide when she asked, "Is it human?"

I handled the skeletal remains as if it were a fragile piece of china. "Maybe, but it could also be primate. They look similar."

Her voice sounded shaky. "I seem to recall that about ten years ago one of the carnivals the 4-H sponsored had a troupe of trained chimpanzees." Grandmother tapped her lip. "Although I don't remember hearing that any of them escaped or died."

I presented her with a puzzled look. "How come I don't remember that?"

"Hmm, I believe that's the year you left to attend veterinary school in Georgia. Yes, you left in August, and the 4-H festival was in September."

I reached up and touched my cheek. I could still feel my mother's smile as she hugged me and said goodbye the day she left for her trip to New York. So many years ago. And now she rested with the sky spirits. Was there a connection between River's prize and my mother's death?

My insides churned. "Either way, I'll notify Dad. We'll need a forensics test to determine if this is truly human or animal."

Getting over my initial shock, I realized my hand was wet and stunk, and that River and his sidekick, Rascal, a teacup donkey, had mud clinging to their bodies. Both reeked of rotting vegetation.

"Let's go in the house. I'll call Dad while you gather up your dishes."

Before opening the screened door, I pointed a finger toward my dog and donkey and commanded them to stay. "The two of you need a bath. I wish you could tell me where you found your trophy. Never mind." River made a move to follow me. "No, no. Stay!"

Both animals plopped in front of the door to patiently wait until allowed to enter the house.

While Grandmother busied herself, I pulled a large plastic baggie from a drawer and carefully inserted the bony hand. Then I searched until I found a small pizza carton and laid the evidence inside. To make sure the box didn't get accidentally tossed into the trash once it arrived at my dad's office, I used a broad-tipped red marker and in large letters wrote: EVIDENCE... DON'T TOSS!

Once I'd secured the skeletal hand, I telephoned the sheriff's office. When his secretary answered, I said, "Hi, Joyce, is my dad available?"

"Sure is. Hold on." And in her usual voice

bellowed, "Henry...Tullah...line one."

"Hey, Punkin, you and Tanti have a good visit?"

"We did. You know she makes the best egg salad sandwiches and cherry pie bites in the state."

"Wish I could've joined you. It's Tiny's day off. You know how it is to be shorthanded."

"Yes, sir, I sure do."

"You didn't call just to chit-chat with your ol' man. What's up?"

I gave him a brief rundown about the skeletal hand and that I was sending it to him via Grandmother. He said, "You say the animals are wet and stink? Stink how, like they were digging in a hole—a garbage pit?"

I thought for a moment. "Hmm, no, sir, more like rotting vegetation from a swampy area. I can only think of one place close enough for River to make his way home without being foot weary, and it's between my land and the old abandoned Rasmussen property."

When he didn't answer right away, I could almost see the wheels turning in Dad's brain. "Yep, I know the place. There's about a hundred acres between your house and the marsh."

"It's been abandoned for more than fifty years. I looked into buying it about five years ago and was told the property is tied up in some kind of trust, and the heirs live somewhere in Denmark."

"Yeah, I'd heard rumors that even the State of Kentucky had looked into purchasing the land as a state preserve and didn't have any luck locating the owner." There was a pause. "I'll check it out in the morning."

The words crept into my mouth. "Tomorrow's Saturday. Since the clinic is closed except for emergencies, I'd really like to go with you. The horses

9

need exercising. Do you mind?"

He chuckled. "It's been a while since I rode Moon. Sure, sounds good."

Grandmother yelled loud enough for her son-in-law to hear, "Hey, I'd like to tag along. Banjo wouldn't want to be left behind while his friends have an adventure."

"Tell your grandmother I heard her. Have the coffee ready. We'll meet you at seven."

"I suppose you want me to saddle the horses, too?"

"Naw. We'll bring donuts and breakfast sandwiches from Patty's. I'll help you saddle after we eat."

"You're the best, Dad."

Afterward, I toted the wicker basket as I walked Grandmother to her car. I settled it on the back seat while she climbed in and set the pizza carton containing the skeleton hand on the passenger seat. She paused a second before turning the ignition. "Lock your doors. After the way Earl Redfern broke into your house, and the beating he gave you, and with Cindi living on the university campus, I worry about you being out here all alone."

"No worries, Grandmother. Earl is in prison. Plus, I've got River and Rascal to keep me company." My reassurance didn't dim the concern reflected in her eyes.

As she drove away from the house, I whistled for my pets and they followed me to the special area I'd had built to administer animal baths. I lathered River and Rascal's bodies and scrubbed them good. Even though they couldn't understand me, I talked as I rinsed. "Who did the hand belong to? It's small, like a woman's. I wonder if the person died as a result of an accident, or was she…" Even before I spoke the word it was almost as if an unexpected breeze whispered, "…*murdered*."

Chapter Two

I didn't sleep well. Maybe that was because I was looking forward to spending the day with my dad and grandmother. Maybe it was because I was exhausted and needed a day of relaxation, or maybe it was because the voice whispered on the wind kept me tossing and turning most of the night. Either way, the horses hadn't been ridden in a while. I rose before dawn and hitched them to the hot walker to work a little of the feistiness out of them.

I busied myself in the kitchen, filling two jugs with ice and water. August weather is extra hot, and a person can work up a powerful thirst while sitting in a saddle. A little before seven, I flipped the switch on the coffeemaker. River's excited yips and his toenails scratching against the floor as he raced to the front door alerted me that Dad and Grandmother had arrived. I yawned and scrubbed the heel of my hand against my eyes as I unlocked the door, opened it wide, and yelled, "Coffee's hot."

Dad waved. He rounded to the passenger side of his 4Runner and assisted Grandmother to the ground. He carried a large paper sack, and Grandmother grinned as she held forward a box of donuts. We feasted on bacon, egg, and cheese biscuits, and enough coffee to float a boat.

Patty Sweet is the owner of Sweet's 'n' Eats. She's

also the vice mayor and Grandmother's best friend. The best friend part pays off because Patty always slips in a little surprise with the original order of a dozen donuts. Today she included glazed donut holes.

I said, "If I eat another biscuit, Gandalf will protest that I weigh too much." Gandalf is a stocky black-and-white pinto Quarterhorse gelding, smart and trustworthy, although like most animals, he has a few cantankerous days. He had belonged to my mother.

Dad stood. He stretched to the fullness of his six-foot-three frame. The Glock was strapped to his waist. "We'd better get a move on. Today promises to be another scorcher. I'll saddle the horses while you and Tanti clean up. Did you pack water?"

I pointed to the saddlebag draped over a chair next to the back door. "Yes, sir. Two half-gallon jugs filled with ice."

He grabbed the saddlebag on his way out.

Grandmother headed down the hallway. "We'll be ready in ten minutes. I gotta take care of nature."

While I waited, I looped the new digital camera with zoom lens around my neck. Second to my love of animals, I enjoy taking pictures and recently converted a portion of my basement into a combo office-studio.

Grandmother is spry for her seventy-something years. She doesn't let the grass grow under her feet. I whistled up my pets and locked the kitchen door. Grandmother's long salt-and-pepper braid swayed back and forth as she marched across the yard to where the horses stood swishing their tails.

For the next twenty minutes we rode in silence until we came to a makeshift gate I had created in a section of rusty barbed wire. Once in a while a bull or a heifer will get out and can't find its way back in. I needed a gate to ride a horse through so I could herd the wayward animal back home.

We continued our ride. I snapped pictures of River and Rascal scampering about, and a herd of white-tailed deer that River startled out of the brush. Kentucky is a relatively peaceful state on the outside, with its flourishing forests and green hills, but looks can be deceiving. On occasion Dad gets reports of black bears and coyotes pulling down a cow or a horse. He's even had a couple of incidents where black bears have broken into automobiles and houses, and one human casualty.

I'm not particularly fond of snakes, and the area we're headed is a breeding ground for cottonmouths and rattlers. The swampy area on the old Rasmussen property is the result of a lengthy, jagged fissure that opened up about a hundred years ago. As the story goes, at the tail end of the fissure, the earth yawned wide and swallowed the house, the barn, and Adolph Rasmussen, Senior. Many locals consider the place cursed. A few townfolks claim to have heard moaning and have reportedly seen Adolph Rasmussen's ghost.

I don't believe in curses, or the ramblings of drunken fools, or teenagers high from toking on pot and trespassing on private property, who claim to have seen ghosts and heard eerie moaning. What I do believe in is the sudden dread that fills me.

River's spine-chilling howls broke through my reverie, followed by Rascal's frantic braying. The little donkey burst from a dense area of the swamp like his tail was on fire. Unfortunately for me, he ran straight toward my horse. Nothing much spooks Gandalf except when a tiny gray donkey runs between his legs. I felt the big gelding bunch and automatically set my boots in the stirrups and leaned into the rearing as Gandalf squealed, rose on his back legs, and pawed the air. I glanced over, and Grandmother and Dad had their hands full with frightened horses.

"Shazam," I cried as I settled the startled gelding. My heart thundered in my ears. Grandmother brought Banjo under control and was walking him in circles to keep him from bucking. I think Dad's weight discouraged Moon, instead, causing the quivering horse to blow and snort.

Grandmother sidled her gelding next to me. "I hope River hasn't been snake bit."

Dad replied, "He wouldn't howl. He'd come running for Tullah. I suspect he's gotten himself tangled in briars."

The hairs on my arms stood up. A strange tightening gripped my stomach muscles. "I don't think it's either." I gigged my horse forward. "C'mon. We need to hurry."

We set the horses at a gallop following an old animal track for about two miles. My concern increased with each of my beloved dog's mournful howls. At the edge of a densely treed area we dismounted and tied the horses to a fallen log. I lifted my camera and clicked several shots at different angles.

"This place gives me the creeps." Grandmother's voice sounded strained. "Tullah, you're white as a sheet."

Dad adjusted the .45 on his hip as if expecting trouble. I felt as if someone was walking on my grave without me being in it. Part of me wanted to turn around, get on my horse, and race away from this place. The other part was held by a voice inside my head saying, *I'm here. We're all here. Find us. Please find us.*

I could feel that the voice was in a deep dark place. I felt it in me, and it clawed its way up my spine. I knew it would come out my mouth like a regurgitation of emotion if I let it.

I called out, "River…where are you, boy? Come…come here."

He answered with a series of yips. I called again, "Come, boy. Come to me."

He answered again, this time with loud and demanding barks.

Dad's voice was filled with concern. "What is it, Punkin…you've got a strange look on your face."

I inhaled. I would never get used to these surprise visits of the mind that iced my blood and burdened my heart. I never had them when my mother was alive. Had she somehow in death gifted me with this curse?

I stood there, listening to the hum of mosquitoes and my dog's whines, and staring into the dark marsh until I became aware of the welling of tears in my eyes. I gripped his arms. "Dad, this is a place of death."

"An animal graveyard?"

The musky odors of rotting vegetation and stale water stifled our nostrils. I coughed to clear my lungs. "No, sir. Human."

"Geehosofat, Tullah! Are you sure?"

I nodded. "Don't ask me how I know. I just do."

"I always trust your instincts." He motioned to Grandmother. "Tanti, hold Tullah's hand, and the two of you stick to me like glue."

We'd taken two steps when dark clouds passed over the sun, and the wind kicked up. Gandalf loosed a long whinny. I looked over my shoulder. He was tugging against his reins. I make a clicking sound in my throat and called his name. He calmed but continued to blow and snort. "Even the horse knows, Dad."

I lifted my camera and clicked a few more shots. Grandmother clutching my hand gave me comfort. She swatted at a cloud of mosquitoes that hovered close to her face. Sweat pooled in my armpits. We moved forward through choked vegetation and stayed close to my father. He stopped and kicked a log with the toe of his boot. Kicking a log is an old Indian trick. If there is a snake under the log or on the other side, it will let you know it's there. Satisfied that nothing slithery waited for us, we stepped over the dead tree and continued toward the barking. The deeper in, the squishier the earth became and the more rancid the stagnant water smelled. It felt as if the mud was a living thing and trying to suck us under.

About two hundred yards in, I spotted River. He lay completely prone as if guarding something. He lifted his massive head, looked at me with baleful eyes, and whimpered. I sprinted toward him, squatted, and bent to kiss his head. I rubbed my hands down his sleek black back. "What is it, boy…are you hurt?"

Mud clung to him from head to toe. I lifted his legs, checking for a possible snake bite. He whimpered again but refused to move. "Dad, help me lift him." I had visions of River's belly being ripped open, perhaps by a boar hog. What greeted us was a grisly surprise.

Dad expelled his favorite expletive. "Geehosofat!"

Grandmother covered her mouth to suppress the

fullness of her scream.

I wrapped my arms around River's neck and hugged him. "Good boy, River. Good—good boy." I carefully lifted a human skull warmed by my dog's body. A worm slithered out of the hollow eye socket. River stood and pawed the mud. He looked at me and then at the black oozing earth. I handed Dad the skull and clicked a few pictures. "I think he wants me to dig."

I was glad I wore gloves as my fingers dug deep. Worms wriggled upward and crawled away. For a split-second I thought about fish bait, and then my fingers touched a solid something. I used both hands to scoop away mud. "Oh, God, Dad."

He knelt beside me and helped clear mucky vegetation from a shallow grave to expose a rib cage and the pelvis and then legs. "It's a woman." I looked around at this dank place. "My guess is she was murdered."

Dad shook his head and simply said, "Yeah."

Grandmother gasped. We looked to where she pointed. "He's found another one."

Dirt, mud, and debris were flying as my dog clawed at the vegetation. I goosestepped to where he stood. They were barely above the surface—dirty white fingertips. I carefully brushed the soil aside to expose a skeletal hand.

In a split-second, he was digging next to my knee. Muddy water soaked into my pants. Dad squatted. He smoothed away the mud that threatened to refill the hole. He said, "Another one. That's three grouped together."

Grandmother crossed herself and uttered a small

prayer. We hadn't expected to find the remains of three women.

River raced off through the marsh. I called after him. He answered with a series of barks. "We have to follow him."

Dad, Tanti, and I struggled through tangles of briar vines that tore at our shirts. River stood next to a stagnant stream, the sides high with brittle grass. A safe haven for cottonmouths. My eyes scanned the area. Dad stamped the dirt with his boots. Grandmother did likewise. If there were snakes they would either greet us or slither away. I preferred the latter.

Years of storms had littered the area with broken trees, and their jagged, dead branches reminded me of skinny arms reaching skyward. The air lay heavy, making it difficult to breathe. I stepped forward and sank to the top of my boot, causing me to land hard on my bottom. My boot hung and held fast when I tried to pull my leg from the hole. Inadvertently, I had unearthed another grave.

Grandmother squelched and took a step forward. "Not another one." She lifted a bone. "I hope it isn't human."

Dad reached beneath my arms and hefted me from the watery prison. "What kind of bone is it?"

I relieved Grandmother of the bone, brushed dirt away from it, and sighed. "My best guess is that it's a humerus, also known as the upper forearm." I turned it over. "Without exact measurements, I'm still fairly certain that when we find the rest of the skeleton it will also be a woman."

Dad's eyes shifted to mine. "That's four. From the way River is whining and sniffing, I believe we've stumbled across a veritable boneyard."

Grandmother whispered, "A boneyard? Henry, what do you intend to do?"

He slapped his face, which left a dead mosquito and a bloody streak where the insect had been feasting. "This is not what I expected to find. Let's place each bone where we found it and mark the spot." He searched around and located sturdy sticks to jab into the ground wherever we'd found the bones. He used his pocket knife to cut strips from his bandana to tie around the top of each stick.

Wiping his muddy hands on his knees, he said, "Tiny and I aren't equipped to handle a possible homicide scene this big." He heaved a heavy sigh. "As much as I'd rather not, I'll contact Mac Draper."

"You mean Mac Draper as in head of the Kentucky Bureau of Investigations? The guy that's always in the news?"

"Yep, the very same." He pulled out his cellphone and punched in the numbers. He listened.

"Hello. Yes, ma'am. This is Sheriff Henry Holliday from Enigma County."

The frown on his face deepened. "Yes, ma'am, I understand that today is Saturday. It's important that I speak to Commander Mac Draper."

Pause.

"Yes, ma'am. I'll hold."

Pause. Dad put the phone on speaker.

"Henry Holliday, how the hell are you? It's your lucky day. I don't usually come in on Saturdays."

I could see the impatience in Dad's face. He wasn't one for making small talk, especially when a homicide was involved, and he cut right to the chase.

"If it wasn't important, I wouldn't be calling you. Listen, Mac, last night my daughter's dog brought home a hand. Part of a skeleton, to be exact. Today we've stumbled across a boneyard. There're three bodies that we know of. I'm thinking there might be more. I know you've moved up in rank, but this is a bit more than I and my deputy are equipped to handle."

The jovialness in the KBI agent's voice had shifted to serious. "It'll be good to get back in the field again, Henry. My team and I'll be at your office Monday morning, ten sharp. It'll be like old times."

"Good enough, Mac. I'll notify the hotel to expect your team. How many?"

"Three and myself."

"One more thing, Mac—the bones are in a swamp. We can only drive in so far. Then whatever equipment you need we'll have to carry in."

"Hmm, what about four-wheel drive?"

Dad snorted a chuckle. "Not unless you want to sink completely out of sight. Too heavy."

Pause.

"What about ATVs?"

"Listen, Mac, it's the State's money. If you want to bring ATVs, then bring 'em. Up to you. Here's the thing—whatever the swamp tries to claim is your responsibility to haul out. You can't leave it to adulterate the land. While you're spending the State's money on useless vehicles, you and your team of experts might want to invest in snake boots and mosquito repellent."

"I'll think on it. Monday morning. Ten sharp."

"I'll set you up at the civic center, where we'll have room to spread out and have air conditioning."

"There is no *we*, Henry. I'm heading this operation."

"I'm the sheriff of Enigma County. *My* jurisdiction."

Dad disconnected the call. He emitted what sounded like a low growl. I decided not to ask him any questions. Not just yet.

I whistled up River. By the time we returned to where we'd left the horses, Rascal rested on the grass. He rose and trotted toward us, pushing at my hands for attention.

On the ride back to the farm, I played today's events in my head like the rerun of a three-act play.

Before Dad and Grandmother left the farm, we agreed to meet at the Whitehorse Saloon for an early supper, and to discuss today's gruesome discoveries.

Chapter Three

At four-thirty, I walked into the Whitehorse Saloon. It took a moment for my eyes to adjust to the dim interior. "Hey, Little Sister, how's my favorite goddaughter?"

I smiled at the big bear of a man approaching me. Charlie Whitehorse is the owner of the Whitehorse Saloon and my dad's blood brother. Not as in by birth, rather as in the traditional Native American ceremony of blood-binding between two unrelated men.

I walked into his outstretched arms for the hug. "Hot and thirsty. Are Dad and Tanti here?"

"Back table. Go on over. I'll bring your favorite—cola with two lemon wedges."

"What's on the menu? I'm starved."

Charlie grinned. "Henry's already ordered. BBQ wings, fried shrooms, my famous Kentucky blossom with a secret sauce."

The Kentucky blossom is Charlie's spin on a deep-fried bloomin' onion, and the secret sauce is—well, secret. Although I'm certain the sauce is a concoction of mayonnaise and ketchup.

"Sounds yummy. You joining us?"

"Thought I might. Nothing better to discuss than bones while eating—right?"

He chuckled and ambled toward the kitchen. My vision had cleared, and I spotted Dad waving me toward his favorite spot in a back corner. Although the saloon is primarily what one would refer to as an old-fashioned juke joint with loud music, loud voices, endless mugs of beer, and an occasional fist fight, everyone in town knows it's the best place to eat any time before eight o'clock each evening, other than Patty's Sweet's 'n' Eats, that is.

Not many people know Charlie attended college on a football scholarship, and was awarded the medal of valor and Purple Heart while serving in Desert Storm. Most people think of him as "that Indian." He and my dad have been friends since the sixth grade. Charlie would give up his life for any one of us. As far as I've ever known, we are the closest to an existing family that he has.

I scooted in next to Grandmother. She gave a little *squee* and said, "I've been chomping at the bit to tell you and Henry of my discovery."

I lifted my eyebrows and cut my eyes toward Dad, who shrugged his shoulders. "Okay, out with it."

"You know me and my inquisitive nature. Well, I couldn't recall any recent murders in Enigma, especially a series of murders—or even in Kentucky, for that matter."

Dad interrupted. "Yeah, same with me. My files didn't turn up anything. I can't remember the last time we had a missing person report. Sorry to interrupt, Tanti."

She fluttered her hand. "Out of curiosity, I put in a call to a friend of mine at the *Lexington Sentinel*. All the old files from the *Enigma Gazette* were sent to the *Sentinel*. She was kind enough to give me her password so I could access the morgue records. Thank goodness for microfiche and digitation. I first searched for Rasmussen and came up with an interesting article dated March 1941. It detailed the mysterious earthquake and the disappearance of Adolph Rasmussen." She pulled out a printed copy of the report and laid it on the table. "Thought you might like to read it."

I glanced at the headline: *Cursed to Death.* The article detailed information provided by ten-year-old Lars Rasmussen, who had barely escaped being swallowed up by the earth. "Hmm," I mused. "Greta Rasmussen supposedly sold her soul to the devil and asked him to destroy her husband and all that he owned in such a way that she couldn't be blamed for his death. Interesting." There was more, and I wanted to read all of it. However, at the moment I was more interested in the bones we'd found. "Anything about missing persons?"

Grandmother spread two Xerox sheets of paper on the table. "Not in the *Gazette*. I found these in the *Sentinel*." She tapped the pictures with a manicured nail. "Lacy Costello, a twenty-seven-year-old waitress from Mayfield, and Melissa Bernard, a dental technician from Paducah, were reported missing, both in March 1963. As you can see, it states no trace of either woman was ever found."

Dad perused each article. "It appears that after years of no evidence, and detectives taking retirement or being transferred to different areas, the cases simply went cold."

Flora, Charlie's waitress, arrived with my cola. "Two lemon wedges, just like you like it, hon." I smiled my thanks. She set a fresh mug of beer in front of my dad and a red wine for Grandmother. Flora said, "Food's almost ready."

We thanked her and returned to the news articles. I squeezed the lemon into my cola and swiveled the straw to blend the juices before I sipped. "Sad. I can't imagine how the families must have felt. I wonder if any of them are still living, family members, that is."

Grandmother tsked. "Such a shame."

Flora and Charlie arrived with the food. As was our routine, we asked Charlie to join us. Usually he doesn't. This time, he did. We brought him up to date on the missing women. Dad said, "Our ol' buddy Mac Draper will be here Monday morning with his crew." Dad winked. "You might want to whip up something special to serve for supper."

Charlie frowned. "Pah, that piece of crowbait. I'll serve him shoe leather. For his crew, maybe something a little tenderer. They can't help it if they work for a weasel."

I dipped a fried mushroom into the bleu cheese sauce. "I take it Commander Draper isn't on the top of your 'best bud' list."

Charlie almost sucked the meat right off a drummie. "Nope, and enough said."

Note to self—ask Dad why Charlie doesn't like Mac Draper.

Grandmother licked her fingers and smacked. She complimented Charlie on his BBQ sauce and asked if he planned to enter it in the 4-H Festival's BBQ Cook-Off again this year. She also said she had run copies of the pictures of each of the missing women. We agreed that with sticky fingers covered in BBQ sauce we'd wait until after finishing our food to take a look at photos.

Shortly before seven o'clock, Grandmother gathered up the information we'd discussed and stuck it in a folder and then into her oversized purse. The Saturday night crowd had begun to arrive, along with the local band, the Kentucky Troubadours, who were loudly tuning their instruments.

Charlie walked us to the door. "If you need a good tracker, I don't think I've lost my skills."

Dad did a mini-salute. "I can't see you taking orders from Mac."

Charlie guffawed. "He's been a peckerhead since that first day in boot camp. Leopards don't change their spots. Watch your back, Henry." He waved and disappeared inside the saloon.

Grandmother and I exchanged quizzical looks. She said, "Let's have coffee at my place. We can reread the articles and speculate."

I was about to agree when my cellphone chirped. "Dr. Holliday."

"Hey, Doc, it's Bob Westerman. I know it's Saturday and wouldn't call unless it was an emergency."

"What's up, Bob?"

"I'd sure appreciate it if you would come out to my place. It's my big red stallion. He's down, and I can't get him up. Also, he's got the scours. I sure hope he hasn't twisted an intestine. We've got a show coming up soon, and I need him in tip-top shape."

I assured Bob not to worry, and that it'd take about twenty minutes for me to arrive. Fortunately, my truck was always equipped with plenty of supplies.

I sighed. "Emergency. Bob Westerman's standardbred has a possible twisted intestine. This is the second time I've treated the stallion for the same thing. It's times like this that I really miss Cindi. Anyhow, I don't know how long it'll take. Afterward, I'll head home."

Dad nodded his understanding. "What's on your schedule for Monday morning? I want you in on this investigation."

"Won't Commander Draper object?"

"His objections don't carry much weight with me."

"Dad, don't we need permission to dig in the swamp? I know it's a crime scene"—I shrugged—"but we don't know how to contact the owner. Won't we be trespassing?"

He patted me on the shoulder. "Way ahead of you, Punkin. I've already called Judge Duval. He'll issue a special warrant. I can pick it up in the morning."

I raised my eyebrows. "On a Sunday?"

"Yep, nothing this exciting has happened in Enigma for a long time. He was happy to oblige."

I opened the door to my truck and, before swinging inside, said, "So far, there's nothing I can't reschedule on Monday unless it's an emergency."

"Good."

"Dad, what's up with the animosity toward Commander Draper?"

The muscles in Dad's jaw worked as if he were considering his answer. I almost expected him to say it wasn't any of my business or that we'd discuss it later. His voice was grim but steady. "Mac was our drill sergeant during basic training at Fort Knox. He had it in for Charlie from the very beginning. When I made it clear that stepping on Charlie was stepping on me, too, both our lives became hell. When we graduated, our unit was deployed to Kuwait, during Desert Storm. Sergeant Macintosh Draper deployed with us as our squad leader."

Dad rarely talked about the war, and when he did, he skirted around serious topics, only to recall some of the more humorous incidents.

I waited.

The jugular at the side of his neck turned blue and pulsed. "Sergeant Draper's overly inflated ego and irresponsible leadership cost good men their lives and sent others home as cripples in both mind and body."

"Is that why Charlie limps?"

He looked off into the distance as if watching an invisible play before he continued. "Yeah. We didn't meet up again until the police academy. Draper was one of the instructors. Let's just say that he never cared who he stepped on to get where he is. If I didn't need him to handle this investigation, he'd be the last person I'd contact."

I stepped down from the truck and wrapped Dad into a hug and whispered in Cherokee, "*Gvgeyuhi e do da.*" (I love you, Father.)

He pushed back. Mist rimmed his eyes. He drew a breath to recover. "You remind me so much of your mother. *Gvgeyuhi u-we-tsi a-ge-ya.*" He patted my cheek. "I'll see you Monday morning." He touched the brim of his hat in a little salute and walked to where Grandmother waited in his truck.

Dad wasn't a man to express sentiments, and when he did it made the words extra special. I blinked back the rush of emotions that assailed me. He'd said, *I love you, daughter.*

By the time I left Bob Westerman's and returned

29

home, it was a little after midnight. Both my armpits were ringed with sweat, and I was ready for my second cold shower of the day. The stallion would live to perform at other competitions, and the bed was calling my name.

A distant rumble of thunder brought false promise of rain. As much as we needed a good deluge, I silently prayed for nature to hold off until we'd retrieved all the skeletons from the swamp. At least, I hoped all the bodies had been buried in the same vicinity. Just like a tiger doesn't change its stripes, a serial killer doesn't change his habits.

I climbed into bed and snuggled against the pillows. Sleep brought troubled dreams. A young woman lay in a muddy grave. She stared up at me through the mire, her eyes pleading. Red fluid dribbled from the corner of her mouth. The dark strands of her long hair gyrated like the goddess Hydra's many-headed serpents. Through the serpents' eyes I watched naked bodies all pleading and reaching for me.

Jerking awake, I bolted upright in the bed. My sheets were strewn on the floor, and sunlight streamed between the curtain's long borders. I'd slept well past eight and needed to hustle if I were to meet Dad at the café by nine-thirty. I'd had too much on my mind to sleep peacefully.

My feet hit the floor, and I raced down the stairs to open the doggie door to let River and Rascal out for their morning business—and then I remembered—today was Sunday.

Chapter Four

Since today was Sunday, I decided to climb back into bed in hopes of catching a few hours of dreamless sleep. No such luck. The first phone call was from Grandmother, inviting me to lunch.

"I didn't sleep well last night, Grandmother. I was on my way back to bed."

"You have time to take a long nap and then come for a late lunch, say two-ish. Besides, I'm inviting Henry and Paul Ritter."

I rolled my eyes upward. I'd prefer lolling the day away. I'm not lazy, but ever since my friend and right-hand assistant left to finish her degree, I've had to burn the midnight oil, and that's been several months now. My search for a qualified assistant had proven fruitless. It seemed no one wanted to live in a small, out-of-the-way, rural town. "I'll bite. Why are you inviting Dr. Ritter?"

"Because he was born here, lived here all of his life, and then came back to practice here after he finished medical school. If anyone knows the history of this town and about the Rasmussen curse, it will be Paul Ritter."

I relented. "Are you cooking?"

"Heavens, no. I'm ordering from the Crispy Chicken. Now, scoot, go back to bed. See you around two."

I yawned my goodbye and padded up the stairs, my eyes closing as soon as I climbed into bed. Just as I was entering la-la land, my phone whistled, jerking me awake. The text ID displayed Deputy Tiny Goodbody's picture. My heart skittered. I opened the message. It read—Tullah, didn't want to call and scare you. No emergency. Need to talk to you about my niece. Call me at your convenience."

Relief flushed over me. Even though we live in a small and practically crime-free town, I always worry about my dad. I walked to the bathroom and splashed cold water over my face, and decided a four-hour nap would only make me feel groggier than I already was. I pressed the redial number.

"Hi, Tiny, what's up?"

"Sorry to disturb your Sunday, Tullah. My sister, Dr. Sunny Sanders, and my niece are moving to Enigma. Sunny accepted the position of Chief of Staff at the hospital. She's replacing Dr. Gannon."

"Uh-huh. I'd heard he was leaving and taking a position at a hospital in Los Angeles. He never did quite fit in around here. I guess he'll feel right at home with the movie stars. Anyhow, that's good news about your sister, although I don't really remember her."

"No, she's been gone a long time. Her husband passed away recently. It was a lengthy illness, and she's decided to come home. Said she needs a slower pace of life. Ella, my niece, just graduated with her degree as a veterinary technician. She's got her own horse, loves animals, graduated with honors, and is looking for a job. Knowing how you need a good assistant, I told Ella about you. I hope you don't mind."

"Tiny Goodbody, you are a godsend. Tell me more

about your niece."

"Well, like I said, she graduated with honors from the Texas A&M College of Veterinary Medicine. She's single, not involved with anyone as far as I know. She's twenty-three years old, and excited about meeting you. Dr. Gannon is vacating his rental, so Sunny and Ella will live there temporarily."

"When do they plan to arrive?"

"On Tuesday. They're driving in from Dallas, Texas. Sunny is pulling a rental trailer loaded with all their belongings, and Ella is following with the horse trailer. They'll need a couple of days to settle in. What about meeting them Saturday week?"

"Sounds good. Is Ella keeping her horse at your place?"

"Yep. Thanks, Tullah."

We hung up, and I headed to the shower feeling like I'd been handed a gift. If Ella Sanders was anything like her uncle, she and I would get along just fine.

I arrived at Grandmother's apartment. Dr. Ritter and my dad sat around the small dining table in Grandmother's equally small apartment. I chuckled. Only my grandmother would set an elegant table and serve fried chicken, potato salad, and baked beans from a fast-food joint, on fancy dinner plates, and with precisely folded gold linen napkins.

We bowed our heads, and Dr. Ritter blessed the food. Grandmother said, "We can talk while we eat. I've already told Paul about finding the skeletons in the swamp." She waved her fork as she talked. "Paul, except for when you were attending medical school, you've lived in Enigma your entire life. I was born in nineteen forty-nine, so I don't remember anything about the Rasmussens. What about you?"

Dr. Ritter wiped his mouth with a napkin and sipped a healthy gulp of iced tea. "I was friends with Lars Rasmussen." He seemed to do a calculation in his head. "It was nineteen forty-three. Lars and I had celebrated our tenth birthdays a day apart. That's how I can remember the date. Lars had an older brother, Adolph Junior. His mother and Lars called him 'Dolphy.' He was about sixteen and hated his name as much as he hated his father."

I was about to ask why when my grandmother gave me the *look* that cautioned me not to interrupt.

Dr. Ritter continued, "Adolph Senior had come from the 'old country,' as he called it. The old country being Germany. Greta, his wife, hailed from Denmark. As I recall, she was beautiful, with hair the color of spun silk and naturally pink cheeks and lips. She was a gentle woman who loved her children, and she suffered in silence the verbal and physical abuse heaped on her by Adolph—a man so mean the townspeople avoided him. Adolph supposedly was a wealthy man when he came to Enigma from the old country. I can't attest to that. What I do know is that, on more than one occasion, my mother doctored Greta's bruised face, broken bones, and miscarriages. When he drank, which was often, the alcohol fueled his meanness, making him even more violent.

"Mother had baked a cake for the birthday Lars and I shared. She was busy with patients and told me to take it as a surprise for Lars. You see, the old man didn't hold with any type of celebration unless he was celebrating the opening of a fresh jug of whiskey.

"Remember, I was only ten years old. I was just in sight of the house when I heard the most awful screaming. I don't remember dropping the cake as I raced to the house. Greta and Lars were begging and pleading with Adolph. They had hold of his shirt and were pulling at him. He was bent over the well. I thought maybe he was drunk and had fallen and they were trying to save him. I was wrong.

"Like an enraged animal, he turned and shook Greta and Lars off his back like they were mere toys. He grabbed Lars by the arm and flung him through the air much like one tossing a ball. I ran to Lars. Tears flowed, and I couldn't understand a word he was saying because it was a blend of German and English all mixed together."

Dr. Ritter trembled. He clasped his hands together and leaned his forehead against his fist. His breath sounded like a sob. We sat quiet. Waiting.

"It's taken me years to shut out that god-awful scream. It was Greta. To this day, I do not know what she was screaming. Lars later said she was calling on the god of thunder to strike Adolph dead. I can tell you that the sky darkened, but I don't know whether it was a tornado that struck just at that moment, or if Thor had actually answered her plea, but the day turned to night, the thunder was deafening, the earth belched and rumbled. Greta screamed for Lars and me to run, and we did, all the way to town.

"When we returned with the sheriff, my mother, and a bevy of townspeople, Greta sat in the dirt, her arms held as if she were cradling a child. Her silken hair had turned completely white and her mind had left her. She rocked back and forth, repeating over and over—'Dolphy…Dolphy…Dolphy.' "

Dr. Ritter's hands trembled. He had to use both of them to guide the glass of tea to his mouth. He used the napkin to wipe tears from his aged eyes. It seemed he had lapsed into a trance.

I had trouble finding my voice. "What happened afterward?"

He spoke slowly and painfully. "Lars told the sheriff that his father was crazy drunk, as usual, but this time his anger was more violent. He'd accused Dolphy of being lazy and of stealing all the money in the cookie jar. He'd grabbed Dolphy by the neck and whether on purpose or by accident snapped it, then dumped him down the well. That's when Greta broke. I guess she'd had enough, and seeing her child murdered for no reason was more than she could bear. I guess she feared Lars might be next."

He hefted a huge sigh. "Lars knew the money was right where his father kept it—inside the hollow of an old oak tree. Dolphy hadn't stolen a penny and never would. He was always too afraid of the old man.

"When it was all over, the ground had opened, swallowing the house, the barn, the well, and Adolph, Senior. That night the rains came. It rained every day for over a month, turning the place into a quagmire. People stayed away, claiming to hear moaning, screams, and crying. They dubbed it 'Rasmussen swamp' and claimed it was haunted.

"Anyhow, we brought Greta and Lars to our house. Mother tended her until her mind was stable enough to travel, and then Mother helped book passage to New York. Years later, I received a letter from Lars saying he and his mother had returned to Denmark, but her mind had remained forever broken until she had finally passed away in her sleep. I never heard from him again, but the taxes on the property have always been paid."

I closed my eyes in thought. What a terrible experience for two young boys. "Lars would be your age. Do you think he's still alive?"

Dr. Ritter raised his eyebrows as partial answer to my question. "We both turned eighty-eight in March. Over the years before medical school, I always sent a birthday card with a note of news. I never heard from him. Then life got in the way, and I stopped writing. Eighty-eight is a long time to live. Whether or not he's alive? Only he knows."

I finished the last bite on my plate. The story hadn't diminished my appetite. "I understand why people think the Rasmussen swamp is cursed. There's a thousand acres of land, and more than a hundred is quagmire and the rest so infertile that nothing substantial will grow on it even during the rainy season."

Dr. Ritter said, "I'm suddenly very tired. Tanti, if you don't mind, please wrap two of the cream-filled donuts. I'll take them home for later."

Although he lived only an elevator ride to the third floor of Grandmother's apartment building, I offered to escort him home. He declined.

We said our goodbyes. I helped Grandmother clear the table and load the dishwasher while Dad looked over the two news articles and the photographs Grandmother had copied from her search at the *Lexington Sentinel*.

Grandmother said, "Thank goodness for these modern technical developments. Without microfilm and digitation I might never have found this information. These were the only two missing person cases I could find, though."

Grandmother and I joined Dad at the table. "You did good, Grandmother. Dad, did you discover anything helpful in the articles?" I asked.

He held up a couple of black-and-white pictures, both slightly out of focus and a bit fuzzy. "These two women disappeared one week apart in March—two thousand twelve. A waitress, age twenty-seven, from Mayfield, and the other a dental technician, age twenty-six, from Paducah."

"Hmm. Were their bodies ever found?" I asked.

He scanned the paper again. "It says Detective Ed Brown worked the case. According to the article, the women came from stable home lives, attended church regularly, and had no known enemies. No, the bodies were never located. Well, this isn't good."

"What?" Grandmother and I asked in unison.

"Apparently Detective Brown retired, and the cases went cold." Dad pulled at his pursed lips. This was a habit of his when trying to come up with a solution. "If he's still alive, maybe he can give us a little more information than what's in these articles."

"I wonder why the Kentucky Department of Criminal Investigations didn't step in and take over?"

"Good question."

I stifled a yawn. "What time do you plan to be at my place tomorrow?"

"I'll give you a call as soon as Draper and his team arrive."

"I have three clients in the morning. If I'm not finished by the time you show up, I'll saddle Gandalf and meet you as soon as I can."

Dad grinned. I said, "What?"

"You know River is the key to finding the skeletons, and he won't go with me."

"And why does that make you smile?" Smack my head. "Oh, gotcha. You can walk Draper around in circles, and he won't know the difference. You are bad, Dad. But, oh, how I like the way you think."

Grandmother lamented. "Drats. I have a council meeting tomorrow. Sure wish I could go with you."

She poured coffee in our cups and set the box of donuts on the table. Between bites, I said, "Patty is the vice mayor. You could let her take charge of the meeting."

She shook her head. "Patty is more than capable of running the meeting." She lifted a donut and took a generous bite, speaking between chews. "You know she's my best friend, so I hate to say this about her. She's all fluff and no filling. She tends to back-pedal when the council members aggressively voice their opinions."

I patted her hand. "Dad and I will update you on all the details so you won't feel left out."

I went on to fill them in about my conversation with Tiny Goodbody. "I sure hope his niece works out."

We all agreed that Dr. Sunny Sanders and Ella would fit well into the community. I finished my coffee, pushed back my chair, and lifted the bag of leftovers Grandmother had fixed for me. I kissed her on the cheek.

"See you tomorrow, Dad."

Chapter Five

An electrical storm isn't the most dangerous of disasters, but it can still damage homes and horse barns, start fires, and even kill livestock in the right situations. Kentucky hadn't seen rain in months, and the extended summer had baked the color of our normally lush bluegrass country to a burnished brown. We have our share of electrical storms, and I worried about Dad and the KBI agents traipsing around in a place that is a conduit for lightning.

I'd finished with my first two patients and hoped the cloud of dust kicking up in my long driveway was patient number three. I glanced at the clock and calculated that Commander Draper and his team should be pulling into Enigma right about now. With any luck, I'd be ready to join them in the swamp.

I stood outside and stared up at the ominous sky. Storm clouds gathered like giant capacitors. Rumbling thunder vibrated the ground. River and Rascal hugged against my legs. Static electricity prickled the hairs on my arms.

Patient number three was a beautiful Harlequin Great Dane with a broken tooth. The owner and I struggled to lift the hundred-and-thirty-pound dog to the exam table. I felt like a contortionist trying to help hold the dog still in order to administer the anesthesia. An otherwise easy extraction, and a caution to the owner to avoid giving Elsa hard, non-bending chew toys, took over an hour.

I helped the owner steady the wobbly dog to the van and then into the back seat. As soon as she left, I immediately cleaned and sterilized the surgery and surgical tools. Then I contacted my answering service to let them know to direct any emergencies to Dr. Cooper.

A little past noon, Dad called to say the commander and team were on the way and that he had a surprise for me. I like surprises and couldn't imagine what he was bringing me.

"The lightning worries me, Dad. It's popping really close to where we're headed."

"I hear you. We'll be in a world of mess if it rains."

"What's the surprise, Dad?"

"It won't be a surprise if I tell you."

After we disconnected, I gathered my snake boots, my kit left over from my forensic days, and my camera. Then I whistled up River and Rascal and sat inside the office to wait while I consumed a sandwich and a cola.

The convoy rolled to a stop in front of the cattle gate, with Dad's 4Runner in the lead. I locked the office door and grabbed my equipment. The dog and donkey followed me.

The moment I met Commander Macintosh Draper I felt myself squirm inside. When he smiled and extended his hand, his smirk reminded me of the way a shark must smile when it sees a swimmer in a black wet suit. Something didn't jibe. River's hackles rose. I reached down to shush the growl.

I clasped Draper's extended hand. "So you're Henry's daughter. Yeah, I looked up your profile.

You've made quite a reputation for yourself."

He glanced around. "No offense to your profession, which I'm certain you're very good at, but I don't need an amateur sleuth traipsing about disturbing important evidence at a crime scene."

It's never a good sign when Dad's left eye tics into a squint. I grabbed his forearm and was about to speak up in my own defense when a female voice with a familiar accent called out, "As I live and breathe... Tullah Holliday."

"Vaneeta! So you're Dad's surprise."

I and my former University of Georgia roommate and colleague exchanged hugs. "Wow, it's been years."

What the slight Dr. Vaneeta Sunreet, forensics anthropologist, lacked in stature, she made up in spunk. She is a true alpha woman. She placed her hands on her hips and stared at Mac Draper as if she might spit in his eye if he crossed her. "Dr. Tullah Holliday and I did our internship in forensic science together." She laughed. "Tullah decided she liked working with the living instead of the dead and preferred animals over people. She's as tough as her famous ancestor." Vaneeta lifted her eyebrows and quirked a grin. "You know, Doc Holliday, the gunfighter. She's the true huckleberry because she *can* get the job done."

Draper's eyes clinched with mine. I simply smiled and turned to open the back door to Dad's 4Runner. One whistle and River and Rascal jumped up and onto the back seat.

Vaneeta didn't wait for Draper to make the introductions. She pointed to each person as she spoke. "This is Sanjiv Patel, my assistant. He's an expert in collecting probative evidence. Detective Carl Rooks, and you already know Commander Draper."

Draper ran a hand over his patent-leather face and spat on the ground close to Dad's boots. There was something disturbing about him, but I couldn't think what it was.

Thunder volleyed across the sky. Dad suggested we load up and head out. I ran to swing the cattle gate wide and waited until the procession pulled through to shut it. Once inside next to Dad, I said, "Draper is a bit past his prime to be in the field. How old is he?"

"In his middle sixties is my best guess."

"He doesn't like me."

Dad grunted. "He doesn't like himself."

We drove a ways in silence. "It's good to see Vaneeta again. I'm glad she's leading forensics. She's as good as they come, and she won't take any guff from Draper. The thing is, I'm not sure how many swamps she's traipsed around in."

Dad patted my knee. "That's why I've got you."

The old 1985 4Runner bounced along the weedy track. I asked, "What do you know about Carl Rooks?"

"Never met the man."

"I hope he's got a lot of experience to go with the gray in his hair. It won't do for him to be a greenie where we're going. He's wearing a business suit and loafers. You suppose he didn't get the memo about boots?"

"Anything's possible."

Dad stopped at the barbed-wire fence. I hopped out and unlatched the makeshift gate and held it wide for the vehicles to pass through. Draper stopped, lowered the window, and asked, "How much farther?"

The blast from the air conditioner cooled my face.

"Not far. We'll stop to unload your equipment, then backpack it in about two hundred yards."

Draper smiled his shark grin, exposing a row of nicotine-stained teeth. A cigarette dangled between his fingers. "Nope, we'll drive right up to where the first skeleton was found."

I steadied my eyes on his. "It'd be a shame to lose this shiny black truck." I shrugged. "Suit yourself. Just don't say you weren't warned when this beauty sinks out of sight."

I waved him through the opening and heard the soft pop of his inhale when he drew a puff on his cig. As soon as the black forensics van cleared the opening, I secured the barbed-wire gate back in place and sprinted toward Dad's truck.

I slammed the door shut. "Draper thinks he can drive all the way into the swamp." I passed on my comment about the truck. "I don't like that guy."

"I'll handle Draper and Rooks. What about Vaneeta and her assistant—you think they'll back Draper if he tries to get all gung-ho on us?"

"I guess we'll find out."

By the time we arrived and Dad had switched off the ignition, the sky had darkened and a dragon's-breath wind had kicked up. There were no sounds except the hum of mosquitos and our own breathing. A heaviness, thick as clotted cotton, weighed heavy against my chest.

Dad exited the 4Runner. He opened the back door to let my pets out. River and Rascal promptly scampered to where I stood. The animals stayed close, as if they sensed an unseen enemy.

Dad pointed to the shadowy interior and spoke to

the group. "Beyond this point the ground is mostly unstable." He pulled six long poles from the backseat and handed one to each person. "You should always bring a walking stick when in a swamp," he said. "Before every step, use the stick to feel the area where you're going to place your foot. Avoid stepping in any areas where the ground feels soggy or where the water is dark."

Dad also pulled out a can of mosquito spray and passed it around. "We've marked the first three graves. River has a sense for these things. If there are more, he'll nose them out for us."

Draper expelled a sarcastic laugh. "Yeah, and what's the donkey do?" He grabbed the can of spray from the detective and applied a liberal amount.

I couldn't help myself. "Rascal is our good-luck charm. A gentle nose nudge can mean he wants you to move away, and a gentle nip usually is a more cautionary 'Get back!' warning, especially if he senses a spirit or a snake. You do know the Rasmussen Swamp is reputed to be haunted?"

Draper lit a cigarette and inhaled deeply. "Don't give me all that hocus-pocus crap. Dr. Sunreet, are you ready to move out?"

Detective Rooks carped, "It's past two o'clock and I'm sweatin' like a pig." He discarded the suit jacket and slung it across the truck's hood. "This place gives me the creeps. Let's just get on with it."

Vaneeta looked at me and rolled her eyes. "Lead the way, Sheriff Holliday."

We entered a dark place, stooping beneath the low-hanging limbs of giant trees. Briars snatched at our clothes and pricked our skin. A floating mat of duckweed covered the water like a thick green quilt, and whatever lifeforms lived in Rasmussen Swamp seemed to have cowered against the heat. I heard the anxiety in Detective Rooks' voice. "You sure we're not lost? Everything blends together and looks the same."

The voices inside my head taunted me. *Find us. We're here…here…here!* I thought about the missing women. I don't know how I knew they were women—I just did. I thought about their parents, their children, their lovers. I paused for a second and inhaled.

I reassured the portly detective. "We're not lost. And Detective, if we need to return tomorrow, I'd suggest you wear boots."

He frowned down at the mud that covered the tops of his leather loafers all the way to the hem of his slacks. "Will do. As soon as we get back to civilization."

We had barely walked five feet more when Rooks' panicked scream shook me to the tips of my boots. His face was ashen, and the veins in his neck pulsed. "I'm bit. It got me. Right here." He pointed to his leg and let loose a string of profanity.

Carl Rooks is a stout man with a paunch that hangs over his belt. A man past his prime. Dad's face was grim when he approached the detective. He probed the ground with his stick. River hadn't barked, and Rascal hadn't brayed.

Vaneeta poled her way to Rooks. Mud sucked at her thigh-high boots. She said, "For Pete's sake, Carl, you're tangled in briars. There's no snake."

Dad opened his knife and sliced through a tangle of thorny vines snagged around the detective's leg. The portly man snatched a handkerchief from his back pocket and wiped his sweaty face. "Six months, six more months, and I'm due to retire to a condo in Florida. This is your fault, Draper. You've had it in for me since I was transferred to your unit. You assigned me to this on purpose. Because of my heart, I'm supposed to work cold cases. Not traipse around in a godforsaken jungle."

Draper said, "You did it to yourself, Rooks. You've been riding your office chair for years...you're weak and you're—"

"Shut up! Both of you. We have skeletons to find. Settle your differences on your own time."

I didn't like the killing look Mac Draper shot my dad. Just about the time he took a step forward, lightning fingered across the sky. Draper crouched like he'd been shot. "Henry, this better not be a wild goose chase." His voice continued to rise. "If it is, I'll have your badge and your retirement. You said there are bodies. Where the hell are they?"

Dad growled, "Ten steps ahead, you'll find grave number one."

I shot Draper a scathing look and pointed my walking stick. Anger tightened my throat. "The other two are there and there." I offered Rooks a bottle of water from my knapsack.

Draper looked away.

In the turmoil, I hadn't noticed that River and Rascal had disappeared. Another streak of white heat cracked across the sky, answered by an earth-vibrating crescendo of thunder. Lightning struck a dead tree, splintering it. Rooks cursed.

Vaneeta loosed a startled squelch. "I've worked in some strange places. Nothing quite like this, though. It reminds me of when I was a little girl in India. Sugar Swamp was vast and dangerous, and filled with predators. In many ways it was as beautiful as its name, but a place I feared. This swamp is not beautiful. It's ominous." She dropped her knapsack of equipment to the ground and knelt in front of the stake where the strip of dad's bandana hung limp.

I said, "The bodies are buried just below the surface, Vaneeta. Whoever killed these women probably figured time and nature would take care of the remains."

She pointed to her assistant. "Sanjiv, you retrieve the second skeleton." She drew on a white forensics suit, a pair of gloves, goggles, and a hairnet. "Tullah—"

River's howl interrupted whatever it was Vaneeta was about to say. I looked at Dad and said, "He's found another one."

Draper flicked the spent cigarette into the dark water. "That makes four." Without caution or using his stick he charged forward, sinking up to his ankles in mud. He loosed a string of profanity as he used his pole to locate solid ground. His feet made squishing noises as he leaned heavily on the pole to free himself. He heaved a deep breath and spewed a few more obscenities. This time he paid attention to where he stepped as he made his way to where Dad had placed a numbered yellow flag to mark the spot.

It seemed that every five minutes River emitted an eerie yowl. Dad acted as our point man and followed every time to where the dog stood nosing the ground. I watched Dad kneel and carefully dig into the soft earth until he located bones. He used a numbered yellow forensics tag to mark each spot.

I handed my camera to Detective Rooks. "I need to help unearth and bag the bones. Why don't you stay with Dr. Sanreet and Mr. Patel and photograph the grave sites."

I didn't miss the relieved look on Rooks' face as he accepted the camera.

I counted the paces between burial sites and called out, "Dad it's exactly ten paces from number one to two, and another ten paces between markers two and three. I'm thinking the killer might have kept track of where he'd buried each victim so he'd know where to place the next one."

Dad nodded. "Smart thinking." He squinted up at Draper. "Back track to see if it's ten paces from number four to three. If so, we've got a pattern."

Draper sniffed and nodded, his expression grim. He called out, "Ten paces exactly."

Dressed similar to Vaneeta and Sanjiv, I squatted. Rascal came and lay next to me. I stroked his head. Without warning, he brayed, jumped to his feet, and scampered toward Draper. He latched onto Draper's pants leg and tugged. Draper cursed and drew back his pole.

I rapidly scanned the area and yelled, "Moccasin."

Cottonmouths are in a constant state of PMS. They are aggressive and will not back off and slither away—rather, it has been known for moccasins to seek you and chase you down. Draper was in danger.

A black triangular head swam toward the slip of ground where Draper stood. He unsheathed his .9mm. By this time I had stood and don't even remember leaping forward. I used the tip of my pole to flip the water moccasin up in the air and across the rivulet.

Draper's eyes flitted back and forth, searching for the reptile. "Why the hell didn't you let me shoot it?"

My dislike for Draper increased. "We're trespassing on its territory."

Ignoring his string of expletives, I knelt to continue shifting sludge away from the bones. I scowled up at Draper, who stood as if he were afraid to move, and I hissed a low warning, "Hurt one of my animals, and it won't be moccasins you'll need to watch out for."

Chapter Six

Rasmussen Swamp smelled of life and death at once, an organic jumbling of decay and expectation. Frogs croaked, and each hour grew more blistering hot.

Clouds bunched, then billowed up and drifted away. Some gray tendrils twisted into tight spirals, and the mosquitos continued to hum. Commander Draper apparently took my warning seriously about hurting one of my animals. He uttered a mumbled oath and moved off.

Vaneeta spoke into a hand-held recorder, her voice matter-of-fact. "Jane Doe Number One appears intact, however, is missing a hand."

Without halting work, I called over my shoulder, "It's at Dad's office. It's the one my dog found and prompted this search."

She nodded and used a tape to measure the depth of the grave. Again, speaking into her recorder, she said, "Twenty-four inches."

Sanjiv Patel used gentle back-and-forth sweeps with a soft-bristled brush to remove debris from the skeleton he was working on. "I've marked this site Jane Doe Number Two." He measured the depth of the grave. "This one is also two feet deep." He lifted a femur and examined it before carefully placing it in the box. "Her bones appear to have been in the ground a long time. This is no recent burial."

"How long do you estimate?" I asked.

"Hmm, off the top of my head, I'd say at least ten years, more or less. We'll know for certain once we return to the lab and begin testing."

I did a quick calculation. "This is two thousand nineteen. That means she was buried approximately two thousand nine."

Vaneeta sealed the lid on the box and labeled it Jane Doe Number One and noted the date and time the skeleton was found, along with soil samples and other types of specimens, her name, case name, and number. "Like Sanjiv's, Jane Doe One's bones appear to have been in the ground for quite some time."

Detective Rooks zoomed in on each burial site and clicked pictures at different angles. "One thing I've noticed in these three spots is no remnants of clothing or other objects."

Draper snarked. "Yeah, it doesn't take a genius to figure out that the environment and time took care of that. Right, Dr. Sanreet?"

I sealed the lid on my box and labeled it Jane Doe Number Three and other pertinent information. I never wish anything bad on anyone because karma always comes back to bite you in the butt. At this moment, I'm fighting my subconscious to keep it from willing fate to knock the high-and-mighty Commander Draper off his high horse.

Vaneeta stood and brushed leaves from her knees. "Actually, Commander, the detective has made an excellent observation. It appears that Jane Doe Number One was nude when she was buried." She cast a glance toward her assistant.

Sanjiv concurred, "The same with Number Two."

I watched Draper's face bunch into a snarl. He definitely didn't like being taken down a peg or two. I said, "We won't know for certain until we test the bones for possible fibers. However, it appears that Number Three was also nude."

Dad placed another numbered yellow marker in the ground where my black Lab had discovered another grave. "We're up to six so far."

Vaneeta set her evidence box aside and slogged to marker number four. She breathed deep against the humidity. "I wonder how many more?"

"That's six too many." I stood and stretched the kinks out of my back. "With seasonal changes, plus what wild animals can do with de-fleshing, I'm surprised we found these four intact. If there are more, I hope the bones aren't scattered."

Vaneeta knelt and proceeded to sluff away the muddy area. "That makes two of us."

A stingy breeze wandered through the trees, gently ruffling the reedy grass. Rascal ambled to the edge of a deep dark creek. He snuffled through his nostrils. My eyes followed the little donkey to the water's edge, where a bullfrog hunkered on a lily pad, a common enough sight and a bright spot on an otherwise gruesome day. I watched until the frog disappeared in one quiet, big-legged leap.

Our team worked in silence. Hot wind rattled dead tree limbs like dried bones. I felt drugged by the heat. My skin was itchy and sticky beneath clothes that stuck to me like a second skin. I continued collecting bones from the shallow grave. Judging from the wider subpubic cavity, this victim was also a female. I measured the depth of her grave, and like the others, it measured two feet.

Except for the murder of my mother, never in my life have I been struck with such deep sadness as that shadowing my soul that day. My eyes shifted to Dad, and I wondered if he missed her as much as I. As if he knew I was thinking of him, he swiveled on his knees, and I saw how the loneliness tugged at his eyes. He simply nodded.

Our small group talked softly of different reminiscences, with little laughter, and continued from site to site, labeling boxes that held the bones of six Jane Does. And then we were quiet, concentrating on the tasks at hand. The silence grew, broken only by the sound of our breathing and the incessant hum of mosquitos, until thunderheads piled and pushed against the horizon, opening the skies to tease us with a few droplets of rain.

River had given up his hunt and lay a distance away from me, watching my every move. His black body was coated with mud and leaves. Nearby, Rascal placidly grazed on a patch of grass.

The heavy flapping of wings and maniacal laughter interrupted the afternoon smothered against gray clouds. Rascal loosed a panicked bray. My knees, stiff from squatting in one position, protested when I stood and ran toward my frightened donkey. A large barred owl swooped down, its talons lifting strands of my hair. I batted at the giant raptor. It swooped past. Rascal screamed in panic and pain. With outward stretched hands, I grabbed the owl's leg and pulled with all my strength as the wings beat around my head. Its maniacal squawking continued. The bird had sunk its talons deep into the tiny donkey's back.

Dad rushed to my aide. He snatched his hat from his head and fanned it back and forth against the owl's head, trying to encourage it to let loose its prey. Blood covered my hands. I held tight to the frightened donkey. I lifted my voice and spoke to the bird in Cherokee, asking if it was a witch bringing bad medicine, then telling it that my people believed owls were wise and good and would lead warriors to the enemy. I called upon this giant raptor to spare the life of the donkey, who is also a good spirit animal.

The sky darkened, lightning streaked the sky, and thunder vibrated the earth beneath our feet. The brown barred owl looked me in the eyes, and I swear it winked at me. For a mere second I felt a strange energy emanate from the bird. It squawked its strange squeaky-toy noise, then loosed its talons and spread its massive wings to disappear into the swamp. I cradled the trembling donkey against my chest.

"What the hell kind of place is this?" Stupefaction covered Draper's face.

"I told you it's reputed to be haunted. It's a place filled with spirits, and not all of them good."

"Bah, hogwash."

Warm droplets of rain splatted the already boggy ground. I ignored his comment and said, "Although we still have a couple of hours of daylight left, we'd better head back to the vehicles. That rushing you hear is a storm, and it's coming in fast. We're in for a gullywasher."

We hefted into our backpacks, each grabbed a box, and we hustled toward the vehicles, hoping to outrun the rain. Rascal loosed a bray and stumbled to his knees. Dad said, "Take my box, Tullah. I'll get him."

He set his box of bones on top of mine and then scooped all one hundred pounds of a bloody, frightened animal into his arms.

River trotted at Dad's side, keeping watch on his buddy. Blood dribbled down, staining the side of Dad's pants.

Kentucky had suffered over a year of drought. Frogs croaking and chirping for rain had replaced the hum of mosquitos in many areas. The wind increased and pushed us almost faster than we could walk. Vaneeta lost her balance and struggled to keep from dropping her box. Detective Rooks hooked his hand under her arm and lifted her upright. He held tight, helping her forward. Within seconds, hail the size of golf balls pelted us.

Dad was in excellent physical condition, but sprinting while toting a hundred pounds demanded extra strength. I noticed him flagging under Rascal's weight, and called out, "You can do it, Dad. Ten more feet."

I lifted the cumbersome containers and set my chin on the top box to keep it from sliding while I surged forward to where Dad's 4Runner was parked. I was forever scolding him about leaving the doors unlocked. This was one time I was thankful he had ignored me. I set the boxes on the ground and snatched open the back door. Dad's face was beet red from humidity and exertion. His chest heaved as he sucked deep for a relieving breath. As spent as he was, he gently placed Rascal on the back seat. River jumped in and settled on the floorboard, licking his buddy's puncture wounds. Dad opened the hatch and loaded the boxes of bones.

He shouted above the wind to the others, "Let's get

a move on. We don't want to get stuck in the mud. Follow me."

By the time we reached the barbed-wire gate, hail sounded like bombs beating on the vehicle's metal roof. Dad said, "Take over the wheel. I'll get the gate."

"No, Dad, I can do it." I had barely finished speaking before his boots were on the ground, his shoulders hunched against the pelting ice, and sprinting toward the strands of fence.

The wipers worked overtime clearing the windshield. I climbed over the center console and leaned forward to see through the gloom, inching as close as possible yet giving Dad room to pull the barbed-wire gate wide. As soon as I drove through, I rolled down the window and motioned the others to go ahead. I pulled off to the side so Dad could hop in. I was moving out before he'd slammed the door. The others waited for me to pull around and take the lead.

It seemed the ground had grown rougher and ruts deeper as we bounced along at a snail's pace. My hands ached from gripping the steering wheel. I hadn't realized how tightly I'd held my shoulders until the cattle gate to my property loomed ahead. Once again, Dad hopped out and opened the gate. He stepped on the running board and motioned me toward my office, where Dad lifted the little donkey from the back seat while I unlocked the office door. Vaneeta followed us into the surgery, where Dad laid Rascal on the metal table. Vaneeta stroked the snuffling animal's head. "I can help."

I thanked her for the offer and assured her that I'd manage. "We've all had a long, blistering day. Take advantage of a hot bath and a short rest in a comfortable bed. I don't know how long this hail will last, but the hotel has a snack bar, chips, cookies, that sort of thing. If it slacks off, I'm sure Dad will suggest we all meet at the Whitehorse Saloon."

Dad nodded. "It'll be the Whitehorse for sure, Punkin. I'll give you a call later."

"A saloon?" Vaneeta arched her eyebrows upward.

I smiled. "It's about the only place with a varied menu. Of course, we could go to the Crispy Chicken. Your choices are fried chicken served with a side of grease, tater logs, coleslaw, potato salad, and baked beans. Or, we could go to Sweet's 'n' Eats. The food is excellent, but mostly breakfast fare, light sandwiches, soup of the day, and the yummiest desserts ever."

At her hesitancy, I said, "The owner of the saloon, Charlie Whitehorse, runs a clean kitchen, and makes the best buffalo wings ever. It's not your typical saloon, except on the weekends. You don't need to decide now."

We both laughed when her stomach rumbled. "I think the decision is made. Buffalo wings it is."

A few hours later, the hail had stopped and the skies had opened to quench a thirsty land. Meanwhile, I shaved Rascal's back and belly. The puncture wounds were deep but not life-threatening. The entire time I ministered to the donkey, the Labrador stayed by my side, keeping watch. To prevent my dog from licking off the antibiotic salve, I wrapped Rascal's middle with a sturdy bandage, then made him as comfortable as possible in one of the horse stalls.

The rain eased to a soft, earth-replenishing pitter-patter. I sprinted to the house. My cellphone chirped. "Hi, Dad, I hope you took time to rest."

"You're just like your mother—a worry wart. Yeah, I'm good. The reason I'm calling is to let you know we'll meet at The Whitehorse. You comin'?"

"And miss the fireworks? Not on your life."

I guess he didn't get the joke because my failed attempt at witticism brought a "*Fireworks?*" response.

I explained, "You don't like Commander Draper. Neither does Charlie. It will be interesting to see how the three of you play nice."

"We're lawmen, professionals. We know the rules. We'll play nice."

"If you say so, Dad. I'll see you in an hour."

As soon as I disconnected, I hit speed dial to call Charlie.

"Little Sister, ah-ho. Henry told me about the owl. Are you hurt?"

"Just a few scratches, nothing serious. Charlie, the owl winked at me. I'm taking it as an omen. What do you think?"

"My people believe the owl animal spirit represents a deep connection with wisdom, good judgment, and knowledge. You, like the owl, have sharp vision and keen observation. Even Tanti knows you possess insight and intuition, as did your mother. The owl is letting you know something is about to change."

"For the good or the bad, Charlie?"

"This I do not know. Now, the reason you are calling me is?"

"Yes, about that. Dad has probably already told you we're meeting at The Whitehorse. Dr. Sanreet and her assistant Mr. Patel only eat vegetables and lamb or chicken. I told them you make the world's best buffalo wings. I hope you have plenty in the freezer."

"For my goddaughter, I would travel far and wide to fulfill your wish."

His words warmed my heart. "Charlie, Dad did tell you—"

"About Draper. Yeah. Henry and I will try to leave the past in the past. If anything happens, it's on Draper, not us."

The moment I walked through the doors, Charlie looked up and thumbed toward a door. He said, "They're in the back room. Even though Monday nights are quiet, I understand the need for privacy. No need for a bunch of curious gawkers to get wind of a boneyard and go traipsing about where they're not needed."

"Have you seen him yet—Draper?"

"Nuh-uh. Flora served 'em. I'm trying to stay clear."

I gave this burly, goodhearted man a hug and strolled toward the room set aside for private meetings. He called after me, "Your usual—cola with lemon?"

"You know me too well, Charlie. What's for dessert?"

"Nothing better than chocolate eclairs from Sweet's 'n' Eats."

"How many have you already eaten?"

He belly-laughed as I pointed to my top lip and then to his. He licked the morsel of chocolate. "Don't worry. I left a few."

Inside the room, jovial voices greeted me with a round of concern for my little donkey. Detective Rooks lifted his mug of beer and chugged a healthy swallow. He wiped foam from his mouth with a paper napkin. "I'm here to tell you, I nearly sharted my drawers when I heard that hysterical crying. I was for certain a woman was in agony, and then that owl swooped down from out of nowhere. Never seen anything like it."

Whatever snide remark Commander Draper was about to make was curtailed when Charlie walked in with two large pitchers of beer in each of his beefy hands. Flora followed with a round tray loaded with baskets of piping hot, spicy wings, onion rings, and garden salads.

"Well, as I live and breathe, if it isn't Corporal Whitehorse. Never thought I'd see a war hero wearing an apron." Draper barked out laughter.

Dad blanched. I placed my hand on his arm. My face heated. I knew how Dad felt as I watched him rip the thin, white, paper napkin into shreds with his fingers.

Dad, Charlie, and Draper reminded me of three alpha dogs circling one another with only a thin veneer of civilization protecting the rest of us at the table from a snarling confrontation. Rooks retreated into his mug of beer without saying a word. Charlie and my dad exchanged the merest of glances that spoke volumes. This wasn't the time or the place to draw blood. They seemed to agree, silently, on a truce.

An angry glint darkened Charlie's deep mahogany eyes. I have to give it to my godfather. He didn't spill a drop when he set the heavy pitchers of beer in the middle of the table. He straightened and said, "Corporal Whitehorse ceased to exist when he mustered out of the Army. These days, it's *Mr.* Whitehorse."

"Uh-huh. See you still have the gimpy leg."

Rooks glanced from Draper to Charlie. Maybe the beer had given him a wisp of a backbone. "What's with the digs, Draper?"

The commander leaned forward and refilled his glass. "Just having a little bit of reminiscing fun. No harm done. Ain't that right, Corporal?"

Neither Dad nor Charlie answered. Charlie half-smiled. "You folks need anything else, Flora will get it for you. Ya'll enjoy your meal."

Draper drained his mug and reached for the pitcher. I watched the expression of disgust on each person's face seated around the table. I know Dad doesn't like when I come to his defense. Next to Charlie, he's the manliest man I know, and has the good sense to back away from an unnecessary fight. The way his jaw was working, I wasn't sure he'd walk away if this jackass kept braying.

Draper refilled his mug. He lifted it toward Charlie as he limped toward the kitchen, and said, "Here's to the Noble Savage."

Charlie's shoulders stiffened as he straightened his full six-foot-six frame, his dark hair draped down his broad back. The war cry rattled the glass on the closed door. Beer sloshed over Rooks' face as the startled man jerked his hand upward as he said, "Shit a whiskey."

Vaneeta clasped both hands over her mouth to stifle the scream, and Sanjiv jumped like he'd been shot.

Draper's eyes widened as his hand dropped to where the .9mm rested at his waist. "What the hell…"

I watched Dad's hand grip Draper's wrist. "If I were you, I'd drop the digs. Charlie's sense of humor died a long time ago."

I didn't hide the sarcasm in my voice. "Commander Draper, you've already encountered the unseen dangers of a swamp. With the amount of rain we've had today, we'll all need our wits about us tomorrow. Snakes will be crawling to higher ground—moccasins, rattlers, copperheads. My little donkey won't be there to warn you. Maybe you should call it an early night."

Dad excused himself. "Think I'll see if I can help Charlie in the kitchen."

Vaneeta's hand trembled as she filled her plate with wings. She fanned her mouth against the BBQ's sweet, spicy heat. "You should heed what Tullah says, Commander."

I didn't miss the *what an idiot* smirk she cut me before she consumed another fiery hot deliciousness.

Sanjiv Patel dipped a napkin into his glass of water and wiped his face with trembling hands. "Dr. Holliday, you mentioned earlier that the swamp is haunted. I'm curious to know why."

Draper's eyes shifted toward the kitchen, and I could tell a little shame was lurking there. Except that he was a man of with a huge ego and would never offer an apology.

Chapter Seven

I related the story about Adolph Rasmussen's abusive nature toward his wife and children, and how Greta Rasmussen had apparently been pushed to her limits when she caught her husband dumping the oldest son's dead body down the well.

"According to Dr. Ritter, who was a child at the time and witnessed the incident, Greta lifted her hands toward the heavens and cursed her husband. She supposedly called on the name of the thunder god, Thor, to punish Adolph and to take everything he owned. According to Dr. Ritter, the sky darkened and the earth split apart, swallowing Rasmussen, the house, the barn, animals, and all the trees. It's the only time an earthquake was recorded happening in Kentucky. Afterward, the rain came and kept coming until the place became a swamp. People hereabouts avoid the area due to numerous unexplained lights and sounds, and some say they've seen the old man's ghost. We even had a group of ghost hunters come out with their specialized equipment."

I lifted my cola and slaked the heat from my throat while enjoying another wing.

"Yeah, and what did these so-called ghost hunters find?" Rooks wanted to know.

"Paranormal activity." I left it at that. Those who believe will, and those who are skeptics will never be convinced otherwise.

"Bah." Draper spouted, "Nonsense. Utter nonsense. The only thing I believe in is what I can see, hear, taste, and touch, and my .9mm."

I looked at Rooks. "You say you were assigned to cold cases. What about missing persons or serial killings? Any information that we might tie to the bones we've unearthed?"

The detective rubbed his hands on a napkin and across his mouth. "'Fraid not. The files are in the building's basement. There are wall-to-wall shelves filled with storage boxes stuffed full of cold case files. I wasn't assigned an assistant and found the task of coming up with a way to organize the cases daunting. My expertise is following live clues, not shuffling through paper." Rooks cast a disgruntled look toward his superior. "Whatever progress I could have made was halted when the commander assigned me to accompany him in the field."

Rooks reached to the center of the table and pulled a pitcher of beer to refill his mug. "I assure you and the sheriff that once the team returns to Lexington, going through the cold case files and searching for a connection to these missing women is my first priority. I have six months left to retirement. I hope to make substantial progress." He nodded toward Draper. "I'll also refile my request for an assistant. Maybe another old guy like me with one foot out the door or a retired cop looking for a way to pass the time of day rather than watching television or sitting down at the local cop bar swapping lies about the good ol' days will jump at the opportunity to be useful again."

I didn't know if the deepening purple on Draper's

face was from the spicy hot wings or from being put on the spot by a subordinate. Either way, I gained a new respect for Detective Rooks.

As if to change the subject and to direct the heat away from himself, Draper asked, "How big is this swamp…how many acres, if you will?"

Dad not being there, I answered in his place, "Rasmussen Swamp encompasses about a thousand acres. It spans most of Enigma County and a small portion of Dixie County. As you've seen, part of it abuts my property."

Draper pondered for a moment. "I'm not familiar with Dixie County. Do you know if any habitable land sits in the county, like subdivisions, hunting lodges, or people who prefer solitary living away from neighbors?"

I gave this some thought. "I don't have much occasion to visit Dixie County. Most of my clients live in Enigma. My colleague, Dr. Cooper, covers most of that area. I could ask him." I went on to say, "I've tried to purchase the swamp. However, according to the tax assessor's office, Rasmussen land is still owned by the family, who reside in Denmark. The current Rasmussen owner keeps the taxes paid. Anyone caught squatting on the property would be arrested for trespassing. My dad is pals with the local sheriff in the other county. We'd know if any squatters had been run off over there. That's not to say that druggies don't roost in the swamps once in a while."

"So you're telling me that no one, not even hunters, go on the land? What about religious zealots like voodoo worshipers?"

Draper's question wasn't unreasonable. "If this

were Louisiana, I might say yes. Of course, we can't discount a couple of panicked hunters that burst into Dad's office a couple of years ago swearing up and down they'd seen Bigfoot."

All eyes at the table focused on me as if waiting for me to elaborate. "Upon their insistence, Dad followed the men to where they claimed to have spotted the creature." At this point, I chuckled. "What he found was two empty gallon moonshine jugs. He let the guys off with a warning of what he'd do if he caught them trespassing again."

I shook my head and continued. "Most locals believe in the Rasmussen ghost, and also believe the swamp is a place of evil, and they stay away. Believe what you want, Commander Draper, but strange things do happen there."

Dad returned. "I hate to leave the party. My deputy just called, and we have a situation that needs our attention." He kissed the top of my head. "Why don't you spend the night with Tanti and meet us at Patty's for breakfast in the morning?"

"Thanks, Dad, but I still need to look after my animals. See you around seven?"

He settled his brown felt cowboy hat on his head. "I'll check in with you later."

After Dad left, Flora came in to check on us. Draper ordered a boilermaker. By the time we were ready to call it a night, Draper had consumed several boilermakers and needed help from Rooks and Sanjiv to escort him out of the saloon and into the truck's back seat.

"If I were a cussing person, there are plenty of names on my tongue to call Draper." Vaneeta expressed her displeasure.

I lifted my eyebrows. "What would you call him if you didn't cuss?"

Without hesitation she blurted out, "He's a tick-eating, butt-scratching baboon."

I hooted. "Wow! That's really low down, Vaneeta."

She crooked a smile. "Looks like I'd better hurry before my ride to the hotel leaves without me." She turned back, her face serious. "For what it's worth, I believe you about the swamp being haunted."

I returned to the bar to let Charlie know I was leaving. I hugged him. "I'm proud of you and Dad for holding your tempers tonight. Draper got pretty obnoxious."

"The man's not worth our spit." Charlie walked me to my truck. We said our goodbyes. "May the Great Spirit keep you safe, Little Sister."

On the drive home, I thought about the victims. Dad had served as Enigma's sheriff for thirteen years. He was elected two months after my fourteenth birthday. Back then, I wasn't exactly thrilled to be the daughter of a lawman. At any rate, Dad inherited the former sheriff's secretary, Joyce Williams. With ten years already on the job, Dad figured she was an asset and kept her on. She is also a lifelong resident of Enigma, and there isn't much that gets past her. Although neither of them could recall any missing person cases since Dad's time in office, and neither did my grandmother or Miss Patty, Dad had Joyce searching through all of the closed files, even the ones from before he was elected. So far—nothing. Zilch. Dead end.

I'd been in such deep thought that I surprised myself when I drove into my yard. River raced from the barn to greet me. It was late, and I was feeling the effects of the long day as I strolled to the corral gate and let myself in to check on my donkey. He greeted me with a series of happy brays that sounded like suppressed sneezes.

"Hey, little guy." I squatted and gave him a hug. He followed me through the door that led through the area where I have holding crates for healing animals, and into the surgery. I pulled up a stool and used a pair of surgical scissors to remove the dressing around his abdomen. I was satisfied that the puncture wounds weren't inflamed. I cleaned the area and applied an ample amount of antibiotic salve to the areas while he laid his head in my lap. I scratched between his ears. "You know, with your middle shaved, you look like a stuffed toy that needs a little re-stuffing."

After cleaning the work area and tools, I locked up. It was still early, and my mind was whirling with questions. The dog and donkey followed me to the house. At the kitchen door, River stopped. A low growl rumbled from his chest, and the hackles on his neck were stiff. I looked toward the swamp. Fireflies were doing their nightly dance, and the night creatures were tuning up for their nocturnal serenade.

River growled again—low and deep. I unlocked the door and stood a moment before entering the kitchen. I placed my hand on the dog's head. "I know, River. I feel it too."

Someone or something was watching. Unease fretted the pit of my stomach. I held the door wide enough for the animals to enter. I closed down and locked the doggie door and turned the deadbolt in place. My eyes immediately went to the metal baseball bat leaning in the corner next to the door. The sight of it gave me a little comfort as I walked to the refrigerator and grabbed a bottle of water.

My pets followed me up the stairs and into the bedroom. Although they each have their own bed, for some reason the dog and donkey preferred sharing the same space. As they did each night, they settled at the foot of my bed.

I followed my nightly routine of brushing my teeth, brushing my hair, and pulling on my favorite oversized T-shirt, then grabbing a mystery book. Tonight I scooted against the headboard and opened my laptop. For the next hour, I detailed the events surrounding the location of six shallow graves filled with skeletons of women. I noted the behaviors of Commander Draper. His negative attitude led me to wonder how he obtained such a high position in the KBI, or what political connections got him there.

Dad is a great sheriff and certainly doesn't need my help, though I do respect and appreciate that he values my input. My fingers flew across the keyboard and could barely keep up with the thoughts crowding my brain:

Who are these women?

What do the women share in common?

If the murders took place in the swamp, in what part?

If the murders took place elsewhere, why relocate the bodies of the victims to the swamp?

Why were the bodies buried in shallow graves and ten feet apart?

Why are these cases still open?

And the big question: will we find more bones tomorrow, and how many?

I yawned and rolled the kinks out of my shoulders. Time had flown by, and seven o'clock would come early.

The hands on the clock read after ten. I hadn't heard from Dad, and I was worried. Enigma is generally a sleepy little town where serious crime doesn't happen. Dad hadn't said why he had to leave dinner tonight. It's unusual for Deputy Goodbody to need his assistance.

I set the laptop aside and turned out the lamp. For a little self-reassurance, I reached under the pillow next to mine. My fingers touch the handle of my Glock. I had barely closed my eyes when my cellphone chimed to signal that I had received a text message. I hoped it was from Dad. I was saddened when I read his text—*Some teenage boy decided to sprout wings and sail off the fire tower. Details pending. See you in the morning.*

I answered with a sad face emoji. The fire tower is at least one hundred twenty feet high and has been abandoned for years. It's rickety, dangerous, and a hangout place where kids go to smoke dope, make out, and get stupid. Dad has No Trespassing signs posted, which are ignored. Deputy Goodbody does periodic drive-bys to run the kids off and issue warnings, which are ignored. In the bone of my bones I knew there was a fatality. The question is—which foolish teenager would not celebrate another birthday?

Chapter Eight

What a way to begin the day. Sad news is never good news. Dad explained that in order to be initiated into the Boodle Street Dudes Club, fifteen-year-old Elijah Tibbets had to not only climb to the top of the tower, he had to climb on top of the roof—blindfolded.

Dad's knuckles were white from gripping the steering wheel as he explained about the incident at the fire tower last night. "Elijah never made it to the top. According to the other boys, about half way up, one of the rungs broke. Being blindfolded, apparently Elijah panicked and let go of the rail to snatch off the blindfold. He lost his handhold and footing and fell. He suffered a brain injury and most of the bones in his body were broken. His parents are pretty torn up over it."

"That tower should have come down years ago, Dad." I know how dangerous the tower is. I climbed it when I was young and dumb. Complaints from Dad and parents to the forestry department have fallen on deaf ears.

"It's coming down. I got wind that Elijah's father and a group of men plan to pull it down tonight."

"Are you going to stop them?"

He kept his eyes on the weedy ruts as we bounced toward our destination. "Nope. Officially, I don't know a thing about it, and neither does Tiny." He cut his eyes toward me. " Or you."

I made a *My lips are sealed* gesture. "Do you think the forestry department will take action against the men?"

"For what, destruction of an unusable, decaying structure that for all practical purposes was abandoned more than twenty years ago and is now the instrument of a second fatality? If they do decide to take action, I'm sure Mike Duvall will intercede."

Judge Duvall was known as a fair-minded, honest judge, tough on crime. It wouldn't make a hill of beans difference to him that the boys were officially trespassing. What would matter was that a young man would never celebrate another birthday, never graduate from high school. Judge Duvall knew firsthand what it was like to lose an only child who tried to climb the tower.

The night's rain had done little to cool the morning. In fact, I felt like I was standing in a sauna, and we hadn't even entered the swamp's interior yet. Commander Draper pulled a bottle of aspirin from his pocket. He swallowed two. He guffawed. "Got a whale of a headache. A little too much of the hair of the dog at dinner last night."

No one commented. Instead we tended our gear. I felt little remorse for this obnoxiously arrogant man. After hearing the news of young Elijah Tibbets' death, I was in no mood for Draper's nonsense. The hairs on the back of my neck prickled. A low growl rumbled from River's chest. He sidled against my leg.

Rooks' eyes darted back and forth. "Dr. Holliday, does your dog know something we don't?"

"Whatever it is, he'll let us know." I slipped my

arms through the backpack's shoulder straps and followed Dad. The others trailed in single file. It didn't take long before we were wading calf deep in dark, grassy water. I was thankful for my thigh-high boots and walking pole. We stopped at where we thought we'd left yesterday's marker.

"Isn't this where we left marker number one?" I gazed down at the indention filled with muddy water. The yellow marker was gone.

Sanjiv Patel said, "I'll go back and count off the steps." He glanced around. "With all the water from last night's rain we may have missed it, or an animal might have carried it off."

He walked back to the edge of the swamp and paced forward counting aloud. "Two hundred." He used his pole to point. "It should be right here."

I studied the area. "The water is too deep and grassy. Like Sanjiv said, maybe an animal toted it off, or if it floated out of the ground we'll spot it sooner or later."

We counted off another ten steps and stopped. "This is a mystery," I said. "Marker number two should be right about here." Instead, we were met with another shallow impression that swirled with muddy water and grass.

I looked toward the dark and uninviting jungle that seemed to beckon me. My heart beat faster and my legs twitched as if waiting for me to take flight. I knew an animal didn't take the markers, just as I knew that whoever was watching me last night was out there, waiting.

We'd barely entered the swamp when Draper lamented, "How do we know today isn't a wild goose chase?" A smack against flesh and a curse indicated he'd slapped a mosquito.

"Yeah," Rooks spoke up. "Who's to say there are more bodies?"

River loosed a series of throaty woofs and stood rigid, gazing toward the dark interior. I followed his line of sight, and pointed. Perched high on the top of a dead tree sat a barred owl. I wondered if it was the one from yesterday. I pointed skyward. "There's your answer, Detective. The owl will tell us."

Draper ridiculed. "You know, Henry, I think your girl is daft." He smirked at me. "No offense, of course, *Doctor*."

Vaneeta came to stand next to me. "You would do well not to scoff at that of which you have little knowledge, Commander. In our country, the people believe that animals may contain the souls of their ancestors and may come back reborn as friends and family members."

Sanjiv Patel adjusted the sunglasses that had slid down his nose. "Yes, that is so, Dr. Sanreet. I trust Dr. Holliday and her belief that the owl will lead us to more bodies."

Draper removed the small bottle from his pocket and downed two more aspirin. "Bah, all of you are nuts."

The great raptor spread its wings and soared. I stooped to cover the black Lab with my body to avoid a repeat of yesterday's attack. The owl extended its talons and swooped to snatch the red ball cap from my head. The breath of its wings fanned my face, and then it ascended upward and circled over the center of the swamp. We listened as its wings flapped the air. It opened its talons and my cap fluttered downward, out of sight.

Clad in jeans and boots, Detective Rooks had dressed more appropriately for today's excursion. He said with a little chuckle that came out as a groan, "I'm city born and bred, and worked some of the toughest hoods in Chicago. I've dodged a lot of bullets to get to retirement age, and I'm not anxious to die in a swamp. Let's get the job done and get the hell outta here."

I loosed River and watched him scamper toward the deepest edge of the marsh. "Go find 'em, River." He stopped and looked back at me. Without speaking, I motioned him with my hand, letting him know we would follow.

Dad had kept silent. Still, I knew by the way his jaw worked that Draper was getting under his skin. He cautioned, "Use your poles to keep your footing."

My mind filled with questions, like how in the world did an arrogant fool like Draper rise to the position of Commander of the Kentucky Bureau of Investigation? And why was a city detective from Chicago transferred to the KBI mere months away from his retirement? Would I ever know the answers to these questions, and did I really care?

The farther we hiked, the darker the swamp grew and the higher the water crept up our boots, until we came to an abyss shaped like an eye. I stood there a long time staring at the hole and wondering what it was thinking of me. I could feel the words creeping into my head, my mind, words that weren't my own. I thought about love and heartbreaks, and desperate passions, and wondered if emotions were like honeysuckle in late August—sad and sweet, hopeful and tragic.

"Punkin, you okay?" Dad touched my arm. His voice was gentle and filled with disquiet.

My voice failed me, and I tried again. "Messages from the dead are given to us on the wings of an owl." I pointed my pole toward the dark eye. "This is where the earth opened and swallowed Adolph Rasmussen and his son Dolphy. It's been over eighty years, yet somehow I know their bones rest at the bottom of this endless pit."

"Then may they rest in peace."

Without looking at him, I said, "That's just it, Dad. There is no peace in this place."

River's wild yips, a loud splash, and a string of frantic profanity, followed by a plea for help jarred me out of my doldrums. We slogged around the eye's perimeter and through tangles of underwater grass that threatened to hold us captive.

Dad yelled, "Draper, where are you?"

"Here...I'm here. I can't get a handhold." Commander Draper clawed at a slick, muddy bank. Dad dropped to his knees and extended his pole toward the floundering cop. Draper latched on. Inwardly, my smarty-pants voice was cheering *woohoo, karma strikes.*

Rooks and I rushed to grab Draper by the arms and hauled him out of the murky water littered with lily pads. Draper rolled to his side and up to his knees. He sputtered, "I saw a flash of red and thought it was your cap. I was standing close to the edge when the bank gave way and dumped me in the drink." He rubbed both hands over his face to clear away the water. "Damn stuff smells like vomit."

We looked to where he pointed and saw nothing. River yipped. He trotted off. We waited while Draper emptied water out of his boots. It was the dog's baying that set us out at a brisk walk. Not more than fifty feet away, my red ball cap lay next to a tupelo tree. The owl and my Labrador retriever had not failed us.

Dad squatted. Apparently the rain had pushed away several layers of debris to reveal a series of mud-covered bones. From the scattering, it appeared the site had long ago been disturbed and animals had foraged on the deceased. The ribcage had been pulled apart, and an arm and hand were missing, as was the skull. The pelvic bone, a leg, and both feet remained. I bit back the remorse and said, "Who would've wanted to do such a thing to all these women, and why?"

Draper harrumphed. "Presuming it was a woman. Maybe it's a man."

Vaneeta knelt beside me. She lifted the pelvic bone. "It's definitely a woman. Without the skull, we may never know who she was."

Rooks exclaimed, "That makes seven. I wonder if the bodies were planted here or if they were killed here?"

At least the detective and I were on the same wavelength. He expressed one of the thoughts I'd written in my case journal last night.

Sanjiv opened his backpack and began the routine of processing the bones and collecting muddy soil samples around it. "Once the forensic entomologist tests the earth and the insects in the soil, we may be able to answer that question, Detective."

River very proudly loped up and deposited his trophy. He sat and waggled his tail, waiting for me to accept the prize and reward him with a pat on the head and one of the doggie treats he knew I kept in my pocket. I rewarded him with two treats and a hug, then placed my red cap on top of my head.

"Dad, Vaneeta!" I held the bone as if it were a precious treasure. "Whoever she was broke her arm and has a rod in the humerus."

"Yeah, so?" Detective Rooks pulled a handkerchief from his pocket to wipe his sweaty face.

I explained to Rooks that just like dental fillings are numbered and placed in a database, so are metal rods and other orthopedic appliances. "It will take maybe six to eight weeks to identify this woman. Hopefully, the bones will give us more evidence, and Vaneeta and her team will be able to determine each woman's age, height, and approximate weight."

Vaneeta squatted there as if it was the only thing she had the energy for. "Yes, and we may also be able to determine how each of them was murdered. Also, with today's advancements in technology, we may employ a forensics sculptor to use three-dimensional reconstruction to recreate the faces, which will further aid in identification." She removed a bottle of water from her backpack and splashed her face, then drank deep.

By dusk, River had sniffed out four more graves. Eleven, all totaled. It was almost as if he knew there were no more to be found. He trotted toward where we had left the vehicles. We gathered our equipment and the boxes of bones and followed. At the edge of the swamp where we had located the first set of bones, I looked back in the distance and thought about how easy it was to lose a body in this watery quagmire, how quickly the scavengers and the weather could dispose of it. A wave of sadness and weariness overtook me. I drew in a deep breath.

When my mother had died and we identified her body, the detective in charge of her case had commented as if he didn't care about her—if nobody remembers you, were you ever really here?

I would never forget my mother, and I made a silent promise to not forget these women, to make certain they were returned to their loved ones. Despite the success of our discoveries, a wave of exhaustion settled over me as I toted my box of bones to Dad's 4Runner.

Propping against the door, I inhaled the scent of this place of death, and the strong earthy odor of low-slung clouds. It would rain again tonight.

From the corner of my eye, I thought I saw something move, and cocked my head toward a sound. Probably the owl again, I thought, and wondered if it was delivering another message. The others heard it too.

Rooks said, "This place gives me the willies."

Was it sobbing we heard, the wind whiffling through the trees, or our imaginations? Thunder rumbled in the distance. Lightning fingered across the sky. It was close. Another strike followed by another, and a quick succession of thunderous claps.

Draper stood next to his truck. He said, "Henry, I'm skipping dinner and heading straight for the sack. Where's a good place for breakfast?"

Dad answered the question and asked about Rooks.

Draper glanced at the detective, who was already inside the truck. Draper relayed the answer. "Says it's too hot to eat heavy. He'd like anything light."

Dad glanced over at me. "What about you?"

"Tell Rooks to meet us at Sweet's 'n' Eats and to relay that to Vaneeta and Sanjiv."

I whistled River into the back seat, then climbed in the front and waited for Dad. I had the sensation someone had just walked over my grave, and I rubbed the prickles on my arm.

Dad slammed the door and started the ignition. "You okay, Punkin?"

"I don't know. It feels like someone is watching us. Strange, but I had the same sensation last night just before I entered the house." I shook myself. "Probably my imagination."

"Imagination or not, keep River and Rascal in the house with you, and the revolver within hand's reach. I'd prefer it if you'd stay in town with Tanti until we know who or what we're dealing with."

I reach over and patted his arm. "Can't. I have a clinic to run."

I told him about Deputy Goodbody's niece. "She's coming Saturday for an interview. I sure hope she's capable. I need a good assistant."

He shifted into gear. "Do you plan to offer her the trailer—same as you did for Cindi?"

I considered his question. "I've given it thought. She might prefer to live with her mother, especially since they're new to Enigma."

"I'd feel a lot easier knowing you weren't out here alone. You could move the clinic to town."

I scoffed. "Dad, I'm only twenty minutes away. It's not like I live in the boonies. Besides, I need the space for my livestock and possible overnight patients."

"Uh-huh, and your nearest neighbor is five miles down the road and never answers his telephone. Sure gives me a lot of comfort." I didn't miss the trace of sarcasm.

We rode the rest of the way in silence. There was no need to let the stress of the past few days incite an unnecessary argument.

Chapter Nine

We rode in silence. When we entered my yard, Draper and Vaneeta stuck their arms out their vehicle's window, waved goodbye, and continued toward the highway and back to the hotel.

Dad and I had both been lost in our own thoughts until the radio crackled. He lifted the mic.

"Go ahead, Tiny."

Static

"We have a ten-sixteen, Henry. I'm responding now."

Static

"What's your twenty?"

Static

"Heading toward the Vickers' residence."

"I'm on my way. Don't go in alone."

"Roger that, Henry."

Dad replaced the mic.

I blurted, "Isn't Lonnie Vickers on parole?"

"Not after today."

My dad jammed the brakes and shifted the 4Runner into neutral. I opened the door and hopped out. River followed. "Be careful, Dad."

"I'll touch base with you once we've got Vickers in custody." He winked at me and sped off.

What I really wanted was lingering in a cold shower before a long, uninterrupted nap without seeing skulls with worms crawling out of the eye sockets. Instead, I checked in with my answering service, then tended the still-healing punctures on my little donkey, fed the horses, and mucked out the stalls.

Later that evening, I met Vaneeta at the café and was surprised to see her sitting alone. "Where's Sanjiv and Rooks?"

"The owner, Miss Patty, said your favorite was unsweet tea with lemon. I took the liberty of ordering." She stirred the ice in her tall glass. "Sanjiv and Rooks ordered sandwiches and donuts to take back to the hotel. They're both pretty spent."

"I know the feeling. It's been a hot and stressful two days. I'll understand if you'd like to take your food to go, too. What time are you leaving in the morning?"

She didn't seem to be in a hurry and said, "Right after breakfast." In spite of the air conditioning, she fanned herself. "It's almost too hot to eat. What's good here?"

"Best chilled cucumber soup in the state, with a side of shrimp salad, a buttered croissant, and topped off with chunks of ice cold watermelon."

Vaneeta leaned forward on her elbows. "Sounds delightful."

We placed our orders, and while we waited, Patty brought us a bowl of Cajun boiled peanuts to enjoy. "Here's a different kind of heat to jazz up your taste buds." She refilled our glasses.

Vaneeta opened a shell and popped the peanuts into her mouth. "Tullah, you were a genius in forensics. I can't believe you gave it up to become a veterinarian, and in a small town."

Before I could react, she held up her hand like a

stop signal. "No offense, Tullah. You're my friend, and I'd never insult you. I'm just puzzled."

I opened a peanut and savored the hot, salty goodness while I considered my answer. It was the longest silence of the conversation. I sat there rife with emotions. "Something changed after my mother's death. Every time I looked at a dead body or performed an autopsy, all I could see was her. Her murder was a bad time for all of us. My dad and my grandmother needed me as much as I needed to be with them."

I flashed back to the chemical- and ammonia-filled lab and cadavers covered with white sheets. The answer was easy. "I love animals, so it was only natural that I followed the path to veterinary medicine. Besides, Vaneeta, I hated living in the city, where there was no quiet, no fresh air, and life centered around the hands on a clock."

Vaneeta grinned as she snatched the last boiled peanut from the bowl. "Sometimes I dream of my village and its serenity. But, unlike you, I would not return."

Patty delivered our food. She kept her voice hushed. "Is it true about all the skeletons being women?"

I lifted my eyebrows. "Word travels fast in a small town. Yes, ma'am. It's true." And then I had a thought. "Patty, you've lived in Enigma your entire life. Do you remember any serial killings here or in a surrounding county, or a large number of women reported missing?"

"Tanti and I were discussing that very thing, last night, especially with her being a retired crime reporter. Tanti has a memory like an elephant." Patty swatted at a wayward fly. "Nope, it's a mystery." She waved the air again. "Dratted flies come in every time the door is opened." She added, "I hope this doesn't mean we need to put extra locks on our doors, especially at night."

I assured her that with Dad and Tiny on the job and on a call even now, the county was safe. Patty flashed a dimpled grin. "Enjoy your meal. And Dr. Sanreet, maybe your next visit will be a lot more pleasant."

Vaneeta purred her appreciation over each spoonful of chilled soup. She thanked Patty and said to me, "I hope the call your dad and his deputy took isn't dangerous."

"Lonnie Vickers is a repeat..." My voice trailed off. "Holy cow, Vaneeta, I just remembered that Lonnie Vickers served time for nearly beating a woman to death, and he's out on parole. In fact, that's where Dad and Deputy Goodbody are now, on a domestic violence call."

Her eyes widened. "You don't suppose this Vickers has a connection to the victims we found, do you? I mean, they are—were—all women."

"As soon as Dad returns, I'll make sure to mention this to him."

For the next hour, we discussed if the murders took place in the swamp, and if so which part, or if the murders took place elsewhere, but then why relocate the bodies to the swamp, and why were they placed ten feet apart except for the last five being scattered.

And then our conversation drifted to Commander Draper. "Are you and your department permanently attached to Draper?" I inquired.

As if her fingers had a memory of their own, Vaneeta folded her napkin into the shape of a bird. "No, we're not. I loathe the man. Rumors keep cropping up that he's retiring. So far, that's all it is—rumors. He definitely dug deep into your dad's friend the other night. What was that about?"

I gave her a brief lowdown about Draper being Dad and Charlie's drill sergeant during basic training and how his incompetent leadership during a battle cost a lot of good men their lives. "He was responsible for Charlie nearly losing his life."

"In my country, we call people like him a *Badamāśa*, a ruffian, which is putting it nicely. Draper is not a nice man. Anyone who lodges a complaint against him suddenly finds himself or herself with charges against them—falsified, of course. Thankfully, he's not my boss."

I steepled my fingers and used them to support my chin. "The governor is Draper's boss. My dad and the governor attended the same college and played on the same football team."

"Why are you smiling like the canary that just swallowed a cat? Tul-lah!"

"Let's just say that what you don't know won't hurt you. What time are you leaving in the morning?"

"Sanjiv and I plan to get on the road early—no later than seven. We've both agreed to make identifying the victims our top priority."

"You will keep me posted?"

"You and your father will know before Draper. This I promise." She dug around in her purse for a notepad and pen. "Write down your email address." She also handed me her business card and said, "Contact me anytime."

Patty trundled over. "More watermelon, or how about tea and a lemon wafer?"

We opted for refills on our iced tea.

The little bell over the door jingled. Patty whispered, "Oh, my lands, it's that poor Ms. Lampson, and sporting a black eye. I don't know why in the world she doesn't put that boy of hers in an institution. Excuse me." She hurried behind the counter.

"What can I get you, Ms. Lampson?"

A hunch-shouldered woman with white hair that reminded me of wind-blown straw, her hands gnarled from rheumatism, approached the counter. I offered a smile when she glanced over at me. She touched her bruised cheek and lowered her eyes to the donut case. "I'll take the last two glazed and ten more."

Patty Sweet said, "Oh, I'm sorry, Edna. I'm all out of glazed. We won't have more until in the morning. I could make you up a dozen assorted—chocolate, cinnamon, and powdered sugar."

The pitch of Edna Lampson's voice reminded me of a frightened bird. "Oh, dear, this won't do. Junior only likes glazed. He'll get upset." She touched her cheek again.

Patty gave me an imploring look. I stood and said, "Why don't I run down to the grocery store. Maybe Pete has a box of glazed."

Her eyes the size and color of old pennies, Ms. Lampson wrung her hand together. "That won't do. Junior will know the difference."

"What if we put them in one of Miss Patty's boxes? Will that work?"

Patty pulled one of her signature boxes from a shelf. "Great idea, Tullah."

I grabbed my purse. "I'll pay for supper when I return."

"Don't worry about it, Tullah, my treat." Vaneeta also stood. "Besides, I'm calling it a night. I'll touch base with you in about six weeks, or as soon as I have the information we need."

I waved and hurried outside, thankful that Vaneeta had been discreet in what kind of information she would send me. By the time I returned with a box of glazed donuts, Vaneeta was gone. Patty transferred the dozen treats to one of her boxes. She also refused to accept money from Edna Lampson.

Edna walked like a woman in physical pain. If her feet were as deformed as her hands, I could understand why. But then, maybe her eye wasn't the only part of her body that was bruised. It was well-known that her son, Junior, was mentally unbalanced, and Edna still worked at the pharmacy even though she was past retirement age.

Patty sat down and lifted her feet to rest on a chair. "I can't imagine what it's like for Edna, raising that boy without a father. And no one to take him in hand when he gets out of control." She shook her head. "Sad case. She's almost seventy, you know."

"When I was in the first grade, I remember, he liked to pick on the younger kids. We were all afraid of him. Then one day he was gone. We heard he had quit school. Of course, I was too young to know that a twelve-year-old couldn't quit school. It's been years since I've seen him."

"Your mother was livid the day he knocked you down and called you ugly names."

I shut my eyes, recalling that day. "I was certain he was going to twist my arm off."

Patty went on to say, "Junior Lampson is a hulking

monster. Over six feet tall and built like a prize fighter. Edna would never admit that he abuses her. She'd be afraid the authorities would take Junior away from her if she complained about him."

"I don't understand. Why would she want to live in fear?"

"Because sometimes being alone and lonely is worse than living with a monster."

"If you say so, Patty."

I made a mental note to find out more about Junior Lampson. Did he have an arrest record?

"Box up a dozen lemon wafers if you have any left? I think I'll surprise Grandmother before I go home tonight."

I accepted the box of cookies from Patty and strolled down the sidewalk to my grandmother's apartment and rang the doorbell. I held the box forward when she opened the door. "Your favorite."

She accepted the small box and sniffed. "Which favorite? You know I have many."

We laughed because for both my grandmother and me anything sweet tends to be our favorite. She said, "You came bearing gifts because—?"

"Because I love you or maybe because I love you and want to pick your brain."

"You can pick my brain if you'll tell me about the bodies." She opened the box and lifted a cookie. "I'll put the coffee on."

"I'd prefer ice water. The humidity in the swamp sapped me dry." I sat in my favorite chair, kicked off my boots, wiggled my toes, and tucked my legs under me. Grandmother handed me a tall glass filled with ice. I drank deep.

"The only thing I can tell you right now is that we found eleven skeletons. Most of them were intact, and due to the wider subpubic angle we've determined all the victims were women." I also filled Grandmother in about the strange behavior of the owl.

She nibbled on a second cookie. "Owls are good spirit creatures. I am glad it was there to show you the way. Tell me more."

"Dr. Sanreet is certain some of the victims were buried more than ten years ago. I think we can safely assume these women were killed by the same person. I'm just puzzled as to why he's never been caught."

Grandmother lifted her eyebrows. "Maybe the killer isn't a man." She shrugged. "If she were strong enough, it could be a woman."

"A woman? Hmm, anything is possible. What would be her motive?"

"Jealousy, lust, revenge, insanity—only the killer knows."

"Grandmother, as a former crime reporter, don't you think it's strange that eleven missing women didn't make all the media headlines?"

Grandmother glanced at me with a raised eyebrow. "Good point, unless the murders were spaced far enough apart that no one would take notice."

"Smart thinking. Any other reason you can think of?"

Grandmother seemed to mull over the question. "There are times when a missing person is found and the authorities are never informed. When this happens, the case remains open and is considered unsolved. Of course, we'll need to practice patience. I'm as much on pins and needles as you are, Granddaughter, about why these missing women never made headlines, especially since there are so many of them."

The whole thing was incredibly disturbing. I wasn't sure why I felt irritated. I stared through the open slatted blinds and watched a yellow butterfly dance over a bed of red geraniums.

Grandmother snapped her fingers. "Tullah, where did you go?"

I hoped my voice didn't sound weary, or condescendingly patient. "Visiting Neverland, I suppose."

She seemingly ignored my comment and said, "I'm almost finished with the article I'm writing. With Kentucky Bureau of Investigations and Kentucky Forensics printed on the doors of shiny black vehicles, people are already asking questions."

I leaned down to tug on my boots. I related about Ms. Lampson's black eye and the donuts. "What do you remember about her son?"

"Junior? Now, there's a case for you." Tanti sighed as she settled in her chair. "Edna was a victim of a brutal attack which left her pregnant and unmarried. The men went to prison. As I recall, two of them died there, and I think the other one is still serving time. Paul Ritter delivered the baby. He tried to convince Edna to give the infant up for adoption. Apparently, it was obvious something wasn't right with the child. Edna adamantly refused.

"Unfortunately, Junior stayed in all kinds of trouble to the point that to keep him from being sent away she withdrew him from school, saying she would homeschool him. Sadly, it didn't solve the problem."

I leaned forward. "What kind of trouble?"

"Oh, it was horrible, Tullah. He liked to hurt things, animals and people. As I recall, the final straw came when he attacked his sixth grade teacher, Julia Hansen. Edna was beside herself when he was sent to the juvenile justice facility. She sold the family's old home place and moved to Dixie County, even though it's about a thirty-minute drive to Enigma."

"She works at the pharmacy, doesn't she?"

"Yes, as a pharmacy tech. It's too bad an intelligent woman like her birthed an emotionally disturbed child. Maybe it was due to the beating she took, or maybe he inherited bad genes from the monsters that hurt her."

I rubbed my shoulder as if I could still feel the painful grinding of bone as Junior twisted my arm. "I haven't seen him since I was a child."

"Oh, she doesn't bring him to town. At least not in Enigma. But, yes, I saw him a few times before she moved them away. He was about twelve years old. Even at that early age he was over six feet tall, with extra-long arms, drooping eyes, and a tongue that seemed too big for his mouth." Tanti wrapped her arms around herself and shuddered. "Creepy."

I weighed Grandmother's words and wondered if Junior Lampson was capable of committing murder. I decided to keep this thought to myself. I adore my grandmother and have no desire to ignite her reporter's curiosity—and possibly put her in danger.

I redirected my thoughts and told her about Ella Sanders. "She's coming out tomorrow for an interview. I'm so overwhelmed with work that it almost doesn't matter if she's inexperienced. If she's truly interested in the position, I'll hire her on the spot."

Grandmother collected our glasses and placed them

in the dishwasher. "If she's anything like her Uncle Tiny, you can bet she's reliable. Are you going to offer her the trailer?"

I laughed. "Dad asked the very same thing. If the timing is right, I will. However, she may prefer living with her mother."

"Pshaw, what young woman doesn't want to spread her wings and live on her own?" She waggled her finger at me. "You did."

I kissed her on the cheek and opened the door. "Point taken, Grandmother."

"Tullah…" Grandmother's voice was serious. "I'd feel better knowing you weren't out there alone."

"Geesh, Grandmother! What is it with you and Dad? I was born on the ranch. Except for a few years, I've lived there my entire life. Until the unfortunate incident with Earl Redfern, there was no reason for you or Dad to worry about my safety."

"Of course. Forgive Henry and me for *loving* you too much."

The tears behind the worry in her ebony eyes made me ashamed of my abruptness. My mother's murder was ever present in her mind. I hugged her. "I'm sorry, Grandmother. I don't mean to worry you. I'll offer Ella the trailer as part of her income. That's the best I can do."

Grandmother smiled and shut the door behind me. On the drive home, my cellphone chirped. "Dr. Holliday."

A hesitant voice responded, "Hi, this is Ella Sanders."

My heart sank. Surely she wasn't calling to say she'd changed her mind about the interview. I returned her greeting. "Are you and your mother getting settled in?"

"We are. Thank you for asking."

Silence.

"Ella, if you've changed your mind about interviewing for the position, I'll totally understand."

"Oh, no, Dr. Holliday, I'm calling to confirm our appointment."

Whew! I felt like I'd dodged a bullet. "Nine o'clock. And Ella, dress casual. Jeans and shirt will do. I'm not a stickler for business attire."

"Great. I'll bring my diploma and a list of my intern experiences. Uncle Tiny speaks really highly of you."

"That's good to know. We consider your uncle part of our family."

We ended the call. My thoughts flittered to Edna Lampson's black eye. I made a mental note to create a list of possible murder suspects with Junior Lampson and Lonnie Vickers as the top two contenders.

Chapter Ten

Ella Sanders is not what I expected, and the exact opposite of her Uncle Tiny, a giant of a man. Blonde hair worn in a short bob, a face covered with freckles and minimum makeup, and about my height, tall. I always use the eyes and body language as my barometer for judgment, whether it's an animal or a human. William Shakespeare once said the eyes are the windows to your soul. I believe the measure of any being's emotions and thoughts can be ascertained through the eyes, and by their body language.

What I saw in Ella's navy blues was honesty, determination, and stubbornness. Today her shoulders were a bit rigid, and her hands were fluttery. This was only natural because she was interviewing for a job. I remember how nervous I was when I interviewed for my first position as a forensics technician. I decided to keep it relaxed as I introduced her to River and Rascal and invited her to the clinic to show her the office, the examination room, the surgery, and where I keep the post-op patients, all the while asking questions about her qualifications and why she decided to follow her mother to a small town as opposed to remaining in Texas. I also led her through a rear door that exited into the barn and stalls where I keep my horses and the long aisle that opened to the corral.

Ella stopped to rub the nose of Gandalf, a black-

and-white gelding. I explained that he was my mother's horse. I also introduced her to Banjo and Moon. "I understand you trailered your horse all the way from Texas. How is he?"

Ella followed me down the aisle, stopping to pat the pinto and the appaloosa. "His name is Jupiter. He made the trip better than I expected. Mom and I stopped often to give him a break from standing in the trailer."

"Is he strictly for pleasure, or do you run barrels with him?"

Her eyes lit, and a smile beamed across her lips. "Jupiter is a great barrel horse. I was a member of the university rodeo team." I saw that she was trying to tone down her smile when she added, "We did win a few championships."

I added my own enthusiasm by telling her about the annual 4-H festival. "It's held at the end of every September. We hold a junior rodeo and one for the adults. Maybe you'll compete this year."

"With the move and getting settled, I'm not sure we'll have time to get ready. I'll give it some thought."

By this time we'd walked outside, and she asked about the travel trailer. "Uncle Tiny said your former assistant lived in the trailer and that she left to finish her degree. Even though you haven't said anything about whether or not you're considering me for the position, I want you to know that I'm not interested in becoming a full-fledged veterinarian." She gave a half-chuckle. "My mom grilled me thoroughly when I told her I wanted to come to Enigma with her. She presented every reason why I should stay in Texas." Ella ticked off the reasons on her fingers, "Job opportunity, pay scale, boredom"—she rolled her eyes—"dating. You know, all that worry-wart Mom stuff."

"I totally understand. Do you drink coffee?"

"Yes, ma'am. I sure do."

"It's cooler in the house. C'mon, I'll make us a pot. Oh, and dispense with the 'yes, ma'am.' Makes me feel old."

"If you don't mind my asking, you seem young to already have an established practice. How old are you?" She flashed an *oops* crooked smile. "Sorry, it just popped out."

"I don't mind at all, Ella. In fact, I hope we'll become friends and that you'll feel free to ask me anything." I drew in a breath and exhaled. "In a few weeks I'll celebrate my twenty-ninth birthday. As for the practice, it was sort of the right time and place to happen."

As I prepared the coffeemaker, I explained that I'd completed a double major in forensic science and veterinary medicine and had actually worked as a forensics technician. "After my mother's death I decided to leave Lexington and return home to be closer to my dad and my grandmother, and I took advantage of the fact that Enigma didn't have a veterinarian and opened my practice."

I removed oatmeal raisin cookies from my favorite horsehead cookie jar and set them on a plate, then filled our mugs. "Cream and sugar?"

"Black."

"About the trailer, if you decide to take the position, why wouldn't you want to live in town with your mother as opposed to living out here?"

Ella dipped a cookie in her coffee and took a bite. "I love my mother dearly. She's my best friend in the world. With that being said, she works long hours and needs to rest on her days off. She tends to forget that I'm twenty-three, and she still wants to smother me. I'm not sure I'm answering your question." She sighed. "I guess the bottom line is that with my father gone, we both need our independence. Mom thinks she's being brave by not grieving, especially in front of me. I guess we're both trying to be strong for each other, when what we're really doing is tiptoeing around each other on eggshells. Does that make sense?"

I suppose this is why I refused to move my practice to town, and why Grandmother prefers living alone in her apartment, and why Dad converted an old space above his office into living quarters. We all needed our freedom. "I do understand, Ella. For the record, the job is yours."

She clapped her hands together and heaved a sigh as if a huge weight had been lifted. "I hesitate to ask…" Her voice trailed off.

My first inclination was that she needed an advance on her pay. I was wrong. "Ask away."

"Uncle Tiny's pasture is only an acre. Not much more than a back yard. Do you mind if I bring Jupiter out here?" She hastened on. "I'll pay board, or you can deduct it from my salary."

I held up my hand. "Whoa. First, yes, you're welcome to bring Jupiter here, and secondly, all you need to do is tend to his upkeep and feed. It'll be nice to have someone to go riding with. That is, when we have the time." I went on to explain that sometimes we have emergencies that keep us up late, and those happen even on the weekends. "We're not much different from your mom when it comes to patients."

We finished our coffee. She asked, "How soon can I start moving into the trailer?"

"Today, if you like. Wouldn't you like to see it before you definitely decide?"

"I suppose, though my mind is made up."

We walked outside, my pets following. Ella said, "I think it's cool that you have a donkey for a house pet. From those puncture wounds, I'd guess either an eagle or a hawk."

"Pretty close. A barred owl." I didn't think it prudent at this point to mention the circumstances of the attack. I'd let her get acclimated before explaining that on occasion I work with my dad solving a case.

I needn't have concerned myself because she beat me to it. "Uncle Tiny says that you have an innate talent for solving mysteries, and that you sometimes work with him and your dad on cases. That's cool."

I unlocked the door to the trailer and handed her the key. Cindi had taken all of her possessions when she left. "You'll need to notify the power company to connect the electric. Go ahead and put the service in your name. You'll need cookware, sheets, towels, and other things. Feel free to add your own decorative touches as long as you don't paint the walls."

She squealed like an excited child opening a special gift. "I'll bring Jupiter out when I start work Monday morning."

"Monday is great. We'll make your official start date Wednesday, to give you a couple of days to get moved in."

"Thank you, Dr. Holliday. I can't wait for my mother to meet you."

I have a good feeling about Ella Sanders. "I'm Dr.

Holliday when we're with clients, otherwise, call me Tullah."

Ella locked the trailer. She tossed the key up in the air, caught it and tucked it in her pocket. We walked to her truck. She stuck out her hand. "I appreciate the opportunity you're giving me, Tullah."

"Just remember, there's not much glamour to the job. There'll be days when you come home covered in afterbirth and horse manure. You'll be bitten, stepped on, and possibly chased. There'll be times when a day feels like it's a week long. All of that and scheduling appointments, too."

"One thing I hope you learn about me is that I'm not easily discouraged. Being a vet tech is my calling." Ella stepped inside the truck. "Thanks again, Tullah. See you Monday."

Chapter Eleven

Dad's face popped up on the caller ID. "Hey, Dad, how'd the arrest go with Lonnie Vickers?"

He snorted a disgusted reply. "He was sitting on the porch, cool as a cucumber. His girlfriend said it was all a big mistake. I asked how her face and arms got bruised. She said she tripped on a throw rug and fell against the kitchen counter."

"So she didn't press charges?"

"Nope. My guess is she's too afraid of what he'd do to her if she did. We offered to take her to a women's shelter in an undisclosed location where she'd be safe. She refused. Kept repeating that she was clumsy and needed to get rid of the rugs, and that everyone knew she was an accident looking for a place to happen. Yeah, right, my ass."

Seriously? Why would she do that? I knew the answer. It was a complex one. Often women stay with their abuser because of low self-esteem, or they love the abuser and believe the abuse will end. Sadly, some women even think they deserve the treatment they get.

"Dad, do you think it's possible Lonnie is connected with the bones we found?"

I heard his heaved sigh.

"It crossed my mind. The thing is, Lonnie's been in prison for three years. Until we hear from forensics with possible identifications on our victims and probable timelines on their deaths, all I can do is consider him a person of interest."

"And that will take weeks. By the way, Grandmother wants to know if you're okay with her printing an article about the skeletal remains."

I could almost see Dad pulling at his bottom lip, something he does when he's pondering a decision. "Sure. In fact, a news article might spook the killer into thinking we're onto him or her."

"Do you think it's someone local?"

"I think it's a person from Kentucky, not necessarily local."

We sat quiet for a few seconds. I related to him that I'd hired Ella Sanders and that she'd asked about living in the trailer. "I hope it sets you and Grandmother at ease that I won't be alone anymore. She's bringing her horse out Monday and will start work Wednesday."

"Good to know, and yep, it does make me feel better."

It warmed me that my family cared so much about my safety. I told him about seeing Edna Lampson. "Dad, she had a black eye and was limping. She was overly concerned that her son would get upset if she didn't bring him glazed donuts, and I mean *specifically* glazed ones."

Henry said, "It's been a while since I've seen Junior. He must be about thirty-three years old."

"I think he's abusing her. Can you check into it?"

"Dixie County isn't my jurisdiction, Punkin."

I persisted. "You're on good terms with Sheriff Dotson, aren't you? Maybe give him a call and ask if he's ever had problems with Junior. On second thought, maybe you could invite him to go fishing, and while you're at the lake do a little verbal investigative fishing."

"Okay, Punkin, I'll give it some thought. Malachi is smart. If I invited him to go fishing, he'd know something fishy is up." Henry laughed. "If the occasion arises, I'll ask him straight out."

"Oh, Dad, you're no fun."

"I can almost see the wheels inside your head spinning away. Why the sudden interest in Junior Lampson? It has to be more than seeing his mother with a black eye."

I rubbed the back of my neck. "Instinct. Like you, I haven't seen Junior in years, and had totally forgotten about him until I saw his mother at the bake shop. I can't explain it, Dad. Something about him feels dangerous. Maybe he's my person of interest." I reach for the gold cross around my neck, the one my mother gave me. For added protection. "Dr. Ritter says Junior is a monster."

"If your mother were alive, you know what she would say?"

"Yes, sir. That inside every person, even the saintly, lies a monster waiting to be awakened. I get it, Dad. I'm just thinking out loud."

"No harm in that. Granted, Junior is or was mean as a timber rattler in August. I'm not defending the boy. From what I understand, he was worse once he returned from juvenile detention. He was born with a lot of strikes against him and deserves the benefit of the doubt until proven otherwise. Unless I have a concrete reason, there's no need to stir up trouble by asking questions about him."

Despite the chill that prickled me from head to toe,

I let out a long sigh. "I can live with that."

We said our goodbyes. I walked outside and to the barn to feed my horses and put them in their stalls for the night. I've found that currying my horses and cleaning their hooves is therapeutic. I can vent my thoughts, voice my opinions, and share my dreams, concerns, and aggravations. The horses listen. Occasionally one of them will nicker, but none of them ever talk back. I laughed at this thought.

I filled their feed bins and water buckets and then shut the barn door for the night. Afterward, I strolled back to the house to make myself a peanut butter-and-banana sandwich and a glass of milk. Once I settled in my recliner, with River and Rascal next to me, I opened my laptop and created a suspect list:

Lonnie Vickers: Prison. Repeat offender for abusing women. Handsome, glib-tongued, evil eyes. Lives in Enigma. Note: He recently beat up his girlfriend, who refused to press charges.

Junior Lampson: mentally unstable, cruel, attacked a teacher, sent to juvenile detention. Lives in Dixie County, approximately thirty minutes from Enigma. Note: his mother appears afraid of him. Did Junior give her the black eye?

I sat there, staring at the computer's screen. Except for my secret instinct, two names certainly wasn't enough to go on.

I clicked off the page and opened the calendar to check my appointments. The entire week was booked solid. I was thankful for Ella Sanders.

I was headed to the kitchen when the email alert sounded on my laptop. I took my time rinsing the soiled dishes before casually returning to the living room. My heart skipped a beat as I opened the email from Vaneeta. I scanned through the usual blah-blah of "it was nice seeing you again, thanks for everything," etc. and then—*Letting you know that Sanjiv and I are giving priority attention to all of the Jane Does. JD Number Three has a filling in the maxilla second molar, and a filling in the mandible first molar. JD Number Ten, the rod in the humerus. We have already entered the numbers in the database. These are the easiest of the eleven. As soon as we get the information, I will contact your father with a blind cc to you.*

I answered her with—*Great news. What about Commander Draper? Are you letting him know first?*

Vaneeta responded—*He will think he is first. I will keep you informed on each JD as we identify them.*

Me: *Don't jeopardize your job.*

V: *No worries. Draper isn't my boss. I've been promoted to Chief of Forensics, officially replacing Dr. Cartwright, at the University. Remember her? Our favorite professor, and the greatest ever at her job. Got the news when I returned on Friday. Anytime you decide to stop treating animals, I'd love to make you my assistant. No pressure, of course. I know how much you love what you do.*

I congratulated her and had to admit to feeling a tiny bit of envy. I shook it off. I am truly happy for my friend. Enthusiasm sparked inside me. Soon Number Three and Number Ten would no longer be Jane Does but real people. We'd know name, age, how she died, and how long she'd been dead for each one, and then, sadly, someone would need to notify her next of kin.

After we disconnected, I pulled my old forensics textbook off the bookshelf. I needed to refresh my memory on methods of identifying human skeletal remains. As I thumbed through the pages, stopping to skim the red-inked notes I'd made in the margins, the women were ever constant on my mind. They had lived a life I knew nothing about and had maybe been at the wrong place at the wrong time. Instinctively, I knew the killer was still out there. Heartbreaking. My equilibrium felt off. Who could have done such a horrible thing? Why?

I was deep in thought when my cellphone chimed. I didn't recognize the number, which isn't entirely unusual since I'm not familiar with everyone who needs veterinary care for their animals. "Dr. Holliday, how may I help you?"

"Tullah, this is Betty Cooper."

Betty Cooper is Dr. Cooper's wife. I wondered if she was calling to invite me to some social event. Otherwise, I couldn't think of a reason for her to contact me.

"'Evening, Betty. What can I do for you?"

"It's Ben, Tullah. He was cleaning leaves out of the rain gutters and fell off the ladder. I'm at the hospital now. He asked me to call to see if you will cover for him. As you know, I book all the appointments, and he has a tech assistant, but Ralph and I are limited in what we can do. Ralph is Ben's age, and has failing eyesight." She hastened on and sounded out of breath. "Ben doesn't trust anyone but you."

I thought about how many times Dr. Cooper and I had covered for each other over the years. I also thought about how overloaded my schedule was since I'd been shorthanded for several months. I found myself saying, "How bad is it, Betty?"

The worry in her voice was evident. "At his age, it's bad. He broke his hip and will need a total hip replacement. Surgery is scheduled for tomorrow morning. The orthopedist says Ben can expect to be out for at least six weeks. We know you're without an assistant and will certainly understand if you say no." Her voice was tremulous but held a note of anticipation. "It's asking a lot."

In the background I heard the beeps and whir of equipment and surmised that Ben had been admitted and was in a private room.

"Betty, of course I'll help. It just so happens I've hired an assistant. She'll start Wednesday. If Ben's tech can handle all of the non-emergencies and routine visits, I'll cover any surgeries and emergencies, which hopefully will be few and far between until Ben is able to go back to work. Is that doable?"

I heard the snuffles and wondered if she was crying. "You are a lifesaver, Tullah. I've been after Ben to retire, especially after his heart attack two years ago. Every year, he promises. He'll celebrate his sixty-fifth birthday in a few months." She prattled on. "Maybe falling off a ladder is a blessing in disguise. Maybe it'll convince him…I'm sorry, Tullah. I didn't mean to bend your ear."

"That's quite all right, Betty. I'm happy to help. Give Dr. Cooper my best wishes."

For a moment after we hung up, I harbored the thought of calling Betty Cooper back and telling her I'd changed my mind. I was feeling cross and out of sorts for not being able to say no. The next minute, I almost whooped out loud. Ben Cooper lived in Dixie County.

His office and practice was in Dixie County. Edna Lampson lived in Dixie County.

I smiled to myself.

Chapter Twelve

I closed the living room blinds to filter out the morning sun's heat. Dressed in shorts and a T-shirt, I wiggled the toes on my bare feet and pushed back in the recliner. The house was a comfortable seventy-eight degrees. It was nearly nine o'clock, and so far my phone had remained silent. Recalling last night's promise to Betty Cooper, I prayed for a quiet, work-free day. I retrieved my mug of coffee from the side table and opened the email on my laptop.

Bold black letters headlined *The Enigma Bulletin*'s Sunday e-newspaper. Grandmother had outdone herself with the attention-getter: *Rasmussen Swamp Grisly Discovery Site.*

In the article she recounted the legend and the curse of Rasmussen Swamp for readers who had possibly never heard the story or who had long since forgotten it. She went on to state that I, my dad, and members of the Kentucky Bureau of Investigation, along with a forensics team from Lexington, had recovered nearly a dozen sets of human remains from the swamp. She detailed the remoteness of the swamp, which accounted for the lack of immediate discovery of the remains.

She also stated that DNA technology would be used to identify each victim, and that it was alleged all the victims were women. Further, Dr. Vaneeta Sanreet and her assistant Sanjiv Patel had discovered dental fillings and a metal rod in separate skeletal remains, which would help expedite the identity of two of the Jane Does.

The article detailed how the bodies were spaced apart and that identity of some of the victims might prove difficult due to recovering only partial remains. She explained that the remains were transported to the pathology department at University Hospital in Lexington.

She also stabbed the heart of the readers by equating each victim as a wife, a daughter, a mother, or sister, and how tragic it was their families never knew what had happened to their loved one.

She said the swamp, having witnessed the senseless human drama, knew the uncaring killer. She ended the article stating that my dad would be heading the investigation and that no stone would be left uncovered until the murderer was found and duly punished.

The way Grandmother worded the article seemed pretty spectacular. She had not minimized the gruesomeness of the discovery. She had certainly not lost her touch as a crime reporter. I would call her later to offer my congratulations.

As much as I appreciated Grandmother's talents as a writer, I could foresee how the article's appearance might bring about several different scenarios. One, the article might spook the murderer, if he was still alive, and cause him to slip up and blow his cover, which would be a good thing. Two, the article could possibly bring out the crazies who kept the telephone lines hot with phony information, especially if they thought a reward was involved. Then there were always the curiosity seekers. These were the worst people because they flooded crime scene areas—taking pictures, hoping to find some sort of souvenir to keep as treasure or to sell. The problem with this last point was that Rasmussen Swamp was dangerous, especially to gung-ho greenies who would go charging in without a compass but couldn't find their way out of a wet paper bag if they got lost.

Idiots weren't my concern. I had enough on my plate with trying to juggle two veterinary clinics. I closed down my laptop and lifted my mug to drain the last drop of coffee. I hadn't yet had my quota of caffeine and strolled to the kitchen to refill my cup.

An idea sprang to mind. I got comfortable again. This time when I opened my laptop, I decided to research missing persons. I was surprised to discover the number of open missing person cases, with an equal number between male and female.

Vaneeta had mentioned that one of our JDs might have been missing for at least ten years, possibly longer. I scrolled down to discover cases open as far back as nineteen ninety-two. Over twenty years. I peered closely at each pictured woman and then read their profiles, wondering if she was one of our Jane Does.

I debated whether to continue my procrastination by scrolling through missing persons files or, since I was dressed, to take a shot at the paperwork at the clinic's office. I settled on the office, where I waded through e-mails that had gone unanswered, and tackled my least favorite office chore, filing. I was in the midst of creating multiple piles of paper when River let out a series of *we've got company* barks.

Behind Grandmother's blue sports car, Ella's truck rambled down the driveway with a horse trailer in tow. I shuffled the stacks of paper into one large pile and walked outside to greet my visitors. The August sun's blinding glare reminded me to go back inside the office to grab my sunglasses.

A tall, freckle-faced woman with ginger-colored hair climbed down from the truck. She extended her hand. "Hi, I'm Sunny Sanders, Ella's mom." Her smile was as bright as her name.

I introduced my grandmother, who said, "Nice to see you again, Sunny."

"I'm excited to return home after all these years. In some ways, Enigma hasn't changed, and in other ways, it has." Sunny Sanders turned to me. "Your mother and I were cheerleaders together in high school." Her voice faltered as if she'd accidentally opened a door and then didn't want to walk through it. "I'm still shocked over her death." And then she apologized for bringing up hurtful memories.

Four years and still my heart ached for my mother. "Death of a special loved one is never easy, Dr. Sanders, as we both know."

Her hazel eyes filled with a sudden rush of tears. "Yes, my husband was a special man." She blinked several times to clear her eyes. "Sorry. His death is still a little raw. Please, call me Sunny." She went on to thank me for taking her daughter under my wing and providing her a place to live. "I'm sure it will take me a while to adjust to the empty nest syndrome."

Ella looked as if she'd been cloned from her mother, and they could easily have passed for sisters.

"Oh, Mom, you'll be so busy at the hospital you'll hardly notice I'm gone."

A long whinny sounded from the trailer. My horses raced to the corral and stretched their long necks in answer to the call. Ella fretted. "You don't suppose there'll be any battles over territory?"

I reassured her. "It'll be more like a group of boys strutting around trying to decide who'll be boss. Don't worry. After they get finished kicking up their heels and squealing, they'll be best buds."

I followed her to the rear of the trailer, helped with the heavy tailgate, and waited for Ella to lead him out. Jupiter was a handsome buttermilk buckskin with a bald face. Ella looked toward the corral where my three horses stood and said, "Which one will be boss?"

Grandmother ran her hand down the buckskin's withers. She smiled. "We'll have to wait and see, but my guess is Gandalf."

We all turned to watch the black-and-white gelding prance around the corral, his head held high like a regal prince, and his tail hiked like a flag. "Ella," I said, "we'll put Jupiter in the adjoining paddock for a couple of days. That way he can get to know the others without feeling threatened."

After we had the horse settled, Grandmother informed us she had brought lunch, and she strolled to the house to wait for us.

I gave Ella and her mother the grand tour, showing them the clinic and facilities. Sunny loosed a whistle. "This is quite a setup you have, Tullah. I'm confident Ella will learn a lot from you."

I glowed on the inside at the compliment. "Ella, my colleague, Dr. Ben Cooper, fell off a ladder and broke his hip. His office is in Dixie County. He's requested that we cover for him while he's recuperating. Of course, this will mean longer hours."

Her response pleased me. "Don't worry, whatever it takes. I'm here for the long haul." She looked at her mother. "This might mean we don't get to spend a lot of time together."

Sunny replied, "I guess we both know how that is. A surgeon's work is never done."

Ella said she wanted to show her new digs to her mother and that she'd brought a few things to leave. "Come to the house when you're finished." I winked. "Grandmother doesn't like to be kept waiting."

We enjoyed a lunch of chicken pecan salad on croissant rolls, homemade bread-and-butter pickles, and chocolate eclairs. As a matter of conversation, I said, "I've known Tiny my entire life and have always wondered what prompted your mother to give him such a name."

Dr. Sanders laughed. "Our mother had a weird sense of humor. My name is Sunflower Goodbody Sanders. My brother's full name is Tiny Seven Goodbody. At least, I could give myself a nickname. Poor Tiny. Mother said she knew he would grow into a giant because he was such a big baby. She figured if she gave him a controversial name, he'd have to fight to prove he was bigger than his name. He was terribly bullied growing up, but I'm so proud of the man he is. Oh, and about his middle name. He was born at seven o'clock on the seventh day of the seventh month. I vowed that my child would have a sensible name."

Ella licked the chocolate off her fingers. She smiled at her mother. "And I'm forever grateful, Mom."

Curiosity pressed me to ask, "Did your parents have odd names?"

Sunny laughed. "My mother's name was Lily Paddington Goodbody. Daddy always called her his little Lily Pad. He had a sensible name—Ralph. God rest their souls. They were fine people." She glanced at her watch. "I hate leaving good company, but Ella and I still have a ton of unpacking to do."

We all stood, and I escorted Ella and her mother to the door. Sunny skipped down the steps. She looked up. "By the way, along with all my other duties, I'm also Enigma's new medical examiner. I read Tanti's article about the remains located in the swamp. Tragic." She shivered. "Even as a kid I thought that place always seemed ominous."

I looked toward the swamp. In the distance, black dots dipped and soared against the sky's brilliant blue. I was certain they were vultures and suppressed a shiver. "I'm looking forward to the forensic reports. My friend, Dr. Vaneeta Sanreet, is heading the cases."

Ella tugged at her mother's elbow. "I'll call the power company in the morning, Tullah. I'll also bring a load and start moving in." She moved away and then turned back and yelled, "If you need me to help out tomorrow—"

I waved. "Don't worry, if we have an emergency, I'll put you to work."

I was champing at the bit for Ella and Sunny to leave. Grandmother had been extra fidgety, and I was eager to hear what she was trying so hard to keep from telling me in front of company.

I hurried back to the house and into the kitchen. "Okay, Grandmother, out with it."

She refilled our tea glasses. "I thought they'd never leave. Lovely ladies, and I did invite them to lunch when Sunny said she was riding out with Ella to bring the horse and to see where she'd be living. I just didn't expect them to lollygag around."

Grandmother followed me into the living room. I expelled an exasperated snort. "Are you going to tell me or keep beating around the bush?"

She set her glass on the coffee table and reached for her purse. She extracted a letter and held it toward me. "It's from Denmark. Specifically from Pedar Nielsen. He's coming to Enigma, and he's the grandson of Lars Rasmussen."

I opened the envelope with a return address from Copenhagen, and scanned the letter. "It's addressed to the tax office. How did you get this?"

Grandmother offered a sly smile. "I'm the mayor, you're my granddaughter, Henry is the sheriff, and you and he found the bodies. Our esteemed tax commissioner thought I should know. She's all atwitter about someone from Denmark visiting our little town. He's interested in looking at the property and will need a guide. Naturally, I thought of you."

I read aloud, "My mother, Heidi Rasmussen Nielsen is the daughter of Lars Rasmussen. As you are aware, my great-grandfather, Adolph Rasmussen, was the owner of a vast property in Enigma, Kentucky. My great-grandmother, Greta Rasmussen, willed the property to her son, my grandfather Lars, who is in failing health. I am well aware of the supposed curse placed on the property by my great-grandmother. As I am not familiar with the area, I wish to hire someone knowledgeable to show me the vast acreage on which we have paid taxes these many years. It is also my desire to visit with my grandfather's old friend Paul Ritter, presuming Mr. Ritter is still living. I bring him a gift from my grandfather. You may expect me to arrive toward the end of August if all goes as planned."

I folded the letter, returned it to the envelope, and scrubbed my hands over my face. "I can't make any promises about guiding Mr. Nielsen. With covering for Dr. Cooper, plus my own appointments, I'm not sure I'll have time, and I can't start Ella off by dumping a load on her the first week of her employment. I sure don't want to give her a reason to resign before she even gets started."

I rolled my lip under my teeth. "Here's a question. Don't you think it's strange that he shows up within days of our discovering the remains of eleven skeletal women?"

Grandmother snorted. "Tullah, don't let your imagination run away with you. Denmark is thousands of miles from Kentucky. Look at the postmark on the envelope. Pedar Nielsen mailed this letter almost a month ago. It's a coincidence, pure and simple."

"Of course, you're right, Grandmother." I then related that I'd had an email from Dr. Vaneeta Sanreet and how she hoped to solve the identity of two victims in a few weeks. "Pedar Nielsen sure picked a heck of a time to visit."

Grandmother tsked as she stood and gathered our glasses. I followed her to the kitchen. She said, "What did you think of my article?"

"You have a way with words. I'm sure it'll draw a lot of attention."

"Oh, it already has. In fact, Henry said his phone

has been ringing off the hook. You know how it is when people get wind of this type of news."

"Yes, I do. I can already hear the gossip machine revving into high gear. I feel sorry for Joyce having to field all the calls from crazies who think they saw something, or claiming to know who the killer is for the reward money. Pffft!"

"Don't worry." Grandmother patted me on the back. "Joyce is an old pro at this sort of thing. It isn't the first time she and Henry have handled a bunch of false alarms."

The kitchen TV was on but low enough to hear. The word *killer* caught our attention. "There's a killer out there," the reporter was saying, "some hideous monster." He speculated, voice dramatic, "The ghosts of these women will not rest easy until their killer is found. And where is he now?"

Grandmother slammed the palm of her hand against the kitchen counter. "Capitalizing on my story and without crediting me! How dare he, and without saying a word to me! Where is the professionalism? I'll call the television station and give the manager a piece of my mind. Scaring everyone out of their wits!"

I envisioned a television crew rushing to the swamp loaded with camera equipment, tromping about, putting themselves in danger, just to make headlines for a story where there are no suspects, no motives, no arrests, and so far no persons of interests. At least none that had been named.

"This isn't good. If he hasn't already, Dad should give Sheriff Dotson a heads-up that Dixie County might be overrun by zealous crews of news hounds." I thought for a moment. "The only way anyone can access the swamp from Enigma is through my property, and I'm not giving them permission. In fact, I'll go to the hardware store to purchase several No Trespassing signs."

Grandmother muttered, "Yes, I foresee a nightmare." She gathered her purse and the tote bag filled with empty containers. "I hope all goes well with Ella." She pursed her lips and squinted at me. "Goodness knows you need a break. You're far too young and beautiful to have dark circles under your eyes."

I opened the door and held it wide with a promise that I'd take care of myself.

Chapter Thirteen

Mending a German Shepherd's broken leg, delivering twin foals, and a jam-packed schedule—it seemed like the week had sprouted wings and flown past. Much to my relief, I'd received no calls from Dr. Cooper's clients. Ella had completely moved into the trailer and had tackled a long-ignored pile of paperwork along with assisting me with patients. My horses had accepted Jupiter with nothing more than a few squeals and nips. By the end of the week, the four acted as if they were best friends.

The quiet weekend I had planned didn't happen. Saturday morning, I pulled the pillow over my head to drown out my phone's chime. Whoever was calling could leave me a message. Except the caller was insistent, and the phone chimed again. I tossed the pillow aside and reached for my phone, squinting at the screen.

I cleared the morning croak from my throat. "Dad, it's barely seven o'clock. What's wrong?"

"Nothing and plenty." He sounded harried. "Joyce called in sick. Ever since Tanti's article went nationwide viral, the office phone's been ringing off the hook, and Tiny isn't due to come in until one. I'd consider it a personal favor if you'd fill in for Joyce. I'll buy your breakfast, lunch, and supper."

If flames could explode from my head, I'm sure

they would. Although I mentally commiserated with my dad, I needed a day off. "You owe me more than food. Right now, I'll settle for biscuits with sausage gravy, a side order of scrambled eggs, hash rounds, and coffee. We'll discuss lunch and supper later."

"You got it, Punkin. Get here as soon as you can, but don't break any speed laws."

I threw on a pair of jeans and a pullover shirt, and tugged on socks and boots. Slapped on a little makeup and pulled my hair into a ponytail. Downstairs, I lifted the doggie door to let River and Rascal out to do their morning business. I sent Ella a text, letting her know how to contact me if a Saturday emergency arose. Not exactly sure how busy or boring the day might become, I stuffed my laptop and a new mystery novel inside my backpack.

The town was barely waking up by the time I arrived at Dad's office. The day was clear and the sun already intense. I dashed up the steps, through the entry door, and down the corridor. I heard the phone ringing. I turned the knob, and the office door creaked open. Dad was sitting at his desk, frowning. He looked up as I entered. His eyes narrowed as he spoke to the caller, "No, ma'am, forensics has not had enough time to identify the remains." He reached for a pen. "Your daughter went missing when?" He scribbled down a date and a name. "Yes, ma'am. I have the information. Someone will contact you if we have a positive match that turns out to be your daughter." He listened. "Yes, ma'am, I'm sorry for your loss. We'll try to be as expeditious as possible. Thank you for calling."

He lifted the coffee mug to his lips and grimaced. "Cold."

I grabbed the cup and rushed to the bathroom to rinse it before filling it with fresh coffee. I also poured myself a cup, since I hadn't had my first dose of caffeine to get me started. I picked up the pieces of paper scattered across his desk and shuffled through them. "What's all this?"

He fortified himself with a healthy slug of dark roast. "Phone calls from hopeful relatives wanting to know if we've identified the remains, and from the usual loonies saying they had information if there is a reward."

When Dad is agitated he paces. He stopped, chugged more coffee, and paced again. He stopped and slammed his fist against his palm. "There's dozens of 'em, and not all of 'em are from Kentucky. What galls me is I've listened to every one of the callers tell me basically the same thing—the investigation of their missing loved one was treated as insignificant."

"Do you think any of these are our Jane Does?"

He shrugged. "For the sake of the relatives, I hope so. No one should ever have to live in doubt for years on end."

I counted as I sifted through the slips of paper. "Fifty. I'll type these up and put them in order by the dates they were reported missing." I looked over my shoulder as I walked toward the reception desk. "Did Joyce say why she's sick?"

"Sinus infection."

The phone rang. I answered, "Sheriff Holliday's office, how may I help you?"

"Tullah, this is Patty. Henry ordered breakfast. I'm just calling to see if you're ready for me to bring it over."

"I can run down and get it. There's no need for you to deliver."

"Stay right where you are. It's the least I can do. Besides, my fit-o-meter keeps telling me it's time for me to get my hundred steps in. I have to keep these old bones moving, you know."

Fifteen minutes later, Dad and I were scarfing down fluffy biscuits laden with creamy sausage gravy, scrambled eggs, and crispy tater tots. Thankfully, the phone had stopped ringing long enough for us to hurry through an undisturbed breakfast.

After clearing the desk and dumping the paper bags in the trash, I separated the lists I'd created by gender, focusing only on missing women.

I walked to the white board in Dad's office and, using a red marker, divided the board into names, states, and dates missing. After I had finished, we stood back and studied the information.

What was supposed to be my relaxing day off had turned into something far removed from that. I thought about a quote from Frank A. Clark. "If you find a path with no obstacles, it probably doesn't lead anywhere." There was a solid truth behind his words, and this morning was about to prove it.

I let out a large sigh and walked over to the coffee bar. I removed the filter and dumped the grounds in the trashcan. I replaced it with fresh dark roast and filled the cylinder with water. The water gurgled and began its rich and savory descent into the coffeepot. "There're so many names, and all from different states."

Dad cocked his head at me. "Sure wish we could speed up forensics. I'm admitting this just once, and only once. I wish you were leading the forensics team.

You'd at least have one or two names for us by now."

His words touched my heart. I could feel my smile becoming self-conscious, but I couldn't make it go away. "True. If we had a few names of the Rasmussen Swamp JDs, we might be able to establish a pattern."

Dad paced again. He stopped at the big window to gaze out at the town. "Yeah, I suspect all the JDs were killed by the same person. Yet I'm puzzled as to why we didn't know about the murders, especially since they appear to have happened in our own back yard."

At that moment, the door leading from the hallway and into the reception area swung open. A woman of undeterminable age stood hesitant. Her arms were bare, fleshed out with skin as thin as tissue paper and covered with yellowish-green bruises. Her eyes were sunken and haunted, and her gray hair, thinning and lank, hung at her shoulders like damp mop strings. Her brown eyes flicked to me, and for a second I could see how nervous she was. She was fighting back tears. For a moment I feared she might faint.

I hurried around the desk to where she stood. "Please have a seat." I gently placed my hand on her arm and led her to a chair. "My name is Tullah. Would you like a cup of coffee?"

She looked at me with those haunted brown eyes. "I need to talk to the sheriff. It's…it's urgent."

Dad stood in the doorway, the sunlight silhouetting him and accentuating his height. "I'm Henry Holliday. How can I help you, Mrs….?" He eased into the chair next to her.

I watched her lace and unlace her fingers, and decided to pour her a cup of coffee anyway. "Cream and sugar?"

She flicked a questioning glance at me like she hadn't understood. I held the cup forward and repeated, "Do you take cream and sugar in your coffee?"

She was silent for a moment. Her voice was reedy. "Cream and four sugars, please."

We gave her a moment to savor a few sips and to collect herself. She wiped the corner of her mouth with a fingertip, and sighed. "My name is Lucille Pickford. My son is Roy."

The moment she said his name, Mrs. Pickford burst into tears. Sobs shook her frail shoulders. I glanced around Joyce's workstation. As if he'd read my mind, Dad said, "Right bottom drawer."

I pulled the drawer open, relieved to find a box of tissues. I grabbed several and leaned across the desk. Dad handed them to the sobbing woman.

Dad said, "Is your son in some kind of trouble, Mrs. Pickford?"

"I-I'm afraid so, Sheriff. He's disappeared."

I'd been in the office enough to know that Joyce wrote down everything a visitor said, especially if they were filing a complaint. I grabbed a pen and a clean sheet of paper.

Dad swiveled to face her. He kept his voice soft, but firm. "What kind of trouble do you think Roy is in?"

"He's a good boy, Sheriff. Honest, he is. He's trying so hard to do right." Her voice sputtered off.

"Why don't we start from the beginning? How old is Roy?"

"He's forty-two."

From the way she had first started, I had envisioned a young teenager. Boy, was I wrong.

"Does Roy live with you or on his own?"

Her wrinkled face bunched into a pasty concern. "He lives with me in the Purvis Trailer Park out on the county line road." Her cheeks pinked as if she were embarrassed about where she lived. "That is, until he disappeared ten days ago. I've called and called his cell phone, and he don't answer. He works at the tire shop, and he ain't showed up for work, either."

Dad's voice remained calm, almost monotonic. "Has Roy ever been in trouble? Does he have enemies?"

She leaned forward and set the empty Styrofoam cup on the edge of Joyce's desk. "The devil is his enemy, Sheriff." She twisted her hands together. "I'm afraid the evil has gotten ahold of him again. There's something that ain't right in Roy's brain. Ever since he was a youngster."

Her tale was gut-wrenching, and I grimaced as she spoke. "Roy's been in and out of prison since he was a teenager. After he finished his probation this last time, that's when we moved here. He promised to stay clean, and he's been a good boy for over a year. Working steady and helping me out with the bills and all."

"Roy takes drugs?"

She answered with a hesitant nod and seemed lost in thought. Dad urged her to continue. "Besides the drugs, what kind of crimes did Roy commit?"

She kept her eyes downcast. Her voice wavered. "Since he was a little boy he likes to hurt things, especially when he's hallucinating. It's the demon in him, Sheriff. He can't help it when the devil takes ahold."

Tears spilled down her cheeks. "I saw on the TV

'bout them bodies you and her"—Mrs. Pickford nodded toward me—"found in the swamp. I don't know if my boy had anything to do with 'em or not. All I know is that he's gone. Didn't take nothing with him 'ceptin' his old junkie car and a hunnerd dollars I had stashed in the cookie jar."

Lucille Pickford held the tissue against her nose and blew. She wiped the tears with the back of her hand, and then she reached into the pocket of her faded brown slacks. "Here's a picture of my boy. It hurts me to the bone to say this—I-I hope he's dead. He's not my good boy no more, and I can't keep livin' with the fear that he might hallucinate on drugs and kill me."

"Did he put the bruises on your arm?"

She pressed her lips together. "He has strong hands."

Dad accepted the tattered photo and handed it to me. "Are you employed, Mrs. Pickford?"

"Not no more. Not since I fell down the steps and broke my back." Her eyes glistened with tears. "It was an accident, don't you see. Roy was havin' one of his fits. He didn't mean to push me. He thought I was a she-devil or somethin'."

She seemed hesitant to continue. "I get a monthly check, but it ain't hardly enough to buy my medicine and pay rent, and buy a few groceries."

Dad's gaze settled on Lucille Pickford. "There's a women's shelter in Lexington. If you're afraid Roy will come back to hurt you, I can have my deputy drive you there. The ladies that run the shelter might be able to help you find a nice place to live where the rent is affordable. If you want to stay safe, you have to promise not to contact Roy so he won't know where to find you."

I had no sentimental attachment to Lucille Pickford. I couldn't imagine how difficult it must have been for her to suspect that her son, her only child, might be a serial killer—it was so drastic, unthinkable.

She placed a balled fist against her chest. Her sigh was audible. "C-could we go today, Sheriff? I-I'm really afraid he might come back."

"My deputy will drive you tomorrow." At her gasp, Dad hastened on. "If you'll feel safer, you can sleep in one of the cells tonight. Tomorrow we'll go by your place and pack a few clothes and other essentials."

"I ain't got much, Sheriff. I sure do thank you, but I don't got any money to pay for sleepin' in the jail."

He offered his hand. She placed hers in his. "Don't worry, Mrs. Pickford. It's all taken care of." She followed him to his office. He said, "We'll keep the door open. The ladies room is through there."

She reached for the barred door and pulled it shut. She didn't know that Dad had to turn a key for it to lock. "I feel safer already." She lay down on the cot. "I ain't had a solid night's sleep in a long time." She closed her eyes.

Dad sat in his chair. He hunched toward his computer and typed. I knew he was pulling up Roy Pickford's criminal records. Without looking up, he said, "I called Charlie before you arrived, and ordered supper. How about letting him know we'll need three orders. Also, call Patty and order lunch."

The phone rang. I answered, "Sheriff Holliday's office. How may I help you?"

I placed my hand over the phone and mouthed, "It's another one." I wondered how many more calls we'd receive from anxious family members. When I'd finished, I added the name to the white board.

At noontime, taking a break from answering depressing telephone calls, I strolled next door to Sweet's 'n' Eats and ordered lunch. As I waited, I couldn't imagine what it would be like to have a son who was a cold-blooded killer.

Patty set a glass of iced raspberry tea in front of me. "Patty, do you know Roy Pickford?"

She wiped her hands on her crisp pink apron. "The name rings a bell. Why?"

I was about to answer when the little bell over the door tingled. Lonnie Vickers strolled in like he owned the place. He offered a beguiling dimpled smile. I merely nodded and focused on my iced tea.

He reminded me of a strutting rooster when he ambled to my table. He pulled out a chair. I frowned up at him. "I don't recall inviting you to sit."

He smiled, ignoring me. He sat down and reared the chair back on two legs. "I usually don't need an invitation. The ladies like me, a lot." His insufferable grin widened. "Your daddy's the sheriff, ain't he?"

"Isn't he," I corrected. "Yes, he is."

I saw Patty tense, and decided to give her an excuse to leave the table. "Would you mind adding six chocolate eclairs to my order?"

She hesitated. I nodded to indicate I was okay.

Lonnie's smile reminded me of a lion sizing up its prey. Without taking his eyes off me, he called out, "Hey, Miz Patty, my girlfriend took a bad spill. Needs stitches over her eye. She's at the emergency room, and I thought a couple of cupcakes might make her feel better. I'll take the two with purple frosting, and put some candy hearts on 'em."

He focused on me. "You pro'bly don't remember me from high school. You were that uppity girl on the rodeo team. Thought you were better'n the likes of me. I always thought there was something peculiar about a girl that liked horses more'n boys. I hear you're some fancy animal doctor. How 'bout that. Little half-breed girl makes good."

He rocked the chair a little farther on its two back legs. The chair seemed precariously suspended. I've always been thankful for my height, especially that day. At that very moment, I lifted the glass of tea to my lips and without blinking stretched my leg and used my boot to nudge the chair leg. It tottered. Lonnie's arms and legs flailed out. His beguiling grin changed to a clownish panic as he grabbed the air to keep from falling backward.

I cocked an eyebrow toward Lonnie as I lifted the glass of tea and sipped through the straw, savoring the icy sweetness.

Patty's new fitness regime was apparently paying off. She scooted behind the chair, keeping it from crashing to the floor. In an exaggerated, breathless voice, she said, "My goodness, I need to warn the cleaning crew about the amount of wax they're using on the floor. Slippery as an eel."

She looked over Lonnie's head and winked. It's all I could do to keep from laughing out loud. Patty set the box of cupcakes on the table in front of him. "That'll be five dollars and eighty-three cents."

Lonnie set the chair down with a thud. He swallowed audibly, then stood and whipped out his wallet, tossing six dollars on the table. He snatched up the box and said, "Keep the change." And then he glinted at me. Just stood there and glared before storming out of the café.

Patty placed her hands over her heart. "My word in heaven, Tullah, he looked at you as if he wanted to take you apart one piece at a time."

To ease the tension, I loosed the laughter I'd held in. "It would've served him right if the chair had tipped completely over. A man who beats up on women is a lowly coward."

"Lord have mercy. He beats up on women?"

I explained about Dad and Tiny being called out to Lonnie's house for domestic abuse. "When they got there, his girlfriend refused to press charges. I'll bet you a dime for a donut that's why she's in the emergency room today."

Patty glanced toward the café door. "He's a mean one, that's for sure. His poor girlfriend." Then she said, "Tullah, you don't suppose Lonnie is the..." She clutched her throat and whispered, "the Rasmussen Swamp killer."

I knew Lonnie Vickers had served time for nearly beating a woman to death. "Anything's possible."

A waitress came out with a large white sack. "Your order, Doc Holliday."

"How much do I owe you?"

Patty said, "It's all taken care of. Henry said to bill the county."

I gathered the bag and thanked Patty and the waitress. Patty said, "I don't trust Lonnie Vickers. Be sure to tell Henry about this little incident."

Although I had an unsettling feeling, I assured her nothing would come of it. "To put your mind at rest, and so you don't go tattling to my grandmother, I promise to tell Dad."

"And I promise to only tell Tanti if the subject comes up." Patty offered a smug grin.

My heart beat a little faster as I left the café and spotted Lonnie standing across the street. His smile dipped into a scowl. He stared at me. His lips moved, but no audible words came out. Although I'm certain I recognized the word "bitch."

I felt his eyes boring into my back as I retraced my steps back to Dad's office. Once inside, I laid out the sandwiches and eclairs as I related the incident with Lonnie Vickers.

Before he could respond, the phone rang. I answered with my usual greeting. A woman's voice said, "This is Dr. Sanders, may I speak to Sheriff Holliday?"

"Hi Sunny, this is Tullah. Hold just a moment."

I pointed to Dad and then to the phone. He picked up.

I listened to the one-sided conversation. Before he replaced the old-fashioned receiver in its cradle, he said to Dr. Sanders, "Whatever you do, keep her at the hospital. And if Lonnie Vickers shows up, call Security. I'm on my way."

Dad rubbed his forehead. He looked at me. "Dr. Sanders reported a female victim arrived in the ER with a broken arm, contusions along the ribcage that suggest the victim was repeatedly kicked, and a concussion. The victim refuses to give her name or the name of her attacker."

"Lonnie said his girlfriend was in the ER. Do you think it's Angela Davis?"

Deputy Goodbody strolled in. He looked at our expressions and said, "What?"

Dad gave him the short version of Dr. Sanders' phone call after a brief mention of Mrs. Pickford, who was still snoozing in the cell. "I'm taking Tullah with me. Maybe she can convince the victim to name her attacker. If it is Ms. Davis, and Dr. Sanders gives a thumbs-up, we'll try to convince her to go to a women's shelter. Stay close to the phone, Tiny."

"Sure thing, Henry. What about the woman in the cell?"

"She'll be here overnight. Oh, and if she wakes up"—Dad pointed to the sack—"her lunch is there. I promised that tomorrow you'd drive her to Safe Haven for Women."

"Gotcha."

On the drive to the hospital, there was a tight silence between Dad and me. "All those women…dead before their time. I know you're a woman, smart and brave, but you'll always be my little girl, and I'll always want to protect you." His voice choked. "I couldn't…didn't protect your mother. I put my job before her."

"Stop it, Dad. You're the sheriff. You couldn't up and leave Tiny to handle an entire town by himself, not even for a week. Mom understood, and frankly, she'd be mad as hell knowing you blame yourself for something you couldn't foresee would happen, something you couldn't prevent." I swallowed hard and softened my voice. "If it makes you feel any better, I'm glad you'll always want to protect me. Just don't obsess over it, okay?"

He studied my face, and I knew he was thinking

how much I looked like my mother. How often he and Grandmother have said that except for my blue eyes, I'm a replica of her. Suddenly he looked so much older than his forty-eight years.

I did my best to assure Dad he had nothing to worry about. "Lonnie Vickers is a coward who beats up on women who are too afraid to fight back."

Even as I said it, I had to admit that between Vickers, Roy Pickford, and eleven skeletons recovered practically from my back yard, I wasn't feeling at all safe. "I forgot to ask, what did Roy Pickford's records say about him?"

Dad wheeled the 4Runner into the hospital's ER parking lot space reserved for law enforcement, and switched off the engine. He frowned, his icy blue eyes stormy with a mixture of concern and anger. "Habitual alcohol and drug offender, possession and distribution of crystal meth with drug paraphernalia, assaulted a victim with a lead pipe, resisting arrest, shoplifting, possession of a deadly weapon…" He squared his jaw and continued. "Registered sex offender, and he was committed to a state mental institution twice. Before that, he served time in a state prison. Roy Pickford is a dangerous man. I'll put an APB out on him as soon as we get back to the office."

"Why was he in a mental hospital?"

"The report said he was diagnosed with psychotic schizophrenia."

"Oh, that's not good."

Chapter Fourteen

A nurse greeted us with a frown as we approached the nurse's station. "Hello, Sheriff…Dr. Holliday. Dr. Sanders said to buzz her as soon as you arrived. She'll be with you in a few minutes."

Dad said, "Has the victim said anything?"

The nurse shook her head. "Not a word. Not even when she checked herself out."

Dad and I exchanged startled glances. We said in unison, "She what?"

The soles of Dr. Sanders' white shoes made a suction sound against the shiny tile floors as she approached. She threw an irritated look at us. "We were getting a room ready when her husband came in with a box of cupcakes. I swear her face turned whiter than the bedsheet. He handed her the cupcakes, kissed her on the cheek, and whispered something in her ear. That's when he looked at me and smiled…a smile that didn't reach his eyes."

"What happened then?" I asked.

Dr. Sanders sucked in a deep breath. "The guy demanded a wheelchair and said he was taking his wife home. When I objected by stating she had a concussion and needed to stay overnight for observation, the woman looked up at me and said she was fine and didn't want to be admitted. He scooped her up in his arms, plopped her in the chair, and wheeled her out."

Dad straightened his shoulders. He pinched the bridge of his nose as if trying to relax the tension building in his head. "How long ago?"

Dr. Sanders lifted weary eyes as she glanced at the large wall clock. "Fifteen or maybe twenty minutes ago. He said her grandmother had died and they needed to leave immediately."

I felt my own jaw tighten. "You said he handed her a box of cupcakes. Did you notice if they were from Sweet's 'n' Eats?"

"As a matter of fact, they were."

"Lonnie Vickers."

Curiosity flashed in Dr. Sanders' eyes. "You know him?"

"Yes, and I was in the café when he bought the cupcakes. Here's the thing, she's his girlfriend, not his wife, and we believe her name is Angela Davis."

Dad cut in. "This isn't the first time he's beaten her up. She's too afraid of him to press charges, or even leave him. I was hoping Tullah could convince her to let us drive her to the women's shelter in Lexington." He adjusted his hat. "Short of chaining her to the bed, if she checked herself out, there isn't anything you could have done to keep her here."

I nodded soberly.

Dr. Sanders shrugged. "I know, but it doesn't make me feel any better." She glanced at the clock again. "I'm sorry. I have a surgery consult in exactly two minutes."

I'm sure she was trying to smooth over her abruptness when she said, "Ella is enjoying working with you."

I edged toward the door. Dad was as impatient to

leave as Dr. Sanders was to get to her surgery consult. I waved goodbye. "She's a fast learner. I'm happy to have her."

Dad pulled sunglasses from his shirt pocket and adjusted them on the bridge of his nose. I did likewise as we stepped from the hospital's cool interior and into the hot glaring sun. Neither of us spoke as we strode to the 4Runner.

"What do you plan to do about Mrs. Pickford?"

Dad backed out of the parking space. He turned in the direction of the Whitehorse Saloon. "Call Charlie and tell him to add one more meal to our order."

"For Tiny?"

"Yep."

"You haven't answered my question about Mrs. Pickford."

"First we'll swing by the tire shop to see if Roy's car is there. If not, I'll ask the owner what he knows about Roy." Dad rolled up to a stop sign and waited for traffic to pass. "I'll have Tiny drive Mrs. Pickford to Lexington in the morning."

Dad reached into his shirt pocket and handed me his cellphone. "Call the office. I need to talk to Tiny. Put the phone on speaker."

"You know, if you had a newer vehicle you wouldn't have to dial. All you'd have to do is say, 'Suzie, call Tiny,' and she would."

He reached forward and patted the dashboard. "Yeah, well I like the beast. We've been through a lot together. Besides, the only time I've ever asked for a new vehicle the answer was, 'It's not in the budget.' "

I let out a large sigh and pressed the call button and waited. "Tiny, Dad needs to talk to you."

Deputy Goodbody's deep bass voice said, "Go ahead, Henry."

"Tiny, check NCIC to see what you can find out about Lonnie Vickers. There has to be more to him than our local records." He went on to explain about Lonnie taking his girlfriend to the ER and then absconding with her. "I'm on my way to Barney's Tire Shop to inquire about Roy Pickford. How is Mrs. Pickford?"

"She's sitting in the cell with the door closed. I gave her one of Joyce's romance novels to read."

"Did she eat?"

"Yep, like she was half-starved."

"Any more phone calls about the missing women?"

"Phone's been ringing off the hook. I think I'm getting cauliflowered ear from all the calls."

Dad and I both laughed. Tiny said, "I'll see what I can pull up on Lonnie Vickers and have it ready by the time you get to the office."

"That's a ten-four."

Dad wheeled off the main highway and drove to the rear of the tire shop. A paunchy man in grease-covered coveralls rolled a large set of metal doors to the ground. He inserted a key in each of the padlocks. He turned in our direction. He shaded his eyes as we stepped out of the 4Runner and walked toward him. "Howdy, Sheriff, did ya need sumpthin'?"

Dad offered his hand and never flinched when he clasped the greasy paw. "I understand Roy Pickford works for you, Barney."

The tire shop owner frowned and scratched under a scruffy chin. "Did. Ain't seen him in 'bout ten days or so." He hawked and spat. "Don't know where he is and don't care, neither. Roy was crazy as a bedbug."

Dad said, "Uh-huh, how so?"

Maybe it was mention of the vermin that caused Barney to scratch other places on his body. "Always talkin' to people that weren't there. Had a temper, too. Bad for business, ya know. My customers, 'specially the women, complained 'bout him. Took him home for supper one night, and my wife said never to bring him back." Barney lifted his arm to expose a hairy armpit. He scratched. "Why? What's he done?"

"Roy's mother reported him missing. Did he happen to mention any special places he liked to visit, or people?"

Barney kept scratching. Maybe it was mind over matter that had me resisting the urge to scratch, too.

"Nah-uh, can't say. 'Cept for talkin' to himself, he—" Barney snapped his fingers. "Yeah, yuh-huh, I remember him tellin' his imaginary friend that he planned to drive down to Mexico to buy some good stuff. Then he told me he was goin' to buy his mama a mansion and he'd never have to work for sumbitches ever again." Barney used his finger to make a slashing motion across his neck, and said, "Roy called himself king and said, 'Off with their heads.' And then he laughed like a danged hyena."

"What kind of car is he driving?"

"Old '57 Chevy. Looks like a piece of junk on the outside. Don't let it fool ya. Got a monstrous V-8 under the hood. It can get sixty from a standstill in the blink of an eye." Barney's eyes shifted toward the 4Runner. "Ain't nothing you got that can catch it."

"Uh-huh. What color is it?"

Barney scratched under his arm. "That's a hard'n', Sheriff. It's all kinda colors, blues and reds and green, mixed up with years of rust."

"Is there anything that would make the car recognizable—like a hood ornament?"

Barney thought for a moment. This time he scratched the top of his head. With all that scratching, I wondered if the man ever took a bath. He said, "Sorry, Sheriff. I just never paid any special attention. Being the only tire shop in town, it's 'bout all I can do to keep up with my work."

Dad pulled a business card from his pocket and handed it to the man. "Thanks for your help, Barney. If Roy shows up, give me a call. It'll set his mother's mind at ease."

Barney stuck the business card in a pocket. "If'n you ask me, and you ain't, his mother'd be better off if he went to Mexico and never come back. You be careful of that jaybird, Sheriff. He's bad news."

I waved goodbye and followed Dad back to the 4Runner. "Do you think Roy went to Mexico?"

Dad revved the engine and shifted into gear. "Mrs. Pickford said all he has is the money he stole from her. He won't get far on a hundred dollars. My guess is he'll try to steal what he needs. If he's still in Kentucky and does commit robbery, we'll nail him."

"Dad, if you had to place money on the Rasmussen Swamp killer, who would you bet on—Roy Pickford or Lonnie Vickers?"

He chuckled. "So that's what they've dubbed him—the Rasmussen Swamp killer." He kept his eyes on the road. "A woman beater versus a psychotic schizophrenic? I believe Roy Pickford could kill and never blink an eye. Then he'd claim the devil made him do it."

"If it is him, and he's caught, he'll never go to prison, will he? I mean, the PD will try to play the insanity card."

Dad kept his eyes on the road. "That's up to a judge and jury."

"Dad, what if it's both of them?"

He pulled the sunshades further down on his nose and peered over the rim. "You mean Roy and Lonnie, partners in crime?" He thought for a moment. "Anything's possible."

"I guess you heard about Pedar Nielsen coming to town."

"Tanti told me. She said he wants to look at the property."

"Yes, and she also suggested that I be the one to show it to him." I tsked. "I hope she isn't planning to play matchmaker. Gads, he's probably old and baldheaded, with a beer belly. Plus, he's from Denmark."

Dad rarely laughs. This time he did. "You've got quite an imagination, Punkin." He wheeled into his parking spot in front of the office. "Besides, what's Denmark got to do with anything?"

"You know the old saying, 'Something's rotten in Denmark.' Maybe there's something rotten about Pedar Nielsen. Maybe he takes after his great-grandfather."

"And maybe Pedar Nielsen is a nice guy whose only interest is looking over the property he owns, and maybe putting a few ghosts to rest. I'll admit that his timing isn't the best, especially with the swamp being a crime scene. Which brings me to a question—if he decides to sell, are you still interested in buying?"

I considered the question. "Given the current

circumstances, I'm not sure."

"What's your interest in the land? It's not much good. Very little of it is arable. Yearly taxes would probably eat a hole in your pocket right quick-like."

It took a moment for my eyes to adjust to the building's darkened interior as I followed Dad down the hall to his office. He'd asked a legitimate question, and I really didn't have a legitimate answer.

He didn't give me a chance to respond, or maybe he already knew I didn't have a reasonable response. He hung his hat in its usual place and marched straight to the coffeepot. "Anything from NCIC on Vickers?"

Deputy Goodbody sat at the reception desk. He opened a file and read the information he'd gathered from the National Crime Information Center. "Lonnie Vickers, thirty-two. He has three moving violations. Involuntary manslaughter. Did a three-spot in Boyd County for domestic violence, drug possession, and did another year up at Ashland for domestic violence and drug abuse violations. He's a real model citizen."

He closed the file and handed it to Dad. "Afternoon, Tullah. My niece is excited about working with you. Sure do appreciate you giving her this opportunity."

"I'm happy to have Ella. She comes with a wealth of updated ideas, which reminds me I need to attend more veterinarian medical conferences." I turned to my father. "Are you putting an APB out on Lonnie, Dad? I mean, Angela's life may be in danger."

"On what charges?"

I shrugged. "I don't know…kidnapping?"

He sat in his chair and stretched his long legs out in front of him. "Nope. Kidnapping won't wash. Angela refused to press charges, and she apparently went willingly from the hospital. Right now, I don't have a reason to arrest him."

I crossed my arms and considered him. "I think I'll drive to Charlie's and pick up supper. I need a break from all this crime stuff."

By the time I arrived at the Whitehorse Saloon, the parking lot was filled and the jukebox was blaring loud enough to wake the dead—no pun intended. Fatigue was catching up with me from the long hours and little sleep. Instead of going inside, I opted to drive around back to the drive-thru window.

"Hey, Tullah, your timing's just right. Flora's packing up your order." The waitress yelled, "Yo, Flora, Tullah's here."

Flora Landy had worked for Charlie for as long as I could remember. She never wore makeup, and her face was a wrinkled roadmap that reflected a difficult life. She was friendly but never invited friendship unless she liked you. And she was tough, never backing down when a drunk kicked up a ruckus in the bar. One thing about Flora, if she liked you she'd give you a genuine smile and a few snippets of conversation. If she didn't like you…oh, well. Today, she smiled and leaned out the window with two large sacks of food. "Hamburgers and shrooms are nice 'n' hot. I put in some extra bleu cheese sauce for you."

I accepted the brown paper sacks. "You're the best."

"I don't suppose you've heard any news from those forensics people about the bones?"

I twisted around to set the sacks of food on the seat. "Nothing yet."

144

She didn't seem to want to end the conversation, which was unusual. Flora wasn't known for idle chit-chat. Her eyes drifted to a haunted look. Her voice wobbled when she spoke, "More'n sixty years ago, my only sister disappeared. She was sixteen. Pretty as a picture and smart as a whip. I don't mean sassy smart. She had book-learning smarts. The sheriff said she probably ran off with her boyfriend. Thing is, her boyfriend was sitting at his mama's kitchen table when my daddy went lookin' to see why Carlene never came home from school. We were poor folks scrabblin' to make a livin' back in the early sixties. Sheriff didn't care. Nobody cared."

Flora's expression changed to hard and her voice bitter. "I was ten years old. Today is my sister's birthday. She'd a been seventy-six. Terrible thing, not knowing what happened to her. I think that's what sent my folks to early graves." Her voice drifted off. "The not knowing." Then she rallied back to real time. "It's a good thing you and Henry are doing."

Just that quick, she shut the drive-thru window and disappeared.

I returned to the office and distributed our supper. Mrs. Pickford stated she wanted to stay in the jail cell. No amount of reassuring her that she was safe and that her son couldn't get at her could entice her to join us.

Between chews, I repeated Flora's story. "Do you suppose we can get Carlene Landy's case reopened and find out what happened to her?"

Dad glanced over at his deputy. "That's a shocker. It's surprising what you learn about people that you've known for years. Tiny, do you know where Flora hails from?"

Tiny had started on his second hamburger. "I believe I heard her once mention being from a small parish in Louisiana. Charlie would have it on her employment records. You want me to ask?"

"Right now, our first priority is finding Roy Pickford and Lonnie Vickers as persons of interest. Sixty years is a long time back to revive a cold case."

"Dad…"

He held up his hand. "Let me finish, Tullah. As soon as we hear from Dr. Sanreet with the identity of the eleven remains, then find the murderer, we'll do what we can to solve the mystery of Flora's missing sister. In the meantime, I suggest we keep it under wraps. There's no need in giving Flora hope where there might not be any." He arched his eyebrows. "Fair enough?"

I wadded up my empty wrappers and stuffed them in the sack. I cocked my head to one side and placed the cup of cola back on the napkin. "Fair enough."

After supper, and much to Dad's disgruntlement, I refused his offer to spend the night at his apartment, arguing that I had animals to feed and I didn't feel easy leaving Ella alone until she got comfortable with her new home and surroundings.

Before driving home, I stopped at the hardware store and purchased several No Trespassing signs. I didn't know when or if a horde of reporters would try to converge on the swamp, but I wanted to make sure they understood they couldn't willfully cross my property.

Chapter Fifteen

In Sunday's early morning dawn, I trotted across the yard and rapped on the trailer door. "Ella, wake up."

It took several moments before I heard shuffling. A sleepy-eyed Ella opened the door and rasped, "Is something wrong?"

"We have an emergency. A young thoroughbred stallion stepped in a hay rake, and the owner can't get him untangled. The farm is at the far end of Dixie County, which is a forty-minute drive. We'll need to hustle."

She rubbed a fist against her eyes. "Okay, give me ten minutes."

I held up the tote bag. "Breakfast."

I sprinted to the office and grabbed my medical kit. I knew my truck was fully loaded with all the necessary supplies. I spoke to my dog and donkey and made sure they had adequate food and water before getting in my truck and driving up to the trailer.

Ella locked the metal door and joined me. While she buckled her seatbelt, I read the address into the GPS and then nodded toward the tote bag sitting between us. "There's protein bars to go with the coffee. Depending on how bad the horse is injured and how long it takes to tend him, it may be a while before we get to eat."

She filled two cups and set them in the console holder. She unwrapped a protein bar for each of us and said, "Did the owner call you direct? I thought you had an answering service for the weekends."

"We do, and they did. I called the owner to get details." I lifted the cup of coffee and sipped before continuing. "It's not clear how the stallion got out of his stall. At least, no one is 'fessing up. However, somehow, and again it's not clear how, the horse managed to get tangled in the spokes of a hay rake."

Ella pulled her phone from her hip pocket and tapped the keyboard. She held the screen forward for me to see the image of a modern hay rake. I glanced at the picture. "Yep, I've seen this type of accident before. I hope the outcome for this youngster is a good one."

"How old is the horse?"

"Two years. The owner says he bought him a month ago, and in his words, 'got him for a song.' Apparently, the horse has excellent bloodlines but has had no handling and is wild and unpredictable. We'll see when we get there."

We rode in companionable silence for a while. It wasn't until we hit the open road that the conversation started to flow again. We spent the last half of the trip with Ella asking questions about my different cases. I liked this girl and saw a bright future for her. I just hoped she didn't decide to take the same road as my former vet tech and leave me high and dry.

The moment I pulled into Calumet Lane I instructed my phone to call Arnold Calumet.

The owner answered, "Doc Holliday?"

"Yes. I'm pulling up to your barn. Where is the horse?"

"We're in pasture number three. My barn manager will meet you out front and show you how to get to us."

"I see him."

At that moment a man dressed in denims, shirt, and knee-high rubber boots raced to the truck. Ella opened the door, and he slid in beside her. I pointed the truck in the direction he indicated. The barn manager said, "We managed to throw a shirt over Cisco's head to cover his eyes. Poor animal was in a sheer panic by the time we found him. There's so much blood it's hard to tell how bad he's hurt."

We reached the site, and I braked to a halt, shut off the engine, and jumped out. Ella grabbed the medical bag and followed. Hands on hips, I assessed the situation. The horse was covered with sweat and blood. It was a puzzle how the animal had managed to not only run a hay rake tine all the way through the upper part of his leg and just under the chest, but to also wedge his hoof between two of the spokes.

I greeted the man standing next to the horse. "Mr. Calumet...Dr. Holliday...my assistant Ms. Sanders."

Calumet held tight to the horse's halter while extending a hand to shake Ella's. He said, "Thanks for coming. I hope it's not as bad as it looks."

At the sound of my voice, the horse tried to move. Apparently the pain and the restriction of his jammed leg caused him to loose several grunts as he tried to dance around. Calumet spoke calming words to the injured animal.

"We'll administer a mild sedative to keep him from jumping about."

Ella opened the bag and handed me a prepared syringe. I made soothing sounds and whispered words known only to the Cherokee. The horse quivered, and I reassured him that I was there to take away the pain. I rubbed my hand down the young stallion's withers, and continued cooing. I ran my hands down his back. The quivering stopped. I quickly and decisively inserted the needle into the chestnut thoroughbred's broad hip muscle.

I handed the empty syringe to Ella and said to Mr. Calumet, "I have a pair of bolt cutters in the truck. We'll need them."

He continued to hold the halter, giving a nod to his barn manager. While we waited, I said, "My hands aren't strong enough to cut through the spokes. You'll need to work fast. Once we've freed Cisco's leg he may try to run. We'll gently lift upward to free him from the tine."

No one spoke as the barn manager grunted and sweated with the effort to cut through the thick iron spokes. The horse relaxed under my hands. I continued to whisper and, as I did, gazed off into the monochromatic landscape, transferring calming thoughts to the animal.

There was a loud pop as the bolt-cutter blades finally cut the metal. "Done."

The barn manager whipped out a bandana and wiped sweat from his forehead. I instructed him to snip off the tine as close to the entry wound as possible. He was quick and accurate.

To Calumet and his manager, I said, "The two of you stand on each side of his head and hold his halter. This is going to hurt, and we can't chance him rearing."

Ella stood back. I ran my hands down the bloodied, slender leg, and held my breath. My heart pummeled in my ears, and I prayed the horse wouldn't panic and rear. I gently lifted his leg. "As soon as he's free, lead him to the rear of my truck."

It pained me to see the injured animal trying to hobble forward—his left foreleg dangled, unable to bear his weight. It took the better part of an hour to completely cleanse the wound to make sure no miniscule flecks of paint had become trapped between the ligaments. It was one of the worst puncture wounds I'd ever seen. It angered me that the owner was more concerned about whether or not the horse would be good to race than he was about the health of the animal.

"The one thing I can guarantee, Mr. Calumet, is that this horse will not run this year. A wound like this can take up to twelve months to heal, unless you want to cripple him for life."

Disgruntlement covered the man's craggy face. I continued, "If Cisco has an excellent lineage, all isn't lost. As a stud he can probably make more than what he'd win at the track." I went on to fill Calumet in on how to change the dressing and apply antibiotic ointment, and finished by saying, "I'll contact your regular vet, Dr. Cooper, and fill him in on today's visit. In the meantime, call me if you detect any sign of infection."

Ella had the truck repacked by the time I'd finished speaking with the two men. I hooked a lead strap to the halter and slowly led the limping horse to the barn. I wanted to see him safely in a stall. Ella followed in the truck and parked in front of the barn's two mammoth double doors.

I shook hands with the men and gave them an appointment card. "I'll see you in two weeks."

****

Dixie County is much like Enigma—rural, with

little industry, and dependent on the tax base of the thriving thoroughbred farms. I pulled into a parking space in front of a decent-looking restaurant called the Pancake House. "I don't know about you, Ella, but my protein bar wore off several hours ago."

"Mine too."

When we entered, a waitress behind the counter smiled and welcomed us. We slid into a booth and picked up menus. The first thing we ordered was coffee and iced water. It didn't take long before our pecan waffles, eggs, and bacon arrived. Between mouthfuls we discussed the horse. I praised her for her professional assistance.

"You did well, Ella. I think we'll make a good team."

Her face pinked, which made her freckles stand out. "How did you know to use the bolt cutters? I looked at the way his hoof was wedged and was honestly stumped."

I said, "I've seen similar incidents, just not quite this bad."

"Tullah?" Ella washed down a mouthful. "I once saw a horse drop dead due to panic. What were you whispering to Cisco that kept him calm?"

"Oh, I can't take credit for what a syringe of sedative did."

"No, I mean before you gave him the shot. It sounded like you were chanting."

I heaved a sigh at the memory. "It's a song my mother used to sing to me. It's part of a Cherokee morning prayer welcoming the new day and saying that our hearts and our spirits are strong."

We sat quiet until I said, "If you don't mind, while

we're here I'd like to visit with Dr. Cooper and his wife. You know, bring him up to speed on the patient, and also see how Doc is getting along with his new hip and physical therapy."

We finished our breakfast. I paid the bill, and we ambled out to the truck. Ella had no way of knowing that my visit was twofold, and part of it was with an ulterior motive.

I drove down Honeysuckle Lane and parked. Ella gasped at the house. "It looks like a cottage right out of a fairytale."

"You'll like Betty and Ben. She's a retired kindergarten teacher, and he, of course, has devoted his entire life to healing animals."

I pressed the doorbell, which sounded like church bell chimes. A short, ruby-cheeked woman with snow-white hair answered the door. Betty invited us in and offered coffee, which we both apologized for declining since we'd recently finished several cups.

Dr. Cooper rested in his recliner. He listened intently, bobbing his head up and down, as I explained in detail about Calumet's colt. He praised my work and thanked us for our quick action. Then I said, "Before we leave, do either of you know where Edna Lampson lives?"

Betty exchanged glances with her husband. She said, "Shipley Road is in the seedier part of Dixie County. Edna's house is at the dead end. Why do you want to know?"

I didn't want to tell a lie. Lying isn't in my nature. I had to think quickly. I explained about the incident in Patty Sweet's bakery and café. "I thought while I'm here, I might go by and check on Ms. Lampson."

Betty reached out and grabbed both my hands. "No. It isn't safe. That son of hers is pure evil in the flesh. He's operating on three brain cells, and actually punches people on impulse for no legitimate reason."

"I've witnessed it, Tullah." Dr. Cooper wore a concerned expression. "That's why Edna lives so far out. As bad as the neighborhood is, no one bothers her. They're afraid of Junior. I've heard that to keep him from wandering off while she's at work, she gives him sleeping pills, and that she has padlocks on the outside of the doors in case he wakes up and tries to get out."

I set their minds at ease with a promise that I wouldn't visit Edna.

****

Once we arrived home, I explained that I was saddling Gandalf and riding out to put up No Trespassing signs all along my fence line.

"Jupiter hasn't been ridden in a while. Do you mind if I tag along?"

"You're sure you want to spend the rest of your day off riding fence line?"

"C'mon, let's get saddled up."

I didn't tell Ella that I also intended to check if Edna Lampson's lot backed up to the Rasmussen property. Five hours later, I had my answer. Edna Lampson's small, dilapidated cottage with peeling white paint and sagging roof sat in the middle of a weed-choked, chain-link-fenced yard, and behind the house sat a medium-sized, rusting, metal storage shed, and behind the weedy shed a gate that opened onto the Rasmussen land. My instincts kept telling me that Junior Lampson was somehow involved with the murders.

Heat had sapped the energy from both of us. I thanked Ella for helping me hang the signs. We were within a few hundred yards of the cattle gate to my yard when a black object swooped down and nearly knocked the hat off my head. Gandalf snorted and sidestepped. I checked him with a pat on the neck and reassuring words.

The object circled around and did a dip and a dive. It was by sheer luck that I reached up and grabbed what resembled a gigantic mosquito.

"What is that, Tullah?"

I turned it over in my hand. "A drone." I glanced toward my house. "Damned reporters." I dropped the black aviation equipment to the ground and commanded, "Up, Gandalf, up."

The pinto gelding reared and reared again, each time coming down on the drone, until I was satisfied it was sufficiently smashed. I stepped out of the saddle and gathered the broken pieces of plastic and wrapped them in the hem of my shirt.

We rode on to the gate. Ella leaned down and pushed it open. Parked in my yard was a black van with the letters WKYB on the door. I trotted the gelding over to where a man dressed in jeans and a blue pullover golf-style shirt stood holding a remote. He wore a sardonic grin as he extended a manicured hand that looked like it'd never seen a hard day's labor. He smiled. "Afternoon, Bruce Webber, reporter for WKYB news."

I ignored his hand. "You're trespassing."

"No, I'm not. Your sign says, "Holliday Veterinary Clinic. That makes it public property."

I dropped the shattered drone at his feet. "I have

No Trespassing signs posted. *That* was in my pasture, which *is* private property."

His upper lip lifted into a snarl. "Do you have any idea how much one of those cost? I'm filing a complaint with the sheriff."

"Go right ahead. Tell him that Dr. Holliday broke your toy."

He slapped his side and guffawed. "Doc Holliday. That's a good one. Next you'll tell me that you're the outlaw reincarnate in a woman's body." He continued to snigger.

"People like you make me tired. However, the sheriff's office is always ready to serve. By the way, the sheriff's name is John Henry Holliday." I cocked an eyebrow.

I stepped down and handed the reins to Ella.

The reporter's snarky grin morphed into a serious frown. He took a step toward me with his fist filled with broken plastic.

Big mistake.

River appeared like a black apparition, his ears flattened and lips pulled back to reveal sharp canine teeth. The hackles stood up on his back, and warning growls rumbled from his chest. Most comical was my little gray donkey trotting up also, as fast as his short legs would carry him.

Rascal brayed a warning and turned his rump toward the man. Before he planted a kick to the reporter's shin, I called him off. Rascal actually looked disappointed when he trotted to stand between my splayed legs. I commanded my snarling dog to heel. He obeyed.

"I think you should hop in your van and leave the

premises, Mr. Webber."

The reporter backed toward the vehicle until he bumped into the front grill. He wasted no time getting to the driver's side door and entering. He rolled down the window and yelled, "You haven't heard the last of me."

I smiled and waved as he backed his truck around and tried to pop a wheelie as he plowed down my driveway.

"You were totally awesome, Tullah. Wow!" Then as an afterthought, Ella said, "Are you worried?"

"Not really."

After unsaddling and cooling off the horses, we each retired to our own home. Inside the kitchen, I opened the refrigerator and poured myself a glass of tea. I also popped the last of my leftover pizza in the microwave.

It wasn't until I settled in my recliner that I realized how tired I was. Nonetheless, I opened my laptop. My heart thumped against my chest. I had received an email from Vaneeta.

Chapter Sixteen

I didn't realize I was holding my breath in expectation of opening Vaneeta's email until my lungs said I needed to gasp for air. I immediately noticed she had sent the message to my dad, with me copied. This brought a smile. Vaneeta was a smart cookie. For caution's sake, she had blind copied Commander Draper and Detective Rooks their own separate emails, allowing Draper to think he'd received top priority on the case. She had promised to notify us first. Still, it was too soon after discovering the remains, and I wondered what kind of information she had for us. I clicked to open.

The subject line read: *Cause of Death-Rasmussen Swamp Jane Does*

While awaiting DNA results, Sanjiv and I focused on cause of death. Results: The hyoid is the U-shaped bone of the neck that is fractured by strangulation. On this basis, our conclusion is that postmortem detection of hyoid fracture is relevant to the diagnosis of manual strangulation in JDs one through ten. JD number eleven is inconclusive at this time due to the missing cervical vertebra.

Sheriff Holliday and Tullah, it is my opinion that whoever killed these women has exceptionally strong hands, principally the thumbs. The hyoid bone in each victim was completely crushed.

Attached is the official report of our findings. I will keep you updated as we continue to uncover the mystery of these victims.

Dr. V. Sanreet

I was so enrapt with reading the information I didn't realize I'd missed my mouth until cold tea wet the front of my shirt. I scolded myself for making a mess. I set my laptop aside, happy it was spared. I drained the last of my tea and gingerly rose from the chair. My muscles were screaming. It had been a while since I've spent so many hours in the saddle, and now I was paying the price. I decided it was time for a long hot soak in the tub with my favorite grapefruit citric bath salts.

I was half way up the stairs when my phone chimed. "Hey, Dad."

"Did you get the email?"

"Yes, sir." I continued up the steps. "Do you think Lonnie or Roy is capable of crushing a hyoid bone?"

"Both men are known drug users. Depending on what combination of drugs they might've used and how sexually aroused they were, yeah, they would have that kind of superhuman strength."

"Have you had any results on the APB you put out?"

"Nothing yet."

"Did Tiny drive Mrs. Pickford to Lexington today?"

"He did. He also took her by the trailer park where she lives to pack a suitcase. While he was there, he did a walk-through of the rooms. The walls of Roy's bedroom were plastered with photographs of women of various ages and in various stages of undress. He also found an empty drug paraphernalia kit. I'm thinking Roy is looking more and more like a prime suspect. With his psychotic history, we need to find him before he hurts someone or himself."

"Once you bring him in, how will you connect him to the murders?"

"When you're working on a case, you have to be open to all possibilities. Right now, big goals start with small steps. I'll run a background to ascertain the dates on all of Roy's arrests, incarcerations, and psych hospitalizations. Until we know the dates of the murders, connecting him or Lonnie to them is like trying to put a puzzle together that has missing pieces."

I understood his position and his frustration. Dad is a man of principles and a stickler for details—although he doesn't mind skewing the details a tad if it helps get positive end results and bring a case to fruition. "Dad, you need another deputy. Even better, you need a deputy with a forensics background. You're working yourself into an early grave."

It aggravated the pure snot out of me that the sheriff's office and jail sweltered in the summer because of antiquated window units for air conditioning and was like an igloo in the winter. Hamburger flippers who never suffered more than an occasional blister on the finger from a hot stove made more money than Dad and Tiny, who often put their lives on the line and worked insufferably long hours. I can't remember the last time Dad took a day off, much less a vacation.

I didn't intend to heighten the pitch of my voice or to get so riled up. "I've already lost one parent. Go to Grandmother and the county commission and plead your case."

"Calm down, Punkin." I knew he was trying to placate me when he chuckled and said, "Since you're familiar with all the perks, you want to apply for the job? I'd hire you in a minute."

I growled and gritted my teeth. "You frustrate me to no end, but I'll always love you."

He said, "Still my Punkin?"

"Always, Dad."

I chewed the inside of my cheek, something I always did when I was aggravated. I changed the subject and related the incident with the reporter and the drone. "His name is Bruce Webber with WKYB. He said he's going to file a complaint for destruction of property and attempted assault."

"Assault? What did you do?"

I laughed. "Not me. River and Rascal. Dad, you should have been here. Rascal backed his little gray rump up to that guy and was ready to plant those tiny hooves against his shin. It's a good thing both of my animals are trained to stand down on command. Otherwise, I think River would have taken Webber apart."

I could almost see Dad grinning even when he said, "I'll check with Judge Duvall about the drone. I'm not up-to-date on FAA regulations. Could be this Webber guy is bluffing about the destruction of property. As for the assault, if Ella witnessed that you didn't sic the animals on Webber and that you called them down, he doesn't have a leg to stand on."

"She videotaped the entire incident on her phone."

"Good. I'll be sure to mention that if Webber comes in to file a complaint."

I stepped into the bathroom, turned on the hot and

cold water, and added a healthy dose of bath salts. "There's something else, Dad."

I related the incident at the Calumet Farm with the young stallion, my visit with Dr. and Mrs. Cooper, and posting the No Trespassing signs.

"Tullah, don't tell me you drove up to the Lampson house." This time his voice held a no-nonsense tone.

"No, sir, I didn't. Ella and I were on horseback when posting the signs." I described the condition of the house, the yard, and the gate. "We were a good eighth of a mile away, yet close enough to see that the gate opened onto land leading to the swamp. And Dad..." I hesitated as goosebumps rippled over me.

"What, Punkin?"

"There was a guy in the back yard. It was too far away to know for sure, but he looked like a hulking hairy beast. When he spotted us, he half ran to the fence and started yelling what sounded like obscenities at us. We had finished hanging the last sign, so Ella and I turned the horses and galloped away."

"What do you mean—he half ran?"

I thought for a second. "Like he was dragging something heavy or maybe something was holding him back. I was a child the last time I saw Junior. Do you think it was him?"

"I'll need to pull up a current photo, or check with Sheriff Dotson to see if he has one on file. Did this person in any way act as if he was attempting to leave the yard?"

"I didn't turn to look. I thought it best we leave as soon as possible."

"If my calculations are correct, the Lampsons are approximately five miles from your house. That's about a two-hour walk between the Lampsons, your house, and the swamp. If the only access to the swamp is through the gate you spotted, then I'd say it'd be highly unlikely that Junior Lampson could tote a body for five miles, bury it, then return to his house, all in the same night."

"Does that mean you're ruling him out as a person of interest?"

"Let's just say that he isn't a strong blip on my radar. Even though there's a fence separating your property from the swamp, you and Ella keep your doors locked at all times."

"Will do."

We said our goodnights. I tossed the phone on the bed and stripped off my dirty clothes and stepped into the bathtub, allowing the steaming water to rise up to my chin. By the time the water had turned cold, I was hungry. After toweling off and changing into my oversized T-shirt, I grabbed my phone, skipped downstairs, made a peanut-butter-and-jelly sandwich, and filled a glass with milk.

Back upstairs, I propped in bed, enjoying my snack while reading my newest mystery novel, so engrossed in the plot I actually jumped when the phone chimed.

"Hello, Grandmother."

Her voice gushed, "He's here, Tullah."

"Who is *he*?"

"Pedar Neilsen, and Tullah, he's married. He brought his wife."

I released a squeal just to annoy her. "Hallelujah. That lets me off the hook. What else?"

Honestly, I really didn't want to know…what else. I was ready to turn out the light and call it a night.

I heard the frown in her voice as she chastised me for being snide, then said, "He and his wife, Inga, are resting tomorrow. Jet lag. Tuesday, we're meeting for supper at Patty's. Six sharp. I'm eager to hear what Pedar has to say about the swamp."

I was eager, too. What if he was announcing that he'd decided to sell the property to a mega conglomerate that was only interested is raping the land for some unorthodox enterprise that would destroy the homes of wildlife and the ecosystem and for what—a profit? I inwardly growled.

As much as I wanted to spout off, I didn't. Instead, I said, "Grandmother, when was the last time you were inside Dad's office?"

"What's this about, Tullah?"

"Poor Joyce is sweltering in front of a desk fan that blows hot air because the antiquated window units don't cool the building. It's a good thing the jail cells aren't full. Otherwise, the prisoners would die of heat stroke. Don't even get me started on the frigid temperatures in the winter. Grandmother, you are the mayor. I know you've only been in office less than a year, but can't you convince the city council to make remodeling the entire building a priority? Have you taken a good look at the front entrance lately? It looks every bit of its hundred years. There's also the little matter of Dad and Tiny needing another deputy. Have you seen the dark circles under Dad's eyes? Between the heat and the long hours with no days off, let's just say I've lost one parent, and I'm not ready to be an orphan even at my age."

"Tu-llah." She splits my name into syllables when making a point. "You are speaking with your jaws clenched." Her voice was quiet, firm, and even. "Calm down, or you'll blow a gasket. I am fully aware that the building is literally falling apart at the seams. In fact, Joyce is on Thursday's agenda. She's addressing the Council and the County Commissioners about all the items you've mentioned."

Grandmother cleared her throat. "I'm letting you in on a little secret. After Joyce presents her case, I'm proposing to the council and the county commission that it would be more cost effective to build a new sheriff's office and jail. I'm prepared for some pushback from the old farts whose foresight is limited to the end of their noses. However, Patty and a few others will back me. My argument is that if we wish to bring industry to Enigma, then we cannot continue to look like an Old West ghost town. In fact, Patty, Joyce, and Flora are my committee to contact companies that provide soft industry to small towns like ours. They've had some excellent response and will present their information to the council and commissioners."

Excitement oozed from Grandmother's voice. "And Tullah, they went to the library and got help putting together a power point presentation to show to the council and commissioners. It's wonderful that at our ages we're learning new technology."

Her excitement faded, and her voice became serious again. "There's simply no money in the budget for another deputy. I'm hopeful that once we bring in industry and our tax base increases we'll get Henry and Tiny all the help they need."

Grandmother gave me the time of the meeting. She also ticked off a half-dozen businesses, plus a movie production company, that sounded like strong prospects. I truly hoped my appointment schedule was light enough for Ella to handle the office by herself. I wanted to attend the meeting.

Chapter Seventeen

Pedar Nielsen was not the short, bald, paunch-bellied man I had envisioned. Rather, he was tall, slim hipped, hair the color of spun gold, and his eyes an odd shade of gray-blue that seemed to know both pain and joy. Honest eyes.

I took an immediate liking to both him and his wife, Inga. She was tall and willowy, with blue eyes and white-blonde hair that formed a halo around her face. She did look a little pale, and I asked if she was still tired from the long flight. She blushed and a dimple deepened with a timid smile when she said she was pregnant with her first child.

Pedar proudly announced, "Inga is a coloring book artist. She designs coloring books for authors who write books for children."

"What is it that you do, Pedar?" My interest was more than mild curiosity.

"By trade, I am an agronomist. However, as a family, we own one of the finest dairies in Denmark. My brother-in-law manages the milking barns and milk production, while my sister oversees the cheese-making operation. My mother runs all of us."

We laughed at the joke. Still, I'm more concerned than ever—Pedar is an agronomist. Before I could ask my question about his plans for the swamp, Patty and a waitress served our meals. Patty had offered to prepare a typical Danish menu in their honor. I think she was a bit disappointed when Pedar and Inga declared they wished to experience an American cuisine, with a request to keep the meal light due to the hot weather.

As usual, Patty did not disappoint with chilled watermelon soup, bacon-wrapped chicken breasts stuffed with gruyere and asparagus, garlic-buttered baby potatoes, and crème brûlée for dessert.

Pedar wiped his mouth with a linen napkin and laid it aside. "Dr. Ritter, my grandfather expresses his regrets that his health kept him at home. He did so wish to visit with his childhood friend." Pedar handed the old doctor an envelope. "He sends this."

We all sat expectant as Dr. Ritter opened the large white packet. It held a letter, which he set aside. His eyes sparkled with tears when he held forth a sepia photograph of two young boys seated together. He pointed, "This is Lars, and this handsome lad is me. We were wearing our first pair of dress knickers and were so proud to have our picture taken." He thanked Lars and said he'd read the letter later.

Lars then placed his hands on the table, his fingers laced together. It appeared from the expression on his face that he grappled for words. "The Rasmussen curse has dominated our lives. Even in the twilight of his years, Grandfather still has screaming nightmares. He still sees the body of his dead brother, and his mother struggling to keep Adolph from dumping the body down the well. Until the day she died, great-great-grandmother Greta blamed—no, punished herself for calling down the curse."

He paused, his eyes sad. "We read about the remains of those poor unfortunate women. It seems the

Rasmussen land is truly cursed."

Inga trembled when she reached over and placed a hand on her husband's arm. She looked at us and said, "A curse is like a dragon. Once the dragon is slayed, it can no longer attack you. We don't know how to slay this dragon and hope you can help."

He laid his hand over hers. His eyes were earnest when he continued. "I am here to look at the land to see its worth, and then I will decide. Grandfather has given me legal documents to act in his stead. He wishes to free our family and those who come after us of this albatross before he dies." Pedar drew a deep breath and exhaled. "Henry, Tullah, may I request that you act as my guides and show me this cursed place that has bedeviled my family for almost a hundred years?"

Dad and I agreed. I said, "We haven't had rain in almost ten days. We can drive the truck as close as possible, then walk into the interior." I asked Pedar and Inga if they had heavy-duty boots. "The swamp has poisonous snakes. The heat makes them extra fractious."

Pedar nodded. "Grandfather spoke of killing the rattlesnakes when he was a young lad. In my country, we have the *vipera berus* which is quite poisonous. I have packed my *botte sauvage* as a precaution."

Inga smiled as she caressed her budding baby bump. "I am afraid that I am not used to your hot weather. Pedar has agreed it is better for me to remain at the hotel."

Grandmother and Patty invited Inga to attend their monthly book club meeting. Patty refilled our tea glasses. "We call ourselves the Bookworm Biddies. Our members would love to have a celebrity coloring book artist as our special guest. Isn't that right, Tanti?"

Grandmother beamed and said, "Yes, but of course we'll understand if…"

Inga's dimple deepened with her smile. "I'd be honored."

Pedar nodded graciously at Grandmother and Patty. "I am also honored that you ladies will look after my Inga while I am away." His jaw ticked as he looked into his wife's keen blue eyes. "Inga is correct. We must find a way to release the land from its curse. I cannot fail my grandfather."

Maybe my brain was having a fanciful moment. I exchanged glances with my grandmother, who seemed to read my mind when she nodded. A worm of excitement crawled through me, leaving delightful prickles in its wake. I said, "Actually, there may be a way. Uma Hoktochee is a cousin who is learned in the old ways of the Cherokee and the Navajo. She lives in Lexington, not too far from here. Though she is old, ninety-two years, her mind is sharp. The Native people had many ways of dealing with curses."

"My granddaughter has an inner sense about such things. It is good that she has thought of cousin Uma. I shall contact her immediately."

Pedar and Inga exchanged wide-eyed glances. He transferred his attention to my grandmother. "Mrs. Crow, I am hopeful your cousin will know how to help us."

Dad's mouth hung open. He glanced from me to Grandmother to the Nielsens and then back to me, as if trying to comprehend what he'd just heard. Then his mouth snapped shut. The crinkles around his blue eyes deepened with his concern. "Tullah, be careful. Dark magic is nothing to play with."

"You and Pedar will be with me, Dad."

"And me, too." Grandmother gave us a conspiratorial smile. She glanced at the large clock on the café's wall. "I must telephone Uma before she retires for the night. Why don't we meet at my apartment in an hour?"

****

Grandmother set our drinks on small square napkins before broaching the subject of her conversation with Cousin Uma. She seated herself and didn't speak. A myriad of emotions played across her face. She tucked a strand of black hair behind her ear. Her ebony eyes were troubled. We waited.

The air conditioner kicked on. A light breeze wafted down from the ceiling vent, cooling the small living room. Grandmother spoke as if she were out of breath.

"Cousin Uma says the only way to break the curse is for a kinsman to collect the bones of the innocent and the evil. The bones are to be buried in a place of sanctity." She held forth a piece of paper. "I have written down the words that are to be spoken over the grave of the evil one."

Pedar leaned forward, bracing his hands against his knees. "According to Grandfather, the swamp is vast." He sighed. "This is an impossible task."

A flash of memory hit me. "I think I know where to find the bones."

All eyes focused on me. Dad's were particularly troubled. Moonlight angled through the venetian blind's slats, casting its pale glow across the brown wooden planks of the floor. I looked over at Pedar. "This is going to sound crazy."

I rose and crossed the room to peer through the white slats into the darkness. Inside my head, I heard the owl calling. I turned and said, "The bones are resting at the bottom of the evil-eye. It's in the heart of the swamp."

Pedar looked between his wife and me. "What is this evil-eye, and how deep is it?"

Dr. Ritter had remained quiet. We had forgotten he was with us until he spoke. "I believe it is where the crevice opened and swallowed everything in sight." His voice softened to a whisper, "Only Greta and Lars remained physically unscathed. I was ten years old and witnessed all of it. I ran to town to get help, and when I returned, the place where the earth had opened like a wide gaping mouth had by that time closed into the shape of an eye. I have never returned to that place."

Pedar persisted. "That still does not answer my question about the depth."

I breathed deeply and closed my eyes. "The water is dark. I'm not sure anyone knows the answer to your question. It could be shallow or unfathomable."

"Then we need to find out. Where might I purchase goggles and an underwater lamp?"

Inga gave a ragged sigh. She cradled the baby bump as if trying to protect it. Her words came out in a rush. "Pedar, no, please. You cannot do this."

Inga's pleading gaze landed on me a second longer than I felt comfortable with. It was no longer excitement that wormed through me, but icy fingers of dread. Cousin Uma's solution to the curse brought little comfort.

Chapter Eighteen

At daybreak, Dad's 4Runner bounced over the
rutted ground toward the swamp. Even at this early
hour the day promised to be a scorcher. No one spoke
as he drove. It seemed all our minds were preoccupied
with today's event. Thankfully, Grandmother had
agreed to remain in town to attend her book club
meeting. Both she and Patty had vowed to treat Inga to
a pleasant afternoon.

After leaving Grandmother's apartment last night, I
had followed Dad to his office where I suggested he ask
Charlie to go with us to the swamp. The more
manpower the better, in case we ran into trouble.

He parked and shut off the engine. Charlie grabbed
the backpack I had filled with frozen water bottles and
packets of crackers and handed it to me. Dad opened
the hatch and issued each of us a long walking stick.
Charlie wore a holster with a sawed-off twenty-two
rifle snugged inside. He called it his "snake-charmer." I
was certain he would need it today.

Dad pulled out a can of insect repellent. We doused
ourselves liberally. He also removed a canvas duffel
bag which he strapped across his back. If we located the
bones, the duffel bag would be their temporary
transport until they were buried in holy ground.

Pedar pointed to the black dots circling in the
distance. "Are those birds?"

"Buzzards," I said. "They're waiting for a sick or injured animal to die before they swoop in and feed on the remains."

Pedar adjusted his sunglasses. "Grandfather Lars tried many times to describe this place. Never could I imagine its vastness." He bent down and snatched a clump of dried wild grass from the ground. He rolled the rooted dirt between his thumb and forefinger, and shook his head. "The soil is poor. It lacks nutrients."

He gazed out over the expanse. "Grandfather Lars said there is a thousand acres. How much of it is arable?"

"Tullah, Charlie, and I have ridden, on horseback, every inch of walkable land, which is about a hundred acres." Dad pointed to the swamp. "The rest is the way you see it—dead or dying trees, pools of stagnant water filled with duckweed."

Pedar hefted his rucksack. "I don't understand. If there is water, then why is the dirt dead?"

Charlie said, "When it rains, the water fills the holes. Swamp water is slow moving. It is stagnant. As far as we know, there are no underground springs to feed the land."

Dad said, "Keep your ears open and your eyes to the ground." He was really saying this for Pedar's sake. "And use your walking pole. What looks like solid ground is sometimes misleading, and you can sink up to your waist."

At the first shallow indention in the earth, Pedar stopped. "Is this what I think it is?"

"Yes," I said, "it's where we found the first set of human remains. We will pass others along the way."

"Sad. Truly sad. How far until we reach the devil's

eye?"

I pointed my stick toward the interior. "About two miles. The first time we found it was purely accidental."

The swamp was anything but quiet. The rustle of leaves in the canopy of trees mixed with chirps and the buzzing of cicadas and mosquitos. A twig snapped and a deer wandered out, looking at us with mild curiosity before retreating to the safety of the swamp. Somewhere in the distance, cows mooed plaintively.

We had walked about two miles when Pedar said, "Forgive me. I do not wish to complain, but I am not used to this heat. It feels as if the air is being sucked from my lungs. May we stop for a water break?"

He wiped a sleeve across his glistening brow. He unslung the pack from his shoulder and stepped toward a fallen tree trunk as if to sit and rest. Charlie whipped the rifle from its holster and pointed toward the ominous rattling.

Between gritted teeth Dad warned, "Pedar! Do. Not. Move."

Blood drained from the blond Dane's face, leaving him looking horror-stricken.

Pedar had apparently disturbed the rattler that had been cooling in the moist shade of a fallen tree. The serpent had coiled within an inch of Pedar's boot. Too close for Charlie to squeeze off a shot without risking a bullet in Pedar's foot. The viper's triangular head arched, its forked tongue flicked in and out, and black beady eyes gleamed pure malice. The whirring rattles added to our ill-omened mission.

I held my breath for fear breathing might agitate the viper. I cut my eyes toward Charlie as he eased a long hunting knife from the scabbard at his waist. It seemed as if he moved in slow motion when he drew back and hurled the weapon. Even as the sharp-honed blade found its mark, pinning the rattler's broad head against the fallen tree, the snake uncoiled and writhed fiercely to free itself from the weapon.

Pedar leaped forward to safety. Charlie grabbed the thick neck with one hand and jerked the knife out of the snake's head. Then with precision speed, he separated its head from its body. He tossed the triangular head, its fangs curved in a deadly grin, deep into the underbrush. Before cutting off the rattles, he held the headless reptile up by its tail, its body nearly as long as Charlie was tall. The viper's girth was as big around as my upper arm. Charlie said, "You were lucky, Pedar. He would have bitten through the leather of your boot." He held the rattles out to Pedar.

Pedar's hand trembled as he accepted the souvenir. "I am indebted to you, Mr. Whitehorse."

I pulled bottles of water from my backpack and handed them all around. Pedar said, "I do not normally scare easily. When we return to town, I will require a stronger drink than water."

Charlie clapped him on the back. He chuckled warm and deep. "I own the best bar in town. I'll buy."

After slaking our thirst, we stored the empty plastic bottles in my backpack and continued deeper into the swamp, even more watchful than before. Each time we passed an open shallow grave, Pedar made the sign of the cross and mumbled what sounded like a prayer.

After the morning's close call, I worried about the Dane, especially since he was looking a little pasty. Clearly the heat was taking its toll on him. I admired the man for not complaining.

I surveyed the horizon, noting the cloudless sky. It was barely nine o'clock and the air inside the swamp's interior was stifling. Our sweat-soaked clothing clung to our bodies like a second skin.

"How much longer?" Whatever enthusiasm Pedar possessed when we began this journey had left his voice.

I tried to make light of his question. "Oh, as the crow flies, not long. But we have to take the scenic route." I used my stick to point through the woods. The terrain had turned rougher as we traveled. Briar vines snagged our pant legs and tangled around our boots, threatening to trip us as we struggled forward. A mere two-mile hike felt like twenty. Soon we emerged from a thick part of the marsh onto a muddy slough. My foot slipped against a large rock, and I came down on one knee and ripped my pants leg. Blood oozed through the abrasion. Dad rushed to my side. "It's not deep, Dad, nothing to worry about. I'll clean it up when we get home."

We pushed farther without taking a break. My knee throbbed, and I was ready for a rest. About fifty yards up the trail, I pointed. "There it is. The devil's eye."

Amid the wild grasses, moss-draped trees hugged the bank, their low-hanging branches dipping into the weed-choked, eye-shaped lagoon. Murky shafts of light streamed. A gust of hot wind swept across the swamp and moaned through the watery fissure. As if in answer, an owl belled in a melancholic fashion from a tree. I looked up, and there on a bare limb sat a great barred owl—my owl. I am certain it looked me in the eyes and winked.

Charlie spotted it, too. He squeezed my shoulder and said nothing. I wondered what message the raptor was trying to send me.

Shadows seemed to play tricks on us as the sun dipped behind the trees, casting long silhouettes that disappeared into the dark pool of water. Dad and Charlie beat their sticks around the edges of the pool to scare out any lurking moccasins. None appeared. That was a good sign.

Hesitancy and perhaps a little fear showed on Pedar's heat-blotched face when he said, "Are you certain this is where the bones of my ancestors rest?"

Dad spoke up. "My daughter has a way of knowing the unknown, as did her mother. I was with Tullah when we first happened upon this place. It was then that she told me the bones of Adolph and his son were here and that they were not at peace. You must trust her."

Pedar raised his brows at me. "But how do you know?"

I pointed to the tree. "He told me."

Still appearing skeptical, he looked upward at the tree. "An owl?"

Charlie said, "We Native people believe that owls are the messengers of good and evil. If Tullah says the owl led her to this place, do not doubt her. If she says the bones of your people rest inside the evil eye, then you must believe her."

Pedar loosed a shuddering sigh. "At this point, what I do know is this place has no value. I can understand why Grandfather Lars never wanted to return here."

I protested. "It does have value. It is a sanctuary for that which you cannot see—the coyote, fox, deer, squirrels and rabbits, possums, raccoons, the eagle, hummingbirds, and owls, and even black bear."

He thought for a moment. "I was speaking in the monetary sense. However, as you are a veterinarian, I understand your logic."

Changing the subject, Pedar stepped forward and dropped to his knees. He lay flat on his belly at the grassy bank and plunged his walking stick deep, until the water rose up to his shoulder. He said, "The stick is six feet. With my arm, that measures approximately nine feet. I do not feel a bottom." He stood, brushing wet debris from his clothes. He smelled his hand and wrinkled his nose. "Even the water smells rancid."

We three stood at the bank, staring into the unwinking, watery eye, and the eye stared back at us. The air was heavy with the putrid smells of rotting vegetation. The water itself was a blackish green. Big rocks were submerged in the gloomy depths, looking like sunken ruins. Resurrection fern lay along tree limbs like wilted feathers.

Meaningless thoughts meandered through my head, and I wondered if the soul of Adolph, Junior, was speaking to me. *"We are who we are when we are born. We become who we make of ourselves as we age. And then, good or bad, we die. I did not know myself. I died before my time."*

"My goddaughter speaks a message from the dead."

I hadn't realized I spoke the words—Adolph, Junior's?—aloud.

Dad hugged me. He remained silent as he held my trembling body.

It was Charlie who said, "There is not enough

room for a man to dive into the depths. If he went head first, he would drown from lack of air because he would not be able to right himself. It is best to leave the bones where they are."

"No, I must do this," Pedar objected. "You heard what the old woman said. We have to remove the bones and bury them in a sacred place. Otherwise, all those before and after me will never know a moment's peace."

Pedar unzipped his rucksack and removed a length of coiled rope, goggles, and an underwater light. He fashioned a loop and placed it under his arms, tightening it around his chest. "I think I will fit if I go in feet first. Give me two or three minutes. Before my lungs run out of air, I'll give a yank for you to haul me up." He sat on the ground, tugged off his boots, and emptied his pant pockets, zipping the contents inside his bag.

"You don't have to do this, Pedar." I sat down and rested my head against my knees. The cicadas' buzzing increased until I wanted to clamp my hands over my ears and scream for them to cease.

He didn't answer. Instead, he heaved in and out, expanding his chest and filling his lungs with air. Charlie grabbed the rope and wrapped it around his waist as he braced his feet apart. Pedar sat at the edge of the dark abyss and dangled his stockinged feet into the water. He adjusted the goggles over his eyes. Without a word and barely creating a ripple, flashlight in hand, he pushed off the bank. The light's beam created an eerie glow as Pedar Nielsen disappeared below the murky surface of the devil's eye.

The cicadas ceased their irritating rattle. The air

stilled. It was as if the swamp held its breath. The rope inched through Charlie's powerful, gloved hands. I was afraid to ask how deep he thought Pedar had descended. Instead, I grabbed my phone from my backpack and set the timer for one minute thirty seconds, and I prayed that it was not Pedar's time to die. It seemed the seconds turned into an eternity.

"One minute fifteen seconds. Shouldn't we pull him up?"

"We will honor him by waiting for his signal."

Two minutes had passed and the rope lay slack in Charlie's hands. We exchanged anxious glances. What if Pedar had run out of air and drowned? I was ready to demand that he reel in the line when Charlie shouted, "Haul 'im up."

Dad and I grabbed hold, adding our strength to Charlie's. My own lungs were near to bursting when Pedar's head broke the water's surface. We dragged him onto the bank, his clothing and blond hair coated with sludge. Pedar lay on his back, staring up at the sky, gasping for air. The flashlight rolled out of his hand.

We sat next to him and waited. He closed his eyes and took long, slow inhalations. When he regained his breath, he said, "The sides of the abyss were slimy to touch and very narrow. It was difficult to see, even with the light." He sat up and placed a finger to the side of his nose and blew, sending out a spray of dirty water. "The rope was twenty feet, and I didn't reach bottom.

He raked fingers through his muddy hair. Rivulets of water dripped from his chin. His eyes were filled with despair. His voice hitched with desperation. "I have failed."

I picked up the flashlight and turned off the beam.

What could I say to convince this despondent man that he was not a failure? "You are wrong, Pedar. The swamp is a sanctuary—a safe haven for living beings. Perhaps not for a sixteen-year-old boy who never had the opportunity to grow to manhood, and perhaps not to your great-grandmother, or to an old doctor who has lived a lifetime with the horrors he witnessed as a ten-year-old child."

I offered a sad smile to Pedar as I removed my cellphone from my pocket. "If you have no objection, I'll call Father Timothy and explain the situation. If he's willing, we can return tomorrow so he can bless this place, and for you to speak the words that Cousin Uma has given us."

Pedar looked at us, his face filled with uncertainty. His gaze settled on Charlie. "What do you think I should do? I mean…all this Native stuff and all."

Charlie clapped Pedar on the shoulder. "My people are of the Jicarilla Apache. During the early times of war, many warriors, women, and children lay alone in the prairie grasses, their bones bleaching in the sun. I believe the Great Spirit Father called their names and they live beyond the clouds with Him. Listen to Tullah. She is wise. Consider her suggestion."

Pedar squeezed water from his socks before he tugged on his boots. He stood and placed his hands in his back pockets. He walked a short distance and stood looking at the sky. It did not take a mind reader to know that he wrestled with his decision.

Charlie rarely speaks of his heritage, preferring to keep it close to his heart. It is only recently that we learned his father was Jicarilla Apache and his mother Aleut.

The cell phone vibrated against the palm of my hand. I opened the screen and held it toward Dad for him to see the email icon. He nodded. I opened the screen and said, "It's from Vaneeta."

His phone buzzed. He unbuttoned his shirt pocket and removed his phone. "I got one, too."

Vaneeta obviously had more information about the remains we'd discovered. I said, "Do we open the message or wait?"

Dad glanced to where Pedar stood with his back to us. "Not the time or the place. Wait."

My phone chirped. I opened the text. Keeping my voice low, I said, "It's from Ella. I'm needed at the clinic."

My thumbs moved rapidly across the keypad. "Situation here stalled. Describe the injury."

Before Ella could reply, Pedar rejoined us. He said, "Call the priest."

I breathed a sigh of relief. "I need to return to the clinic. My assistant has a patient that requires my attention."

"Of course. I am sorry to take you away from your hospital. Let us go."

I sent Ella a text letting her know that I was on my way.

The trip out of the swamp took less time than hiking in. As soon as we stowed our gear and climbed into the 4Runner, Dad turned on the air conditioning. He said, "Hold on. We're in for a bumpy ride."

We secured our seatbelts. I think Dad hit every pot hole between the swamp and the first gate. Charlie jumped out and swung the gate wide. I took the opportunity to scroll through my phone's directory and dialed Father Timothy's number. I put the phone on speaker.

As soon as he answered, Dad was back on the road—or I should say jostling over the rough terrain—which made talking on the phone difficult. I explained the reason for my call. It never occurred to me that Father Timothy might refuse to go traipsing through the woods to bless a watery grave. He didn't disappoint and asked what time he should be ready.

Dad glanced into the rearview mirror. "Pedar?"

"Same as this morning."

Dad nodded.

I said to Father Timothy, "It gets awfully hot in the swamp. Is six too early?"

Father Timothy replied, "Not at all. I'll come armed with my Bible and snake boots. It's been a while since I've had the opportunity to go hiking."

"Good. Dad will pick you up. We'll also treat you to supper at The Whitehorse."

Father Timothy chuckled. "Now, that's an offer I can't refuse. Chicken wings, I hope."

Pedar leaned forward. "Many thanks, Father. There will be an extra offering in the alms box before my wife and I leave Enigma."

Dad stopped at the last gate. Charlie hopped out to open it. For a man of forty-seven, Charlie is still agile as a cat. He leaped on the truck's running board and waved Dad onward.

I was out of my seatbelt by the time the vehicle rolled to a stop in front of my clinic. I opened the door. "See you in the morning."

"What about supper tonight? Mine and Inga's treat."

"As much as I'd like to commit, sometimes these emergencies take hours. Thanks all the same."

"Another time, and thank you."

I said goodbye and slammed the door. Ella stood keys and medical bag in hand, waiting for me. She said, "We have a twenty-year-old Shetland pony bleeding profusely through the nostrils. It's in Dixie County. I've already notified the owner that we're on our way."

I smiled to myself. Ella was a keeper.

The stars were out by the time we returned home. The old pony had suffered a severe kick to the head by a larger horse. After determining there were no fractures to the skull and no bone chips lodged in the pony's sinus cavity, we stanched the hemorrhage and assured the owner and his young daughter that her pony had a few more good years left.

As eager as I was to read Vaneeta's email, a hot bath was my priority, and then food. On the way home, I put in a call to Charlie for BBQ sandwiches. We swung by the saloon's drive-thru window. When Flora handed our orders out the window, she smiled. "Charlie said to tell you he'd see you in the morning and to enjoy the eclairs."

Good ol' Charlie. He knew how much his customers, including me, loved Patty's eclairs, and he always ordered extra to serve with meals at the bar. It was just like him to sneak a few in as a surprise.

I thanked Ella for handling the clinic on her own today. She said, "It's exciting, and I'm learning so much from you."

I parked under the carport. We said our goodnights. I could tell by the slump of her shoulders that Ella was as exhausted as I as she strode across the yard toward her trailer, her sack of food clutched in her hand.

Dressed in a baggy T-shirt, refreshed from my bath, and sated with food, I was glad to finally get cozy in my recliner. I opened my laptop and clicked on email.

The subject line read: *Identification: Rasmussen Swamp Victims*

Our forensics odonatologist and orthopedist have successfully identified ten victims via dental records and orthopedic appliances. At this time and until we research DNA further, results for JD #11 remain inconclusive. Attached is the formal report. Commander Draper and Detective Rooks have also been notified. I will keep you updated as we continue to solve the mystery of the last Rasmussen victim's identity.

Dr. V. Sanreet

After I had reread the email at least a dozen times, I sent Dad a text asking him to call me. The phone rang almost immediately.

He said, "I know how tired you are, Punkin, and thought you might pack it in early, especially since we're starting before sun-up tomorrow morning. What was the emergency Ella couldn't handle?"

I explained about having to drive to Dixie County to treat a Shetland pony's bloody nose. "Ella was afraid the pony had suffered epistaxis, which is blunt trauma to the head and often causes death. She hasn't had that much experience with this type of condition."

"Smart girl. She was right to contact you."

"Dad, using the information Vaneeta sent, I've created a chart and already emailed it to you. We have a pattern, of sorts."

I heard his email alert bong. He said, "Hang on. Give me a minute to look it over."

I had my screen open, too.

Dad finally said, "Other than the victims' names and a pattern indicating the killer likes women in their twenties, we don't have much to go on. Joyce is researching the NCIC files to locate photos of the women and other information pertaining to their cases."

"Will you keep me informed?"

"It's police business, Tullah."

"I know, Dad. It was my dog that found the skeletal hand and brought it to me, and it was my dog that led us to the bodies. This gives me a vested interest in the case."

Dad chuckled. "You present a good argument. You should have been a lawyer, or maybe a detective."

I audibly yawned.

"What you need is a good night's sleep. Try not to stress over today's events or tomorrow's ceremony."

"G'night, Dad. See you bright and early."

I shut down my laptop and dragged my weary bones upstairs. River and Rascal followed. They settled on their bed. I envy my animals. They were already asleep and snoring. I plumped my pillow and rolled to my side, reaching to turn out the lamp.

Chapter Nineteen

Sometimes I uncomfortably awaken with a low-level dread in the pit of my gut. That was one of those mornings. I hadn't slept well.

I sipped a cup of coffee as I sat on the porch swing watching for Dad's 4Runner to come rumbling down my drive. I felt tense and didn't know why. The answer was soon to arrive.

Charlie's white Suburban pulled close to the porch. My godfather rolled down the window, and his smile was fleeting when he said, "Henry and Tiny have important business. I'm afraid you're stuck with me."

I left my empty mug on the swing, grabbed my backpack, and trotted down the steps. River and Rascal followed. The passenger side door opened, and Father Timothy stepped out to make room for me between him and Charlie. I climbed in and was surprised to see a couple of unexpected guests in the back seat. Father Timothy set my backpack on the floorboard between his feet.

Charlie hopped out and opened the Suburban's back doors. He motioned, and the animals leaped inside. He commanded them to stay, and being the obedient animals that they are, they settled in for the ride.

Grandmother leaned forward and patted my hand. "Good morning, Tullah. Is that pleasure or displeasure on your face?"

"Neither...well, I mean...surprise and a little pleasure, I guess. It's a long hike to the devil's eye, and I'm sure Pedar has already told you about his close encounter with a rattler."

I tried to smile when I looked at the old man sitting next to her. "Dr. Ritter, are you sure you're up to this?"

He grumped, "No, I'm not sure. I just know that I have to do this for Lars and for me. Besides, I walk my mile every morning. You youngsters don't need to fret on my account."

I was surprised to see Inga seated next to her husband. She held a medium-sized potted plant in her lap. Apparently, she knew I expected an explanation and said, "It is called a swamp rose. I have been assured it is hardy and produces beautiful pink flowers. The man at the nursery said the roses have a wonderful aroma." She lifted her shoulders in a demure way. "Greta used to tell us that Dolphy had such a green thumb." She slipped her hand inside her husband's. "She always said Pedar inherited his love of plants and the soil from his Uncle Dolphy. So I think it would please Greta to know we are planting this rose to honor Dolphy."

I agreed that it was a generous gesture. "And what about you, Grandmother?"

Dr. Ritter's voice held an edge of defiance. "Tanti is here because I asked her to come with us."

Grandmother's face colored slightly. I'd often wondered if she and Dr. Ritter had a secret thing going between them. The way he came to her defense made me wonder even more. However, she said, "I'm here in my newswoman capacity."

Charlie climbed behind the steering wheel and glanced at me. "Are we ready to roll?"

I nodded, turned in the seat, and strapped the seatbelt across my chest. No one spoke. I was glad, because agitation itched my scalp. Charlie stopped at the first gate. Father Timothy had apparently appointed himself as the official gate opener.

I reached inside my pocket and handed him a key. Mine is the only gate with a padlock. The ones that separated my land from the swamp were barbed wire stapled to a fence post and with a barbed wire loop to hold it closed.

While we waited for the priest to unlock the gate and give the signal to drive through, I said, "What is the business that Dad and Tiny are on?"

Charlie shifted the truck into gear. "He got a call from a hospital in Louisville about a patient named Angela Davis. The hospital said she was in pretty bad shape and had requested they get in touch with Henry. He and Tiny left about an hour ago."

I glanced at my watch. It was now six-thirty. I remembered her two black eyes, the puffy upper lip, and the mass of bruises on her arms the day Dr. Sanders notified us. "Poor Angela. If only she had listened. If only she had accepted our help."

He reached over and patted my hand. "Frightened people often make bad judgments. You can't help those who refuse to help themselves."

Two more gates and we arrived at the same familiar spot. Charlie switched off the engine. Father Timothy opened the door and stepped to the ground. He grabbed my backpack and offered me a hand of assistance. "This bag is heavy, and cold. If you don't mind my asking, what's in it?"

I wasn't used to seeing Father Timothy dressed in denims, the legs tucked inside a pair of cowboy boots. A black man in his fifties, with gray at the fringes of his curly hair, a kind man with gentle hazel eyes, his five-foot-eleven frame towered over my five-foot-nine. I accepted his hand. His rosary graced the front of his traditional short-sleeved black shirt with white clergy collar.

"Frozen water bottles," I answered. "By the time we're thirsty, they'll be thawed enough to drink. There's also breakfast bars. The humidity has a way of sapping the energy right out of you."

Charlie opened the back doors. My dog and donkey hopped out, ready to romp. Charlie removed the walking sticks and handed one to each of us with the same cautionary warning to watch where we stepped. I explained that we'd see the gravesites of the bodies we'd uncovered. Inga's fair complexion was looking even paler in the morning heat. I didn't want her swooning when we happened upon a gravesite.

Inga was the one I worried about the most, especially since she was in the critical stages of her pregnancy. What if she fell, or got overheated, or snake bit? These questions plagued me. At least Pedar had relieved her from the burden of carrying the potted rose. We hiked forward single file, with me in the lead and Charlie bringing up the rear to make certain no one lagged behind.

Inga mused, "This is certainly a noisy place."

"Yes," I said. "The swamp makes its own kind of music."

I decided to take it slow, respecting the ages of my

grandmother and the old doctor. We passed several of the gravesites. Each time, Grandmother stopped to snap photos with her cellphone. We'd walked about an hour when Grandmother let out a little yelp. Her foot had become entangled in a briar vine, and she'd taken a tumble. Inga's and Dr. Ritter's faces were beet red from the humidity and perhaps the exertion. Although Inga was svelte, I wasn't sure how physically fit she was.

"Tanti?" Dr. Ritter bent from the waist. "Are you hurt?"

Charlie lifted Grandmother like she was a sack of fluff. She rewarded him with a pat on the chest. She smiled at Dr. Ritter. "Only my pride. Now, don't fuss."

I unzipped my pack and doled out the water and breakfast bars. Inga poured a little water in her hand and splashed her heated face. She expelled a delightful squeal and cried, "Look, look, look."

Two marsh rabbits hopped from behind a fallen tree. Inga's screech seemed to frighten the poor animals. They sat frozen for a moment before scampering into the bleakness of the swamp.

"Forgive my inquisitiveness, Dr. Holliday. Has your father learned the identities of those poor women whose bodies you found?"

I reminded Inga that I preferred she call me Tullah. I didn't want to reveal any information that Dad might want to keep under wraps until the time was right. "He's waiting on forensics to complete their DNA testing."

Inga said, "I can't image the anguish their families have suffered." She bit into the breakfast bar and chewed, then washed it down with a healthy swallow of water. "In a way, Pedar and I can relate. I mean, not knowing for certain where…" Her voice trailed off, and she didn't finish. I suspected Pedar had filled her in about yesterday's venture and his failed attempt at finding the bones of his ancestors.

Grandmother rolled the chilled bottle across her forehead. "How much farther? Not that I'm complaining, mind you."

"About a half-mile." I collected the empty water bottles and paper wrappers. Rest period over. A pumpkin sun gave off a splintered glow through bare limbs of surrounding trees as we hiked deeper into the swamp.

A half-mile should have taken ten or so minutes. With Dr. Ritter flagging fast and concerned about Grandmother and Inga, I kept the pace slow. Thirty minutes later we arrived at the devil's eye. A solemn place.

Following the same routine as yesterday, Charlie and I beat the grassy edges of the pool. No one spoke. Inga edged closer to her husband. She stared about at her surroundings. "There is only sadness here."

A sudden creepiness descended, and I wanted to leave this place. River emitted a low, throaty growl. The hackles on the back of his neck stiffened. The moment felt ominous.

Grandmother sidled next to me. Her voice was a husky whisper. "What is it, Tullah?"

A shudder wiggled up my spine, and my secret sense told me to get out of the place. "I don't know, Grandmother."

River let out a snarling bark. Pedar, still holding the rose bush said, "What is wrong with the dog?"

My little donkey made no sound except from his

usual sneezing bray when he's upset. River looked about and growled low and menacing. I squatted and wrapped my arms around the Labrador's neck. "What is it, fella? What's got you spooked?"

He regarded me with his large chocolate-brown eyes. At this moment, I wished I spoke dog language. I stood. Charlie wore an old-style gringo holster with a hammer thong. He removed the leather cord from the .44 caliber strapped at his waist. He said, "I don't mean to hurry you folks, but we need to get on with the ceremony."

There was worry in Pedar's voice. "What do you think is out there?"

Charlie lifted his face to the wind and sniffed. "Bear…maybe."

Father Timothy removed a small bottle from his pants pocket. He said, "It truly looks like an evil eye." He unscrewed the cap and walked to the edge of the ominous pool of water. "This is holy water," he explained as he emptied the container. The contents created small swirls on the water's surface. He extended his hand and made the sign of the cross, and then in a loud and clear voice, he prayed, "Saint Michael the Archangel, defend us in battle. Be our protection against the wickedness and snares of the devil; May God rebuke him, we humbly pray; And do thou, O Prince of the Heavenly Host, by the power of God, thrust into hell Satan and all evil spirits who wander through the world for the ruin of souls. Amen."

He motioned Pedar forward. Inga joined her husband. Pedar removed a slip of paper from his pocket. He glanced at each of us and then at the dark pool. "Since I am unable to retrieve the bones of

Adolph Rasmussen, Senior, and of his son, Adolph Rasmussen, Junior, and move them to a place of sanctity, I pledge the Rasmussen Swamp as a place of sanctuary for all God's creatures who call it home. For now and for eternity."

He unfolded the piece of paper with the words my cousin Uma had given him to break the curse. His voice was reverent as he read, "In the name of Greta Rasmussen, wife of Adolph Senior, mother to Dolphy and Lars Rasmussen, I, Pedar Lars Nielson, the great-grandson, break that bondage of bitterness, that bondage of guilt, that bondage of resentment, that bondage of worry. To keep from becoming slaves to the past and hurtful memories, I and the generations after me choose to forgive Adolph Rasmussen, Senior, for the wrongs he committed, and we beseech Thor, son of Odin, to respect our offering of forgiveness in the name of Greta Rasmussen, who called down the curse."

He removed a pair of gloves from his back pocket and pulled them over his hands. He knelt and lifted the rose from the pot. "As an offering of eternal peace, I, great-grandson of Adolph Rasmussen, and in the name of my great-grandmother Greta and her son Lars, plant this rose to remind all those who may venture into this corner of the world that a swamp is also a place of peace and beauty."

He then stood and stepped off ten paces, and next to a white oak tree he used his hands to dig a hole large enough to plant the rose. He scooped dirt around the plant, then walked to the pool of water, filled his empty plastic water bottle, and used swamp water to nourish the swamp rose.

It was a meaningful ceremony, and I truly hoped it

would bring peace to Pedar's grandfather Lars, and to the future generations. Dr. Ritter added his own words of commemoration.

The sky darkened, turning gunmetal gray. I heard the whispers. Some would say it was the wind. I knew better. It was a warning. A warning of what, I didn't know. "We need to go—now."

"Why—what's happening?" Pedar rushed to his wife.

Charlie hefted the revolver from the holster. Rascal came bursting out of the woods and kept running. My instinct said the little donkey was hightailing it to the truck. I placed my thumb and forefinger in my mouth and gave a shrill whistle. I called River's name. He didn't answer.

"Tullah, lead the way. I'll bring up the rear." Concern filled Charlie's voice. His eyes darted back and forth, looking for an unseen enemy.

"Don't worry, Saint Michael will defend us." Father Timothy crossed himself as he stood between Grandmother and Dr. Ritter, and linked arms, acting as ballast to two aging ships. "Even so, we should do as Charlie says."

A singular howl had us hustling from the devil's eye. A long alto whine pierced the morning air like a soul in agony.

Inga sobbed. "We did not slay the dragon. We awoke it."

"Wolves?" Pedar stood in front of his wife like a stalwart shield.

Charlie gripped the revolver's butt. He said, "No wolves in Kentucky. My guess is a pack of wild dogs."

Concerned for my black Lab, I once again

whistled, and called his name. I gave a quick look about, and said, "Pedar, help Inga to the car." Worry rose for my grandmother and Dr. Ritter. The look on the Dane's face spoke volumes as he scooped his wife into his arms and trotted forward.

I squinted toward the narrow trail leading from the swamp's dark interior. They appeared like ghostly apparitions watching us through the dark shadows. The sun's glare obscured my vision. A chill grabbed me like a cold clutch of death. I'd seen what wild dogs running in packs did to horses and cattle, dogs, and people.

Charlie's shoulder bumped against mine. His voice low and even, he said, "Keep walking backwards, Tullah. As long as we face them, we might be able to get to the truck before they attack."

"What about my dog? They'll kill him."

"River stays away to protect you. Smart dog, him. He knows the pack will attack if he comes to you. Keep walking. He will come."

We back-pedaled as fast as we could without tripping over fallen limbs and getting tangled in briars. We heard Father Timothy shouting, "Here…hurry… you're almost here."

Then the first dog, apparently the alpha male, a broad-chested Rottweiler, leaped in a black blur. Charlie braced his feet apart. He aimed and pulled the trigger. The .44's roar reverberated through the open space. He raised his arm in defense and knocked the dying beast sideways, and yelled, "Whatever you do, Tullah, don't run. Keep moving backwards as fast as possible."

Three more mongrels, growling and slavering, raced forward. Like an eighty-pound cannon, River plowed into a brindle pit bull's side, sending him and the beast sprawling. The other two dogs joined the fray. They looked like coyote hybrids. Before I'd even thought, I waded in, screaming, whacking with my walking stick, and landing fierce kicks to a mongrel's head. My big black dog fought with ferocity. The three animals slashed and snarled and ripped, flinging white saliva and blood around them.

Another blast echoed in my ears. A pit bull lolled sideways, its charcoal eyes glaring from Charlie to me, blood spurting from a gaping hole, and then it collapsed. Its chest gave a final heave.

The remaining dogs backed off, lips drawn to reveal sharp, yellow, canine teeth. Like most gangs with their leaders dead, the followers made a half-hearted attempt at bravado until Charlie fired over their heads. The beta dogs, all mixed breeds, tucked tail and slinked off. One member, a Rottweiler mix, turned, snarled, and charged forward, and then apparently changed its mind and trotted after its companions.

River's hind legs trembled as he struggled to stand. Pedar and Father Timothy raced to where we stood. Pedar held River's head while the priest carried the dog's bleeding rear. The swamp grew deadly quiet.

Charlie beseeched, "Are you hurt bad, Tullah?"

I quivered both inside and out as I looked at my bitten, bleeding hands and a flap of gaping flesh in the calf of my left leg. My voice shook as I spoke. "I'll live. Let's take those two with us. I'll need to examine the brain tissue to check for rabies."

Charlie reached for the walking stick and handed it to me. He scooped up the heaviest dog. "Can you make it to the truck? It'll only take a minute to come back for the other dog."

I leaned heavily on the sturdy pole. "I can make it."

Charlie opened the tailgate. Father Timothy and Pedar, with great care, laid River inside. It took a bit of coaxing to convince the little frightened donkey to crawl from under the vehicle. When he did, he practically jumped into the bed of the SUV, where he lay next to his friend.

Charlie dumped the dead Rottweiler's body over the hood of the truck. He and Pedar went back to get the other dog, which they laid next to the first body. He removed the bandana from around his neck. I sat with my injured leg extended out the door. He grabbed a bottle from my backpack and rinsed blood from my hands. The puncture wounds were deep and would need attending. He ripped the leg of my pants up to my knee. "This is gonna hurt. I gotta see how bad it is."

I nodded. The cold water felt like a thousand needles piercing the gaping hole in the calf of my leg. For a man with hands the size of meat hooks, Charlie had a gentle touch as he lifted the hanging flap of flesh over the wound. I placed my finger to hold it in place while he wrapped the bandana around my leg and tied the ends in a knot. "This'll do until we can get you stitched up."

Father Timothy said, "I'll drive, and Pedar will open the gates. No arguments, Brother Charlie. It's the least we can do. You've saved us from a frightening situation."

My hands shook as I typed a text message to Ella, giving her bare details of the attack on River and requesting she have the surgery ready. She responded immediately with a teary-eyed emoji.

Dr. Ritter gasped; his face was beet red. The pulse in his neck beat rapidly. I prayed he wouldn't suffer a heart attack. "You will need surgical debridement of your wounds. We'll leave River in Ella's capable hands, and then it's straight to the hospital for you."

I objected. "It's important that I remove the brain of both dogs to examine for the rabies virus. Otherwise, I'm in for a series of painful shots. Ella can stitch my leg."

I heard the tears in Grandmother's voice. "I've never felt so helpless in my entire life. Tullah, watching those animals tearing at you and River..." Emotion quieted whatever she was about to say.

Inga sat stone silent. She gripped her husband's hand as if her life depended on it.

Father Timothy peered at us through the rearview mirror. "What made them attack? I mean, we weren't provoking them."

I gritted my teeth against the throbbing pain in my hands. "We were in their territory. It's as simple as that. What galls me the most is the irresponsible owners. If people no longer want their pets, then why don't they take them to the pound rather than bringing them to the country and dumping them out? Dogs turned wild and running in packs are more dangerous than bears."

Father Timothy drove through the last gate and parked as close to the clinic as possible. Ella braced the door open and rolled out the gurney. She did a quick exam of my hands and leg. "You'll need antibiotics and stitches. I've already alerted my mom. She's waiting at the hospital."

"But you can—" My objection fell on deaf ears.

"No, I can't. Tullah, your eyes are glazing over.

You know our antibiotics are for animals."

She was right, of course. I wasn't thinking straight, and with that I'd lost the argument of staying.

Charlie and Pedar each hauled a dog from the truck. I said, "There's a freezer in the back with plastic bags on a shelf above the freezer. Put them there until I can perform a necropsy on them to determine if either have rabies."

As bad as my hands and leg hurt, I followed Father Timothy and Pedar as they carried River to the surgery. I soothed my bloody dog and thanked him for coming to my rescue. "You'll be good as new, fella." He whimpered and made a feeble attempt to lick my cheek.

At my hesitation to leave, Ella gripped my arm. "Trust me, Tullah. I'll take extra good care of River."

Dr. Ritter stepped forward and said, "I don't imagine surgery on an animal is that much different than on a human. Ella, may an old doctor assist you?"

I read the relief in her eyes. She smiled and said, "Let's do this. I've got the surgery ready."

I regretted leaving my dog, but searing throbs had me gritting my teeth. Charlie assisted me as I climbed inside the Suburban. By the time we arrived at the hospital, staying at the clinic was an argument I was glad I didn't win.

Chapter Twenty

On the ride to the hospital, to keep my mind off the pain, I focused on Dad and Tiny's sudden trip to Louisville. I wondered if they had arrested Lonnie, how badly hurt Angela was, and whether she'd agreed to file charges against Lonnie.

Charlie drove like the tires on his vehicle were on fire. He skidded to a stop in front of the emergency room door. I believe he would have lifted me and carried me inside if I hadn't insisted that I was capable of walking in on my own two feet.

"At least let me get you a wheelchair."

"Charlie, I love you with all my heart. No wheelchair."

He pierced me with a dark-eyed frown when I hobbled toward the double doors. "You're as stubborn as your ol' man."

Of course, when my leg refused to support my weight and collapsed, Charlie was there to lift me into his strong arms.

Dr. Sunny Sanders met us. She said, "Let me look at your hands."

I held them up, turned them over, and then back over. She said, "You already know we can't suture the puncture wounds."

I nodded.

She made a motion with her hand, and a tall, lanky

male nurse grinned as he approached with a wheelchair. "Now about that leg…"

Charlie still held me. I frowned at the approaching male nurse. "I can walk."

Dr. Sanders cocked an eyebrow and said, "My hospital. My rules. All patients get first class limo service. Now sit. This is Jeffrey. He's your escort." She added, "Where's your dad?"

I spoke between gritted teeth. Pain was reaching my *beyond tolerance* level. "Out of town on a case."

She smiled at my grandmother. "Don't worry, Tanti, we'll take good care of her." She pointed. "The coffee bar is there. Help yourselves."

I reached and touched her arm. "Dr. Sanders, Inga Nielsen is in her first trimester of pregnancy. We had to do a little running this morning. I'd appreciate it if you'd check her over first."

Without hesitation, Dr. Sanders summoned a nurse, who arrived with a wheelchair. She gave an order. In no time Pedar was wheeling Inga down a long hall.

By evening, we were seated at our favorite table inside The Whitehorse Saloon. Dad and Tiny had returned from Louisville. I didn't know if Dad's grim expression was from concern for me or if it was bad news about Angela Davis. Either way, I knew I'd have to wait.

Inga had been given a clean bill of health, my tetanus shot was updated, and the puncture wounds on my hands were covered with antibacterial lotion and wrapped with sterile bandages. The torn flap of skin on the calf of my leg had been thoroughly cleansed, sealed with staples, and wrapped. As much as I longed for a beer, I knew mixing alcohol with pain meds would make me extra loopy.

Best news of all came from Dr. Ritter. He arched his bushy brows. "Rather than wait, as soon as Ella and I tended to River's wounds and made him comfortable, she assisted me with the brain abrasion of the two dogs that attacked Tullah. It is with profound relief that I can report we found no evidence of rabies."

He held his mug forward in a salute. "No painful shots for you, my girl."

Glasses were raised, and a round of loud cheers filled the bar. The news hit me in the pit of the stomach, filling my eyes with happy tears. For once in my life, I tolerated Dad and Grandmother's hovering.

Inga finished off her plate of French fries, then helped herself to Pedar's. She wiped her mouth. "I still do not understand why the dogs attacked. We weren't molesting them in any way."

I explained that when neglectful people abandon their dogs, such as those we encountered today, the animals become territorial, attacking intruders. "Even tame, well-trained dogs can attack when their home territory is threatened." I added, "Also, if you noticed, the breeds that attacked us are considered most dangerous and most likely to attack when they have lost contact with humans and become wild."

Dr. Ritter spoke up. "All I know is I'm glad Charlie had his gun. It could have been worse."

Father Timothy raised his glass. "Hear-hear, I'll drink to that." He smiled at Inga and Pedar. "I truly believe the dragon you spoke of has been slain, albeit in the form of wild dogs."

His comment brought a round of chuckles. He clasped the cross that dangled at the end of his rosary and continued, "With all confidence, you can return to your homeland and set your grandfather's mind at ease, for the curse no longer exists."

The small group of friends grew silent. Flora delivered fresh mugs of ice-cold beer to the table and refilled my glass with cola and with a side of sliced lemons. She and another waitress cleared the table and asked if we were ready for dessert. From Patty's bakery, of course.

"Whatcha got?" Doc Ritter asked.

"Special for a sourpuss ol' doctor, lemon bars." Flora rarely makes jokes. Even though I'm not sure she was entirely making a joke.

Flora delivered a batch of yellow lemon curd on squares of buttery graham cracker crust and topped with powdery sugar. She helped herself to a square, smiled, and said, "Don't mind if I do." And then she returned to the kitchen.

I was eager to call it a night. Not because of pain but rather because I was eager to hear about Dad's trip to Louisville and what happened to Angela Davis. I was about to shove back my chair with the excuse of needing to retire for the evening. I knew Ella wouldn't hesitate to drive me to Dad's office if I asked.

Before I could excuse myself, Pedar used the edge of a fork to tap the side of his mug. He cleared his throat, and stood. "May I have everyone's attention, please?"

Inga reached up and clasped her husband's hand. She said, "I don't think it's necessary that you stand. These are our friends, and such formality isn't, well, necessary."

He obeyed and declared she was absolutely correct.

He cleared his throat once more. "I have spoken with Grandfather Lars and filled him in on today's events. If you could only know him, you'd know that he demands that all details, even the most miniscule, not be left out. Our conversation also took another turn.

"I do not know when Inga and I will visit Enigma again. Grandfather is satisfied the curse is broken and extremely relieved. He says he will sleep with good dreams tonight for the first time since he was a small lad.

"The reason for my long-winded speech is to let you know that we do not wish to keep Rasmussen Swamp. I have an appointment to meet with an estate attorney to conduct the proper transactions."

His comment brought a round of expectant gasps. It was as we'd feared—he intended to sell the land, and since it was useless for agriculture, he'd seek out an enterprising corporation to build condos on it or a housing subdivision.

"Please," he hastened on, "let me finish. Inga and I didn't know what to expect when we arrived in Enigma. Would we be greeted as outsiders, adversaries? On the contrary, instead, you embraced us as friends." He turned to me. "Tullah, you have opened my eyes to the beauty of the swamp. Tanti, your cousin Uma gave us the special words to break the curse. Father Timothy, you tromped into a swamp without hesitation to pray a prayer to rebuke Satan's evil. Charlie, you became our Saint Michael, protecting us from the demon dogs. Doctor Ritter, my grandfather looks forward to your visit, and we are pleased you have agreed to accompany Inga and me on our return to Denmark.

"And to end all this longwindedness, Grandfather

Lars is donating the entire one thousand acres to Enigma, Kentucky, for conservation purposes. This way the land will remain protected forever. Also, Tullah, you pointed out that the swamp is home to a variety of birds and animals." He chuckled. "Even snakes. Tullah, an easement is given to you to come and go from your property to the swamp for the duration, as long as you own your current property, but no public access to the land. The land is not to be used for any purpose other than a habitat for wildlife." He waved his hand about. "Of course, there will be other specifics which will be detailed in the final paperwork."

He stood straight and tall, reminding me of a stalwart Viking clad in modern-day clothing. He said, "Mayor Crow and friends, how say you to my proposal?"

Grandmother clasped her hands to her breast. "Pedar...Inga, on behalf of the City Council, the county commission, and the residents of Enigma County, I thank you for this generous gift, and gladly accept it."

I said, "Do we continue calling it Rasmussen Swamp?"

Pedar's brow wrinkled. "Rasmussen sounds harsh. I think Dolphy Preserve has a nice ring to it."

Joy and profound relief filled me, and I'm sure everyone around the table felt the same way. A curse broken and the mystery of what would happen to the swamp answered. Now to solve another mystery...who committed the murders and buried the bodies in Rasmussen Swamp?

Chapter Twenty-One

The tantalizing aroma of crispy bacon coaxed me out of bed. Still groggy from the last pain pill, I stumbled to the bathroom, shed my T-shirt, and stepped into the shower, allowing tepid water to bead over me. Fifteen minutes later, I limped down stairs to the kitchen. Grandmother was drowning a stack of waffles in melted butter. She set the platter and a bottle of maple syrup on the table. I barely remembered her plan to spend the night.

Dad looked up from his laptop and winked. "'Mornin', Punkin. How's the pain?

I accepted the cup of coffee Grandmother handed me. "Better," I lied. "What's got you riveted to your laptop?"

He half-turned the screen. "Joyce sent a file with photos and names of ten of our victims. Vaneeta's still trying to get a DNA match for number eleven."

I leaned forward for a better look and winced when I tried to lift a mug of coffee to my lips. Now that the circulation in my hands was waking up, the puncture wounds throbbed.

Grandmother set a brown prescription bottle in front of me. I gave her a questioning look. She said, "I know you didn't ask. Remember…eyes are the windows to the soul, and this morning yours are telling me you are in pain. So don't be stubborn. Take a pill."

She uncapped the bottle and shook an elongated white pill into the cap. She held it forward and with a cocked eyebrow said, "No arguments."

Believe me, I didn't argue. Dad had closed his laptop and helped himself to a couple of golden-brown waffles. His fork, loaded with buttery maple lusciousness was midway to his mouth when his cellphone rang. It's one of those irritating old-timey telephone *bah-rings*. He scowled and lowered his fork to reach for the phone secured in a leather case at his waist.

His scowl deepened when he looked at the caller ID. "Sheriff Henry Holliday, how may I help you?"

He listened. His mouth straight-lined into a scowl. "When?"

The furrow in his brow increased my curiosity about who was on the other end of the conversation and what they were saying to elicit such a serious frown from Dad.

He listened some more. "Yeah, send the body to the forensics department, Lexington University Hospital. Attention Dr. Vaneeta Sanreet."

His head bobbed up and down. I drew a much-needed slug of Grandmother's special coffee. It's really regular coffee except she always sets an eggshell in the filter to mellow the flavor, a holdover from the olden days when coffee had to be percolated on top of a stove.

Dad finished the conversation. "'Preciate you contacting me. If the need ever arises, I hope I can return the favor."

Grandmother was busy cutting my waffle into bite-size pieces. There are times when I really enjoy being spoiled, and this was one of those times. That is, until she speared a couple of morsels. I rescued the fork from her hand and smiled. "Thank you, Grandmother. I can feed myself."

Dad grabbed his fork and filled his mouth. He knows I have an insatiable curiosity even though his telephone conversations are none of my business. I was certain he was deliberately taunting me by concentrating on his food. My plan to outwait him failed. "What was that about?"

He chewed on a healthy bite of bacon and acted like he was ignoring me. "Dad!"

He grinned as he wiped his mouth with a napkin and drew a healthy swallow of coffee. He leaned forward on his elbows. "That was Sheriff Omar Lopez from Laredo, Texas. Roy Pickford is dead."

I didn't mean to slam my mug against the table at the news. "Oh, no, there goes our prime suspect in the Jane Doe murders."

"Yep, tough break."

"What happened? I mean, how did Roy die?"

"According to Sheriff Lopez, a couple of fishermen found Roy's body floating face down in a lake at a popular vacation resort. According to the Laredo coroner's report, the official cause of death was... drowning."

I scoffed. "C'mon, Dad, do you believe that?"

"I said that was the official report. Lopez also said Roy's body was a mass of bruises. It looked like he'd been worked over with a tire iron. Unless the autopsy shows different, Lopez won't have a reason to further investigate. It'll be ruled accidental death due to drowning."

I harrumphed. "How did he know it was Roy?"

"Fingerprints. There was no ID on the body. Once his fingerprints were run through the database it showed the active warrant I have out on Roy. Thus, the phone call."

"Poor Mrs. Pickford. How do you think she'll react once she learns about her son?"

Dad emptied his cup and refilled it. "Like most mothers, would be my guess."

"When do you plan to tell her?"

Dad studied the crumbs on his plate. "As soon as Vaneeta performs the autopsy and releases the body. Probably in a week or so."

"Do you suppose Mrs. Pickford has money to bury him?"

"Probably not. We can release the body to the county coroner and let the state pitch in to either cremate or bury. Whichever she chooses." Dad snagged another slice of bacon. "Tullah, how'd you like to go with me to tell Mrs. Pickford?"

"Yeah, sure, I'm up for that." I was thoughtful for a moment. "Drowning. Huh. Sounds too nice and tidy."

"What's your theory, Henry?" Grandmother cradled a cup in her hands. She leaned back in the kitchen chair.

"We know Roy was headed to Mexico. We know Laredo is a border town. We also know from his mother and his employer that Roy was a psychotic loon. My guess is he got way in over his head in a drug deal. Maybe his mouth overloaded his brain. Maybe he came up on the short end of the money stick, and maybe he infringed on a local drug capo's territory, and whoever the head honcho was took offense, had his goons work Roy over and then dump him in the drink."

"Whew." Grandmother stood to gather dishes. "That's a whole lotta maybes, Henry. Do you mind if I write an article about Roy's demise and our theory that he was a lead suspect in the swamp murders?"

"Go ahead. If there's another killer, such an article might shake his confidence and cause him to slip up."

Grandmother said, "Speaking of killers...you said Joyce sent you photos of the murdered women."

Dad pushed his empty plate aside and opened his laptop. He turned it so we could see. I said, "They're all young and beautiful. What do their profiles say?"

"I haven't had time to give them my full attention. I've asked Joyce to print duplicate copies." Dad looked at me. "Tullah, you're good at solving puzzles. On days when your appointment schedule isn't heavy, I'd appreciate it if you'd help me build a profile grid on each woman to see what connections, if any, they had to each other."

"Great. When do you want to get started?"

"Today's Saturday. What about today and tomorrow?"

Dad stood to help grandmother clear the table and load the dishwasher. I sent Ella a text letting her know I'd be spending the rest of today at my dad's office if she needed me.

She texted back that she was at her mother's if I needed her. I answered with a smiley emoji.

On our drive to town and with the distraction of the telephone call about Roy, I'd forgotten to ask about Angela Davis. "You haven't mentioned Angela. How is she?"

Dad kept his eyes on the road. His shoulders lifted in a shrug. "You've had enough on your mind, like being chewed up by wild dogs. I figured news about Angela could wait."

"You're always looking out for me. I love you for that. Anyhow, you can tell me."

I watched his knuckles turn white as he gripped the steering wheel. "She was a nice a young woman. It's too bad she didn't have a good judgment of men." His eyes were sorrowful when he glanced at me. "By the time Tiny and I got to the hospital, she was gone."

I gasped, suddenly aggravated. "You don't mean she up and left with Lonnie again."

"No, what I mean is that she didn't make it. He'd beat her with a baseball bat. She died of a brain hemorrhage." He sat quiet for a while. I didn't push for more information, knowing he'd give it to me in due time, and I felt ashamed of myself for thinking the worst of Angela. He said, "Before she died, she managed to scribble a note and signed it. The nurse said Angela made her promise to give the note to me."

Again, I waited for him to continue. He cleared his throat. "The note said, 'Sheriff Holliday, if I die before you get here, Lonnie did it. He killed me.' She managed to scrawl her name legible enough to be admissible evidence. The nurse said she'd bear witness that Angela wrote the note and that she had also requested it to be delivered to me."

He reached over and gently lifted my injured hand into his. "She was somebody's daughter. I hope they loved her."

I swallowed back the sob that rose in my throat. "What about Lonnie?"

"He's in custody at the hospital. Charges are for premeditated manslaughter." Dad released my hand.

My eyes widened in dismay. "Why at the hospital instead of the jail?"

Dad offered a sad smile. "Angela managed to grab a pair of scissors. I don't know where she was aiming, but Lonnie won't read so well for the rest of his life. She jabbed him in the left eye."

"Good for her. May she rest in peace." I stared out the window. I couldn't shake the anger I felt toward Lonnie Vickers. "Dad, in your professional opinion, do you think either Roy or Lonnie killed the women and buried them in the swamp?"

He released a heavy sigh. "Roy's brain was fried from psychotic drugs, and Lonnie is plain mean. I don't know that I could choose one over the other. Hopefully the women in the pictures will tell us."

Dad wheeled into the parking space reserved for him. He opened the back passenger door to the 4Runner and helped Grandmother to the ground. Then he raced around to help me. Pain shot through my injured leg, and I let out a yelp. "I'm okay, Dad. Don't embarrass me by carrying me inside like a baby."

"Just like your mother. Stubborn to the end."

Grandmother grabbed her tote bag. "I'm going home. I'll let Charlie know to expect us for dinner. I'll be ready when you're ready." She kissed me on the cheek, then turned in the direction of her apartment.

I didn't refuse Dad's assistance when he helped me hobble up the stairs to his office. As soon as we walked through the door, Joyce was up and around her desk. She embraced me with a gentle hug. "My lord a'mighty, Tullah, I mean this in the kindest of ways, but child, sometimes I think you're an accident lookin' for a place to happen. Although, gettin' attacked by wild

214

dogs isn't an accident, that's for dang sure."

I limped to a chair and sat down. "Joyce, it's Saturday. Why are you working?"

The crow's feet at her eyes crinkled into a smile as she handed Dad a fat file. "I promised I'd have this information for Henry today." She gathered up a purse that was large enough to pass for an airport carry-on. "Now that I've fulfilled my promise, I'm off to my bridge club. See ya on Monday, Henry."

When she was out the door, I said, "What are you going to do when she retires?"

Dad placed his hand under my elbow and gave me a boost. "Beats me. She practically runs the office singlehanded. One thing for certain, she'll leave here feet first before she retires."

Tiny strolled out of his office. "I thought I heard voices." His leathery face creased into a grin as he gave me the onceover. "From the town gossips, I expected you to look a lot worse."

I merely shook my head and found a comfortable chair.

"Knock, knock!" Patty Sweet called out. She walked through the reception area and into Dad's office. She set one of her signature boxes on Dad's desk. "Tanti said you'd be working." She tapped the box with a manicured fingernail. "Chicken salad sandwiches and cream horns. A little snack to keep you fortified until supper." She commissioned Tiny to set the box in the little refrigerator where we keep drinks and other goodies. As quickly as she came, she left, saying Tanti had invited her to join us at Charlie's.

Food didn't appeal to me at the moment. I was still replete from waffles and bacon. Dad thanked her, I waved, and Tiny opened the box and helped himself. He grinned as he wolfed down the food.

Dad gestured toward the long conference table. "Tiny, help me move this so Tullah can spread out the pictures without having to get up and move around."

It's little considerations like this that further endears my dad to me. I secretly wish he'd find a woman worthy of him. I shook away the thought and opened the two file folders Joyce had created—one with photos, a second one with information from NCIC.

I flipped through the pictures. "Each photo is labeled with the victim's name."

Dad said, "Good. Give Tiny and me a few minutes to attach the photos to the murder board."

I waited. Then he said, "Roxie Gilbert."

I flipped through the papers and read, "Roxie Gilbert, age twenty-four, exotic dancer, disappeared March 2004, from Indianapolis, Indiana. Reported missing by her roommate."

He called out, "Lacy Costello."

Again, I searched the stack. "Lacy Costello, age twenty-seven, waitress, disappeared March 2013, from Logan, West Virginia. Reported missing by her sister."

"Victim number three," he said, "Megan Hobart."

I read, "Megan Hobart, age thirty, pet groomer, disappeared March 2018, Paducah, Kentucky. Reported missing by her husband."

As I read off the information, Dad used a red dry-erase marker to write the info under each woman's name. Under Violet Goff's photo, he wrote: age eighteen, college student, disappeared March 2015, Perryville, Missouri. Reported missing by her mother.

We continued. "Annalee Robards, age twenty-two,

hooker, disappeared March 2008, Springfield, Illinois. Reported missing by her pimp."

He gave me another name, and again I read. "Marianne Royce, age twenty-two, hooker, disappeared March 2006, Cincinnati, Ohio. Reported missing by her pimp."

My brain clicked, and it was as if a computer was firing all the neurons. It was difficult to contain the excitement in my voice. "Dad, do you see it?" I pointed. "There. We have a pattern."

He stood back, hands on his hips, scanning the board. Finally, he said, "Well, I'll be damned."

I shifted restlessly in my chair. "So far, these five victims all disappeared in the month of March." I pointed again. "Gilbert, Royce, and Robards, all disappeared two years apart, all even numbered years— 2004, 2006, and 2008." I studied the board for a bit longer. "The thing that's throwing me off is these women all disappeared from different cities and states. I don't get the connection on that."

Dad crossed his arms over his broad chest as he studied the board. "Tiny, bring out that big roll-down map we have of the United States, and pull down the one for Kentucky, too." Dad trotted to the reception area. I heard him opening and closing desk drawers. He yelled, "Found 'em." He returned holding a box of pushpins.

He handed the box to Tiny and said, "Mark each state as I call them out. I have a hunch."

"What's your hunch, Henry?" Tiny asked.

"Let's wait to see if it pans out."

My knee started to jump, something it does when I get excited. Dad commanded, "Tullah, call out information for the next name."

We went through the all the names and discovered there was a two-year gap between Jane Doe Numbers One through Five and a one-year gap between JDs Six through Ten. All the victims were reported missing in the month of March. All were in their twenties when they disappeared except for JDs Eight and Ten, who were eighteen and nineteen years of age.

An email from Vaneeta stated that JD Number Eleven apparently suffered from scoliosis and had undergone corrective surgery. Apparatus in the lower lumbar led to the identity of Leah Calvert, age nineteen, waitress, disappeared March 2017, Mayfield, Kentucky. Reported missing by her mother.

When we'd gone through all the names and Tiny had pinpointed the locations of their disappearances, we sat back to observe the map.

The victims ranged from Missouri, Illinois, Indiana, Ohio, West Virginia, Virginia, Tennessee, and North Carolina. The oddities were Leah Calvert and Megan Hobart, who went missing one year apart. Both lived in Kentucky, each approximately a thirty-five-mile drive from Enigma.

I tilted my head from side to side. "It resembles an eye. North Carolina is the only state that doesn't border Kentucky."

Dad scratched the side of his face and down under his chin. He said, "The North Carolina victim lived approximately five and half hours from Enigma, Kentucky."

Tiny cupped his chin for a second. He grabbed a ruler from his desk and walked to the map and measured. "It's quite a drive from the places they lived in Missouri to here. About seven hours is my best guess, and the Illinois one is about six hours."

Dad paced back and forth in front of the picture board. He stood back and finally said, "My hunch is the murderer resides in Enigma or Dixie County, and lives close to the swamp. He's probably in good physical condition, to be able to tote a body several miles, bury the body, and then return to his house, all in the same night."

Tiny poured three cups of coffee and handed one to each of us. He walked to the refrigerator and pulled out the box of sandwiches. He opened it and held it forth for me to grab one. Dad said, "You're looking a little pale, Punkin. Are you in pain?"

I hated feeling like an invalid, and I certainly didn't enjoy the wooziness that came over me when I took a pain pill. The truth is the calf of my leg throbbed with reoccurring spasms in the muscle. I nodded my answer. He handed me my purse, and I dug out the little brown bottle, popped a pill, and waited for relief to come.

Being in pain didn't diminish my appetite, especially when the food came from Patty's café. While we noshed on our sandwiches, we tossed about the thought of a killer living in our own back yard.

I lamented, "My primary suspect is dead. That leaves Lonnie Vickers."

Dad reared back in his chair, stretching his long legs to prop on his desk. "I checked Lonnie's arrest records. He was serving time for assault and battery in aught eighteen and nineteen, and serving time for petty theft in aught four. A serial killer doesn't break his pattern."

I studied the board. "But this serial killer did. Look

at the dates. The first five victims went missing two years apart. Then for some reason he started kidnapping them a year apart. I wonder what happened to change his pattern."

Dad pursed his lips, and wrinkles furrowed his brow. "Tiny, run a check on the women to see if any of them have a record, even if it's as inconsequential as a speeding ticket. Maybe we'll find a connection that will tie the killer to the women or vice versa."

"You got it, Henry."

"You're frowning. What's on your mind, Punkin?"

"I don't know, Dad. We keep talking about how a serial killer doesn't change his routine." I pointed at the board. "Look. Two of his victims were hookers, and the third an exotic dancer. Then he picks a singer, and a waitress. Those five would suggest he trolled night clubs or bars. Then he picks a beautician, a teacher, and a college student, then a lab technician and a pet groomer." The pain pill was kicking in, and I found it difficult to concentrate. "Dad, do you mind if we call it a day? I'm really done in, and I have a busy schedule tomorrow."

He stood up, and I did, too, but I barely remember the drive home or him helping me upstairs to the bedroom and pulling the quilt over me.

Chapter Twenty-Two

I awoke fully clothed. It took a moment to clear my head and remember that Dad had driven me home. I grimaced as my bare feet hit the floor. I must have really been zonked out, because I didn't remember him removing my boots. I unzipped my jeans and stepped out of them. The calf of my leg was still tender to touch. I removed the bandage. Dr. Sanders did a fine job of closing the torn flesh. The areas around the fang punctures were puffy and an ugly shade of yellowish blue. I hobbled to the bathroom and showered, cleansed the wounds, applied antibiotic salve and a fresh dressing around the calf of my leg, and did the same for my hands.

Dressed and ready to greet the day, I hobbled to the kitchen and opened the doggie door to let River and Rascal out to take care of their morning business. The rich aroma of dark roast coffee greeted me. My chest swelled with love. Last night, Dad had prepped the coffeepot and set the automatic timer. I poured a cup and stood gazing out the kitchen window.

Ella was striding across the lawn toward the clinic. I glanced at the clock to see if she was early or if I was late. I savored the coffee while waiting for a leftover waffle to toast. I thought about the murder board we'd set up at Dad's office. Technically, this was Commander Draper's case and his responsibility to notify the families so they could claim the remains of their loved ones. I went through some sort of mental debate about my attitude toward the KBI agent. Whether Draper was good at his job or not, I'd pinpointed him as a narcissist. I hoped he was tactful in his approach toward the bereaved families.

The cloud cover hung heavy this morning, with the promise of rain. A shiver prickled the hair on my arms as I left the comfort of the kitchen. September had crept in and brought with it a hint of fall. With River and Rascal at my heels, I limped across the yard toward the clinic.

Ella sat at the reception desk. She flashed me a concerned smile. "How's the leg?"

"Hurts like the dickens, but it looks nastier than it really is."

"I'm sure glad those dogs didn't have rabies."

"You and me both. How's our day looking?"

She glanced at the large calendar on her desk. "Unless we get an emergency, we have a Great Dane in for a shampoo and flea dip, clipping a cat's dew claws, and a puppy needing its shots."

I nodded and gripped the calf of my leg when I sat. The moan slipped out before I could call it back. Ella's eyes furrowed. "Tullah, why don't you go home and lie down? I'll call if an emergency arises."

As Dad was fond of saying—*Tullah, you are stubborn*. There wasn't a good reason for me to stay at the office. Ella was absolutely correct when she said she could handle the non-emergency clients. There was just something inside me that refused to give in to pain. Maybe it was the combination of my Cherokee and Irish bloodlines that equated giving in to surrendering.

Before I could respond, the phone rang. Ella answered, "Good morning, Holliday Animal Clinic, how may I help you?" She listened, then said, "Yes, she's right here. One moment."

She handed the receiver to me. "It's one of Dr. Cooper's clients."

I smiled my thanks. "Doc Holliday speaking."

The man's voice sounded harried. He was practically yelling in my ear. "Hank Kellen, here. I'm in Dixie County." He recited his address. Ella wrote it down as I repeated it. He raced on. "I have a two-year-old thoroughbred filly. Dogs spooked her, and she got tangled up in barbed wire. We managed to cut her loose from the fence, and then like a dang fool she took off runnin' with all that wire wrapped around her. Every time I or my brother tries to get close enough to catch her, she runs again. I'm tellin' you, Doc, she's bloody all over, and hurtin' bad. How soon can you get here?"

"I'm not real familiar with Dixie County, Mr. Kellen. I'll set my GPS for your address. Thirty-five minutes is the quickest I can hope to get there."

He didn't sound pleased when he said, "Aw right. Onct you get here, call if you can't find my place. It's a bit off the beaten path."

I hung up and immediately notified my answering service that I had an emergency and would be out of the office for at least three hours. I also asked them to notify today's clients to let them know I would contact them to reschedule their appointments. By the time I'd disconnected, Ella stood by the door holding my medical bag. I hobbled to a supply cabinet, unlocked it, and withdrew a tranquilizer gun and a couple of darts filled with sedative appropriate to knocking out a horse.

I handed Ella the keys to my truck. "You drive. I'll navigate."

Once inside and buckled in, I spoke the address into my voice-activated GPS. Ella slipped the truck into gear, and we were on our way. No matter in what aspect of medicine you might be involved, there's always one job you dread. I'm sure for some vets it's the more gruesome, like bear maulings or coyote attacks, but for me it's always having to cut deeply embedded barbed wire out of an animal. As of twenty-eight minutes ago, this was the second time I would have to use a tranquilizer gun. I prayed my aim would be accurate.

We pulled onto the highway and turned right to travel toward the highway road sign that marked the direction to Dixie County on County Road 319.

Ella held to the sixty-five MPH speed limit. We rode in silence for about fifteen minutes. I was thankful I had brought my cup of coffee with me. The caffeine and the pain pill fortified me.

"Tullah..." Ella's voice interrupted my escape into silence.

"Yes?"

"Were you scared when the dogs attacked you?"

I thought about her question. Was I scared—yes, no, maybe?

"Not at first. My adrenalin was pumping overtime. I didn't have time to think about being scared." I reached down and rubbed my throbbing leg. "Even when I got to the hospital the shock of being mauled still hadn't set in, mainly because everyone was making such a fuss over me. Afterward, the pain medication numbed my brain." I shrugged. "But, yeah, I've had a couple of sleepless nights when I relive that massive brute with sharp teeth charging me."

"I hope that never happens to me."

"Don't let it worry you, Ella. We can't control fate."

A man's voice with an English accent said, "Turn right five hundred yards."

Ella gasped. "You programmed the GPS to have a sexy English accent?"

We both laughed.

I said, "Things get really dull in Enigma."

"You are a hoot, Tullah."

The English accent said, "Turn right."

Ella was still laughing when she slowed to make the turn. We traveled another fifteen minutes discussing the damage barbed wire can do to animals, and the necessity of using this type of fencing. Ella kept her eyes on the road. "I thought most thoroughbred ranchers used composite fencing to avoid such accidents."

"All the ranchers that I know in Enigma use railed fencing. I've never met Hank Kellen. He may be small potatoes."

We passed the road that turned off to the Kellen farm. The sexy English accent said, "Missed turn. Recalculating. Recalculating."

Ella slowed. "I didn't see it. Did you?"

I turned to look over my shoulder. "Looks like someone took out the road sign."

Ella checked the sideview and rearview mirrors, then executed a perfect three-point turn. In seconds we were headed in the correct direction. I looked at the instructions Mr. Kellen had given me and knew the

GPS would get confused, since dirt roads aren't usually programmed on maps. I turned the system off. "Kellen said to go about five miles. We should see his sign that says Kellen's Achin' Acres."

We spotted two young boys standing on the side of the road. "Pull over. We'll ask if they know the Kellens."

Ella slowed to a stop. I rolled down my window. "G'morning. Can you tell me how much farther to Hank Kellen's place?"

One boy, about ten, extended his arm and pointed. "Jes' a little ways up the road."

"Why aren't you boys in school?"

The other boy, about seven or maybe eight, drew a shirt sleeve under his nose. "Bus is late. It'll be 'long directly."

"Okay. Thanks for the directions. You boys have a great day."

I waved, and the boys waved back. I opened my phone and dialed Kellen's number to let him know we were less than five minutes out.

We'd driven about two miles when Ella said, "There it is." She made a left turn, and we bumped along on a windy, rough-rutted road until a barn, badly in need of paint, and a shotgun-style house came into view. Two elderly cowboys, one wearing a battered western-style straw hat, and the other a faded, sweat-stained ball cap with a Kentucky Wildcats insignia on it, stood in front of the barn.

The older of the two men stepped forward and extended his hand. "Hank Kellen. This here is my brother, Luke. Shore do thank ya for gettin' here soon as ya could."

Luke spat a stream of brown tobacco spittle. He wiped his mouth. "Yep, mos' folks miss the turn-off."

The brothers were hardscrabble men past their prime, with big dreams and little money to make those dreams come true. The kind of men who scrimp and save to buy that one prize filly or colt, hoping this is the one that will change their tough luck into gold. I hoped they weren't betting all their odds on the injured filly.

I introduced Ella and asked about the horse. Hank handed me the lead rope he held in his calloused hand. He said, "She's down at the lower forty. We can't get near her, so we come up here to wait till you arrived."

"Is the ground solid enough to drive on?" I asked. "I'll need the equipment in my truck." What I didn't say was that my leg wouldn't hold up to walk the distance to the lower forty acres.

"Oh, yes'm. Follow us." The brothers climbed into a truck that looked as beat up as its owners.

Once inside my truck, I said, "I hope this has a good ending, Ella."

She drew in a breath as she followed behind the brothers. "Yeah, I know. This doesn't exactly look like a thriving horse farm."

"Oh, no, look, Ella." I pointed to a palomino thoroughbred filly. "Look at her eyes. She's scared to death."

"I can see her quivering from here. Gosh, Tullah, there's so much blood."

Ella parked next to Hank's truck. I opened the passenger door and pulled out the tranquilizer rifle. Ella opened my medical bag and handed me the two inject darts. I loaded the rifle with one dart.

"Hank, what's the filly's name?" I'd rather hand

inject her than risk missing with a dart and possibly causing her to run. Her beautiful yellowish-brown coat was pockmarked with blood. The barbed wire had wrapped around her girth, front foreleg, muzzle, and around the left pastern.

"Her registered name is Seattle Sue. We call her Suzie."

I needed to take a hard line with the brothers. They didn't strike me as men who liked to take orders, especially from a woman. "Hank, Luke, Suzie is scared and she's in pain. This makes her a flight risk. Right now, she doesn't trust either of you. To keep her from hurting herself more, I'm asking the two of you to stay in the truck. Once I have her tranquilized, I'll signal you."

The brothers exchanged skeptical glances. Finally, Hank said, "Yes'm. You're the doc."

I opened my bag and withdrew a syringe filled with xylazine. "Ella, as soon as I have her quiet, come running with the wire snips and my medical bag."

She nodded her understanding.

I draped the lead rope over my shoulder and eased toward the frightened horse with my hands extended, palms up, and all the time speaking softly in Cherokee. I told her I understood her pain, and that I too, was in pain. I assured her that I would not hurt her, and that I had medicine to heal the wounds. The minutes seemed like hours until I had limped close enough to touch her. I stood still and continued to reassure her that I was her friend. She relaxed. I reached out and ran my hand down the white blaze that extended from her forehead to her muzzle. I snapped the lead rope to her halter.

With the greatest of cautious ease, I inched the

syringe from my jeans pocket and administered the injection. I continued stroking her forehead and talking to her until her muscles unbunched and relaxed.

"Ella," I whispered loudly and motioned her forward. She parked the truck within inches of me. She handed me my medical bag.

Hank and Luke parked next to my truck and hopped out. Hank sputtered, "I ain't never seen nothing like it. You've worked some kind of magic on her, Doc."

I merely smiled and wished someone could work magic on my throbbing leg. "Hank, take the wire cutters and start clipping in short sections. Ella, ease the sections off and hand them to Luke." I admonished Luke not to toss the barbed wire on the ground where other animals might step on the sharp barbs.

"Doc," said Hank, "why ain't she layin' down?"

I sighed. "I gave her enough sedative to calm her but not knock her out."

"Hmm, that's smart. Wouldn't've thought of that myself."

It took the better part of an hour to remove all the barbed wire. I cleansed every puncture wound while Ella filled the holes with antibiotic salve. I also gave Suzie an antibiotic injection.

"Doc?" Luke bent down to examine Suzie's legs. "She ain't crippled, is she?"

I assured him that none of the tendons in her legs had been torn. I said, "I see you have a hot walker. Give Suzie at least a week before you continue her training. Wash her daily with this antibiotic soap, and then use the salve. Call me immediately if there are any signs of infection."

Ella walked the horse to the barn while I followed Hank and his brother in the truck. Hank took the lead rope and led Suzie to a stall. I was satisfied with the cleanliness of the barn. All the other horses looked to be in good health.

"How much do we owe ya, Doc?"

I quoted him the amount. Hank whistled, but didn't blink an eye when he pulled out his wallet and handed me a credit card. "She's our golden goose. We're bettin' she'll win the Derby as a three-year-old. Then my brother and I can happily retire."

Luke sighed, the only sign that he wasn't made of wood.

I wished the brothers the best. "Dr. Cooper said he'll be back in his office next week. I'll send him a full report."

I tried to suppress the flinch as we shook hands, and the two hardscrabble brothers disappeared inside the cooling shade of the barn. Ella helped me load the truck. She drove down the dirt drive to the main road. We passed the area where the two young brothers had stood waiting on the school bus, and went on to the highway.

"It's past noon, and I'm starved. What about you, Tullah?"

"My toasted waffle wore off an hour ago."

"What about the Pancake House? The last time we were here, the food was tasty."

"Sounds good to me."

Ella spotted the large marquee and swung the truck into a parking space. My leg was screaming. As soon as we were seated and the waitress brought us glasses of water, I popped a pill. I wet a napkin to cool my face.

We read over the menus. A waitress took our orders, then brought our iced teas.

"I don't know about you," Ella said, "but I'm ready for cooler weather."

The waitress brought our ham-and-cheese omelets with a side of hash rounds. She set the plates in front of us. "Be careful what you wish for. Kentucky can get mighty cold. My name's Lottie. Let me know if you need anything."

I agreed while I doctored my crispy taters with ketchup. We were enjoying our omelets when Lottie groaned and said a loud, "Oh, no!"

I sat facing the door and turned my eyes to see what had caused her alarm. His mousy brown hair draped over his shoulders like greasy worms. His face was broad, almost as if it had been stretched to fit his oversized skull, with a wide brow, a crooked nose that suggested it may have been broken and set wrong, and a mouth with lips that looked as if they had been filled with collagen. There was a dramatic caved-in spot on the right side of his forehead, filled with thick scar tissue. His wasn't exactly a handsome face. It was filled with creases that made it difficult to guess his age. He had to duck to keep from hitting his head on the lintel of the door, which made him taller than six foot seven. He looked straight at me. His startling hazel eyes caused a distinct unease to settle in the pit of my stomach.

Ella leaned forward. "What is it, Tullah?"

"Him."

She shifted slightly in the booth and followed my eyes to the behemoth of a man. She turned back to me. "My goodness, he's a giant. Do you know him?"

"I'm not sure. Maybe, from a long time ago."

The waitress who had gasped said, "Louie, call Mrs. Lampson and tell her that crazy-assed son of hers is out."

"Today's Monday. She's working."

The waitress raised her voice. "Then call Sheriff Dotson. We don't want a replay of the last time Junior was here."

Louie's name tag indicated he was the manager. He walked to the soda machine and filled an extra-large to-go cup with cherry cola, placed a lid on top, and stuck a straw in it. He leaned against the bar and held the Styrofoam cup forward. "Hey, Junior, here's your favorite. It's on the house. You don't have to pay. Take it and go on home. We don't want any trouble out of you."

The hulking giant grabbed the cola and made a non-sensible guttural sound. He closed his lips over the straw and grinned. I can honestly say that I felt my blood freezing in my veins when Junior Lampson ambled over to stand at our booth. In the most casual way, he lifted my ponytail and let it sift through his fingers, and then he bent down to smell the top of my head. He sounded like gravel when he spoke. "My special." He laughed and repeated, "My special."

I batted his hand away. "Don't touch me."

Junior laughed. A braying sound. "You special."

Louie, the manager, spoke loudly into the phone. "Yeah, Sheriff. Just like last time. He's harassing my customers. Hurry."

Chapter Twenty-Three

There was no escape. Junior's massive body blocked our only way out of the booth. Ella picked up the steak knife and held it like a weapon. She said, "Look, goon, leave us alone. Go away."

So this was Junior Lampson. The waitress had said he'd escaped—again. I wondered how his mother kept him contained while she was at work. One thing for certain, he was built like a brick wall, and there was no shoving past him. When Ella called him a goon, he laughed, snorting through his nose. The insult had apparently rolled off him. That, or he didn't understand her meaning.

Apparently the sheriff's office was nearby, because Sheriff Malachi Dotson strolled in casual-like. I've known Malachi since I was a child. Older than my Dad by five years, eyes the color of charcoal with skin to match, and as tall as Junior Lampson, Malachi had a reputation for being a tough cop, especially if you got on his wrong side. I knew the gentler side of him.

He smiled as he touched the bill of his navy-blue Dixie County Sheriff ball cap. "Afternoon, Tullah. How's Henry?"

I returned his smile. "Works too many long hours, drinks too much coffee, and doesn't get enough sleep. Does that answer your question?"

Malachi snorted. "You are certainly Tanti's

granddaughter. Not afraid to speak your mind." He winked. "I think my wife and daughter would agree that your assessment of the job fits me to a tee."

Malachi lifted the Styrofoam cup from Junior's meaty hands. He set the cup on the counter. "Louie, another cola for Junior. Make it to go, and put it on my tab."

The restaurant manager was quick to comply. Malachi hitched up his tan pants and adjusted the revolver at his waist. "Your mother working today, Junior?"

Junior grinned through droopy eyelids. "Yu-huh."

Louie handed the cup of cola to Junior. Again, Junior closed his thick lips over the straw and sucked like he was siphoning gas from a tank.

Malachi said, "Did she leave the door unlocked?"

"Na-uh." Junior set the cup on the counter. He clapped his hands like a gleeful child, and then he flailed his hands back and forth. "I 'scaped." He giggled. "Mama be mad…Mama be mad."

"How did you escape?"

Junior's face went blank as if his brain had turned off.

Malachi prompted. "Are you bothering these ladies?"

"Na-uh," Junior's carnivorous grin emphasized an oversized canine tooth. He pointed at me. "Her special."

Malachi said, "You okay, Tullah?"

"Yes, but he keeps saying 'special.' I have no idea what he means."

"He probably doesn't know either. You and your friend enjoy the rest of your meal. I'll take care of

Junior." He said to the waitress, "Lottie, bag up a couple of glazed donuts."

The waitress immediately did as requested and handed the sack to the sheriff. He gave Junior a stern look. "Come with me, Junior, and you can have the donuts."

Junior grabbed for the bag. "Mine. Donuts."

Malachi held the bag out of Junior's reach. "Be a good boy and come with me. If you don't, no donuts."

"Where are you taking him, Malachi?" I wanted to know.

"I'll hold him in a cell until Edna gets home from work. Don't worry about paying for your meal. It's on me." He tipped his hat. "My best to Henry, Charlie, and Tanti. It's been a while since we could all get together."

He cupped Junior Lampson by the elbow and shuttled him out the door just after Junior reached over and grabbed the cup of cola to continue sucking on the straw. He seemed to have forgotten about Ella and me.

Lottie came over and refilled our glasses. "We have apple pie. Made fresh last night. None of that store-bought stuff. It's on the house and comes with a scoop of vanilla ice cream."

Ella and I nodded our acceptance. I mean, who would turn down homemade apple pie? When she walked away, Ella said, "Geez, where are the guys in white jackets and butterfly nets when you need them?"

I replied, "Did you see his eyes?"

"I wasn't really paying attention to his eyes. What about them?"

"They were dead. No emotion. Something for you to remember, Ella, whether human or animal, look at the eyes. You can gauge their emotions as either dangerous or passive. Knowing this could keep you from getting hurt."

"Thanks, I'll certainly remember that."

Lottie brought our pie a la mode. I lifted my spoon and filled it with pie and ice cream. "Has that guy caused trouble before?"

"Oh, yeah." She made a circular motion with her finger to indicate crazy. "He's not right in the head. A birthing accident, from what I've heard. His poor mama works in Enigma." Lottie's eyes widened. "Hey, you might know her—Edna Lampson. I swear she needs to put that boy in an institution. Well," she prattled on, "he's not a boy. 'Bout thirty-two or three, I think. Occasionally, Edna brings him here for ice cream and donuts. I hear she keeps him locked up when she's at work.

"Anyhow, he managed to get out of the house and came here. There were two young girls, pretty things, and he grabbed one of them, the red-haired one, by the arm and tried to drag her out of the booth. He kept saying, 'Special.' She threw her drink in his face, balled her fist, and punched him and started screaming at him. He went berserk, pulled one of the stools completely out of the floor and threw it through the window. He's a hulking monster. It took Malachi and two deputies to subdue Junior."

"What happened? I mean to Junior?"

"Oh, nothing that I know of. Like I said, poor Edna. She's gettin' a little long in the tooth, if you know what I mean. She can't keep working forever."

A bell tinkled. Lottie looked up and greeted the customer. "Welcome to the Pancake House. I'll be with you in a minute." She bustled off with a menu in her hand.

Ella and I finished our pie. Ella excused herself and went to the ladies' room. I checked in with my answering service. "Email the information to me." As soon as the email alert sounded, I called the client and scheduled the puppy's shot appointment for four o'clock. Once Ella and I were settled in the truck, I said, "We have a couple of hours to spare. Let's take a detour."

"Okay, where?"

"Shipley Road. It's on our way."

She turned the ignition and backed the truck out of the parking spot. "I remember passing it on our way to the Kellens'."

As she drove, I thought about that day in first grade. It was recess, and I was jumping rope with my friends. At the age of twelve, Junior was already as tall as most men. He seemed to enjoy picking on the younger kids. Even the boys in the sixth grade avoided him. I have no idea why he singled me out. But he did. I flexed my shoulders. I could almost feel where he'd planted his massive hand and shoved me, face down, into the dirt. I had rolled over. He reached down and grabbed the front of my shirt, his other hand drawn upward.

It was my mother's turn to volunteer as a room mother that day. She had brought cupcakes for my classroom. She was like a warrior woman when she spotted Junior. It took her, the teacher, and the principal to break Junior's grip on my shirt.

I felt the truck shift as Ella maneuvered the turn. Shipley road was rough. Obviously it hadn't been graded in quite a while. The bumps and ruts jarred us as she drove. The cloud of dust obscured our vision as we continued. The heat outside was oppressive, and I was thankful for the truck's air-conditioning. Piles of garbage littered both sides of the dirt road. It was a sad landscape. Shanty houses with peeling paint, sagging roofs, and broken windows, and yards adorned with discarded toilets, old refrigerators, and rusting vehicles.

Ella looked at me, a little worried. "Tullah, where are we going? I don't feel safe."

I bit the underside of my lip. The vision of Junior Lampson leering at me, the gap between his two front teeth, and smelling my hair left me uneasy and unmoored. I reminded her of the day we had visited Dr. Cooper and his wife. When I had inquired about Edna Lampson's residence, he had commented that she lived in a seedier part of the county, and had warned me to stay away.

"My leg is screaming. We won't stay long. I promise. I want to see where Edna Lampson lives."

She frowned at me and gripped the steering wheel when we hit another deep rut. "Why?"

I stretched my legs and focused on my boots. They were badly in need of attention. "I'm not sure, Ella. I have a hunch."

"About what?"

In the event that I was wrong, I wanted to keep the idea to myself. Still, I also didn't want to lie to Ella. I said, "It's really not my place to get involved with Edna Lampson's business. Maybe if I see where she lives, take a few pictures, and report today's incident with Junior to social services, maybe they will remove Junior and put him where he isn't a danger to others. I'm afraid it's only a matter of time before he hurts his mother."

"Don't take this the wrong way, Tullah. This is Dixie County. I'm sure if he was concerned about Junior and his mother, the sheriff would have already taken some kind of action to get the ball rolling." She drew a deep breath. "Instead of taking matters into your own hands, tell your dad."

"Yeah, you're probably right."

Her short-lived smile faded when we came to a house at the dead end of the road. It was the same house I'd noticed the day Ella and I were out riding and posting No Trespassing signs. A sad house with a rusted chain-link fence surrounding a yard thick with weeds. Round iron bars encased the front windows, and the front door. I imagined all the windows were covered in bars.

"It looks like a prison." Ella shifted a glance toward me.

"Stay in the truck. I want to take a quick peek at the back yard." I slid from the truck, leaving the door partially open. Needles of pain stabbed the wound in the calf of my leg. I took a moment to steady myself. Junior said he had escaped. I wanted to see how he got out. If he could get out during the day, then perhaps he could also get out at night when Edna was sleeping.

I had maybe taken three steps toward the house when two long-tailed, brindle pit bulls crawled from under the front porch to lunge against the fence, lips turned back over yellowed teeth, saliva drooling from snapping jaws, ears flat against their heads. The larger of the two pits planted its hind feet in the fence wire, trying to climb over. Visions of the dog that had attacked me caused me to step back. My heart thudded against my chest as I scrambled into the truck. I felt my entire body shaking.

"Oh, my God, Tullah."

"Exactly."

"They could've torn you to shreds."

"I know."

"Can we go now?"

"Yes."

Ella backed around and pulled forward. I turned to look through the rear window. The dogs were barking and lunging against the fence. We bumped and bounced along the same way we had come in, and never met another vehicle. I said, "Apparently Junior and Edna are on friendly terms with the dogs."

"I can understand why they would keep such vicious animals. Honestly, I'd be afraid to live in this neighborhood, especially at night."

I agreed with Ella. Yet my curiosity hadn't been satisfied. I thought about the eleven women who had been murdered by hands strong enough to crush their hyoid bones. Roy Pickford was dead. If he was the killer, then we had zip—no way to prove he did it. Lonnie Vickers had a firm defense for at least two of the years that the murders had taken place. Prison was about as solid an alibi as you could get. I kept thinking about Junior's dead eyes. And what did he mean by "special"? I hadn't crossed him off my suspect list yet.

By the time Ella drove under my carport and parked, we spotted the car parked in front of the office. I glanced at the radio clock. Three o'clock. An eight-week-old Yorkie was waiting to get his distemper and parvovirus shots, to be followed by our 3:30 appointment and then the puppy I'd just scheduled for four p.m. Due to rescheduling our morning patients for the afternoon, time flew. We performed an emergency operation on an elderly Great Dane that had tumbled down a flight of stairs and fractured her hip.

By the time we shut off the lights and locked the doors, it was dark outside. Ella helped call in the horses for the night and put feed in their buckets, and we said goodnight. I thanked her for being my chauffeur today.

On the walk to the house, River loosed a throaty growl and then lit out toward the gate that separates my land from the new Dolphy Preserve. A barred owl sat on a fence post. It took flight. River jumped upward as if trying to catch the raptor. I wondered if it was the same owl from the swamp. My aching leg distracted me from the thought, and we returned to the house.

Being hungry and too tired to cook isn't a good combination. I heated the oven and placed four strips of bacon on a cookie sheet lined with parchment paper. While the bacon cooked, I toasted two pieces of bread, slathered one slice with mayonnaise and the other with mustard, then adorned the bread with thin slices of tomato. The oven timer alerted me that the bacon was ready. After assembling my sandwich and cutting it into two portions, I collected my glass of cola and my sandwich. I settled in the recliner and opened my laptop. I emailed my treatment report and the photos that Ella had taken of the Kellen brothers' filly to Dr. Cooper. I then opened my boneyard notes and detailed my suspicions about Junior Lampson.

River stood at the kitchen door, his hackles raised and emitting throaty growls. I decided to see what was bothering him. I attached the leash to his collar, grabbed the metal baseball bat, and opened the door. It took a few minutes for my eyes to adjust to the darkness. The horses were inside the barn. Nothing moved inside the corral. I checked toward the office. All clear.

River tugged at the leash and whined. I held tight. "Show me, River."

He strained against the restraint, pulling me toward the pasture gate. He made a sound that was a cross between a woof and a whine. I scanned the area. I blinked. "What the…"

Perched on top of the gate fence post sat a barred owl. We stared at each other for what seemed an interminable time. "Why are you here?" I asked.

The owl turned its head and looked over its right shoulder. It then lifted itself and ruffled its feathers. Sat again and continued to stare at me. Many Native Americans believe owls bring warnings from the grave, or serve as messengers of the dead. My voice sounded loud in the night. "Did Junior Lampson murder those women?"

The owl's golden eyes widened. It looked at me and blinked. Shakespeare has always been one of my favorite authors. I have no idea why, at that particular moment, I recalled a passage from Shakespeare's *The Winter's Tale*—"I have heard, but not believed, the spirits o' the dead men may walk again."

So intent was I on watching the owl that when my phone chirped it startled me, and I jumped. The owl vanished almost as if the night had swallowed it.

I wasn't surprised when the phone showed Dad's ID. "Hi, Dad."

"How's the leg?"

"Hurts." I hobbled toward the house.

I filled him in on today's events, leaving out the part about Junior Lampson. "I have something to tell you, but you have to promise not to yell at me when I'm finished."

"It's that bad, huh?"

I limped up the steps and into the house. "Well, yes and no. Promise?"

"You're not a child. I can't paddle your behind."

"No, but you can yell pretty loud."

He chuckled. "Okay, I'll keep an open mind. What?"

I related the incident with Junior Lampson at the Pancake House. "Sheriff Dotson took control and escorted Junior to the jail until Edna got home from work and could come get him."

I could almost hear Dad's teeth grinding. He said, "What is it that you're not telling me, Tullah?"

He only called me by my name when he was annoyed. I drew in a deep breath and released it, then proceeded to tell him about going to Edna's house, the bars on the door and windows, and the two pit bull dogs.

Silence.

"Dad?"

"I promised I wouldn't yell." His voice raised an octave. "What the hell were you thinking of, Tullah?"

I lifted the second half of my sandwich and took a large bite. I hoped chewing would somehow inspire me with a believable answer to his question. I sort of mumbled, "I don't know." I forged forward by saying, "Don't you think it odd that Edna has bars on every window and on the front door of her house?"

"Under the circumstances, not really. Listen to

me—Edna Lampson has more than many times refused to place Junior in a facility. She's afraid he'll be mistreated, and honestly, she's not far from wrong. When he was sent to youth justice detention, he got into a lot of fights and ended up in the hospital with a shiv in his chest. Malachi and I know about the containment bars on her house. She can't afford to place Junior in a private situation, or hire anyone to babysit him while she works. Until he becomes a nuisance, commits a crime, or hurts someone, my hands are tied. Dixie County is not my jurisdiction."

"But, Dad…"

"There are no buts, Tullah. I know you want to believe Junior killed those women. I can't arrest him on gut feelings or instinct. I have to have solid, concrete proof."

A wave of aggravation cemented me to my chair and forced me to admit that he was absolutely right. I decided not to tell him about the owl. I drew a deep breath and let it out slowly. More than a couple of emotions tore at me like the needle pains stabbing the calf of my leg.

"Punkin?"

From the tone of his voice I almost knew what he wanted to say. A man of few emotional platitudes, he couldn't quite spit it out. Ever since my mother's murder he, Grandmother, and I had been protective of each other, probably obsessively protective. "Yes, Dad?"

"If an iota of evidence points in Junior's direction, I won't ignore it. At this time, I have other leads to follow." There was a slight pause, and then he said, "Still my best girl?"

"You know it." To lighten the seriousness of the conversation, I said, "Sunny Sanders is a beautiful, smart woman, and she's single. You should ask her out."

I laughed to myself. It sounded like he had spewed whatever he was drinking and was now choking. "You mean *out* as in a date—*out*?"

"I'm certainly no expert on the subject, but yes, I believe it's still called dating."

"I'll give it some thought."

As soon as we disconnected, I pulled up the file where I had scanned the pictures of the eleven women and scrolled through until I came to Jane Doe #5, identified as Savannah Deer from King, North Carolina. An attractive woman with high cheekbones, dark eyes, and black hair pulled back into a ponytail that draped over one shoulder, she was age twenty-seven, married, and a first-grade teacher. I enhanced the photo and said to my pets, "She's definitely Native American."

River and Rascal lay at my feet. River looked up at me with his soulful brown eyes as if he understood what I'd said. I leaned down to tickle the top of his head, and then gave a little love to my donkey. I checked the time and wondered if Vaneeta was still awake. I sent her a text—*Vaneeta, how long will it take you to verify the ethnicity of Savannah Deer, JD#5?*

I was surprised to receive a speedy answer— *Tullah, by examining the morphology of each victim's skull, we have determined ethnicity. Savannah Deer is Native American. However, as you know, DNA cannot determine which tribal nation.*

I returned with an immediate message thanking her for the quick response. I felt an unease tightening in my chest. I thought about all the skeletal remains lying forgotten in shallow graves until we'd unearthed them. I thought about Cousin Uma speaking of seeing ghosts of past ancestors. She once said she truly believed the dead never leave us. I now understand why I heard the whisperings from the swamp, and why the owl continues to visit me. Savannah Deer is speaking to me from the grave, and the owl is her messenger.

Chapter Twenty-Four

Saturday, with fall in the air, and my stitches were itching like crazy. I sat on the edge of the toilet seat, propped my leg on the tub, and used a surgical staple remover to remove the staples. The area had healed well, and the puncture wounds had scabbed over.

Grandmother and Sunny Sanders, Ella, and I were going to take the horses for a morning ride. As a precaution against opening or irritating the scar, I wrapped a simple bandage around the calf of my leg before I dressed and pulled on my boots.

A horn beeped, and River and Rascal sounded their happy greetings in reply. I looked out the bedroom window and spotted a cloud of dust following my grandmother's little blue sports car as she parked under the oak tree in front of the porch. Ella trotted around the corner of the house. She waved and smiled.

It would feel good to get back in the saddle again. Since Lars Rasmussen had granted the swamp and all its land to the county of Enigma, Grandmother was eager to inspect the area on horseback. I trundled down the stairs to open the front door. Grandmother, as usual, had a large tote bag with her. I was certain it was filled with snacks. Have I said how much I love her?

After a round of hugs, she patted the bag and said, "Lunch and water. The straps will fit nicely over the saddle horn."

We strolled toward the barn to saddle the horses. Sunny, Ella's mom, expressed concern about the wild dogs, and Ella spoke up. "Oh, Tullah took care of that first thing. She called animal control in both Enigma and Dixie County. They came immediately and rounded up about fifteen mixed-breed mongrels." She quirked a mischievous smile as she winked at me. "Of course, they weren't able to catch the bears."

The expression on her mother's face caused Ella to respond, "Just kidding, Mom."

Conversation ranged from plans for the upcoming 4-H Festival to Dad's ongoing investigation into the unsolved murders. Sunny said, "Tullah, has there been a follow-up on Angela Davis? I've thought about her often."

I slipped the bit into Gandalf's mouth and buckled the bridle's cheek strap. "I'm sorry to say that she's dead." I went on to explain about the beating, her written statement addressed to Dad, and that the last I'd heard was that Lonnie Vickers was in the lockup section of a hospital recovering from where Angela had stabbed him in the eye with a pair of scissors.

Sunny expressed her sorrow over Angela's sad demise. We all voiced our opinions about men like Lonnie and frightened, abused women like Angela Davis. We led the horses from their stalls and out of the barn into the morning's tawny sunlight. Normally, Grandmother would ride Banjo, her brown-and-white pinto, but she'd decided to ride Moon, Dad's appaloosa. Sunny, who admitted she wasn't an experienced rider and was a little nervous, would then ride Banjo, who was about as mild mannered as a horse could be, while Moon tends to be a little feisty, especially if he hasn't been ridden in a while.

I cupped my hands to give Grandmother a boost up. Moon is long-legged and over sixteen hands, too tall for Grandmother to lift her foot to the stirrup. I handed her the tote bag, and she looped the straps over the saddle horn.

I led Gandalf to the gate and held it wide for the others to ride through. I didn't lock it. I mounted, and adjusted my weight in the saddle. Sunny said, "Are we riding into the interior of the swamp?"

Gathering the reins, I said, "No, ma'am. The month of September is when copperheads have their babies—lots of babies, and they're everywhere."

Her eyes widened. "Gotcha."

"We'll ride the eastern perimeter, cut a wide circle to the west, and end up right back here." What I didn't say was that I had an ulterior motive for working from east to west. The western section would take us past Edna Lampson's house, and I intended to ride as close as possible to the property. My curiosity still begged to know how Junior escaped, and whether there were iron bars on the rear windows of the house.

We set out. Grandmother, Ella, and I had our hands full with energetic geldings that wanted to frisk and crow hop. "Grandmother, are you okay?"

She nodded. "You know, I'm thinking of Cousin Uma. She'd enjoy being with us today." She waved her hand as if brushing away a fly. "Don't worry about me. I can handle this cayuse."

I turned in the saddle to check on Sunny. She gave me thumbs up. Moon was minding his business and being a good boy. I really wanted to give Gandalf his head and let him have a little run. Instead, I held him to the course, knowing he'd soon settle down.

River and Rascal trotted along beside. I was confident River would let us know if any predators were lurking about.

Along the way we spotted a bald eagle perched high in a tree. A doe peeked out from the edge of the swamp, then scampered back into the shadows. If I was ever thankful that Banjo was steady and calm, it was when a swamp rabbit darted between Jupiter's legs, setting the frightened gelding into a tizzy which transferred to Moon. Grandmother's expert hands brought the big appaloosa under control, while Ella and I had our hands full, but Banjo was like, *Come on, guys, it's just a rabbit.*

We continued our course, settling the horses into a walk, then a trot, and back to a walk. Grandmother lifted her camera and snapped away at the scenery. The sun had brightened to burn off the morning chill. We'd ridden for the better part of two hours when we heard the yodeling. River's hackles rose on his neck. I commanded him and Rascal to stay.

Ella looked at me and asked, "Coyotes?"

I nodded as I scanned the area to see if I could catch sight of them. "I doubt if we'll spot them. Basically, coyotes are cowards. They're more apt to attack a lone animal or human, especially a child." I patted the twenty-two rifle snugged in the leather rifle boot. "I have this, just in case."

Sunny wiped away sweat and rolled the sleeves of her shirt up to her elbows, then gigged Banjo alongside Moon. "Tanti, I could sure go for a bottle of water."

Grandmother reached into the tote bag and handed her a bottle. "Tullah, Ella, what about you?" She smiled. "I also have donuts."

I glanced at the sky. The sun was straight up. It was noon and time for a snack. "Why don't we take a break? Here's as good a place as any." I dismounted, and the others followed.

Ella pointed to a group of oak trees. "What about over there? It's shady, and we can prop against the trees."

Grandmother answered for me. "Snakes."

That's all she had to say. No one argued. I uncapped my bottle of water and let it dribble into my cupped palm for River and then Rascal to drink. I did the same for Gandalf, emptying the bottle. Grandmother presented me with one of her knowing smiles and reached into the bag to hand me another bottle. It is the custom of a good warrior to tend his animals before himself.

It was the slightest sound, like a hushed whisper. River whined as he belly-crawled and laid his head in my lap. Rascal did likewise. I cocked my head and listened.

"What is it, Tullah?" Grandmother cocked her head to one side. She looked toward the swamp.

I lifted my sunglasses and squinted toward the marsh. "Maybe the humming of bees. Maybe the wind." I stuffed the rest of the donut into my mouth and wet my hands with water to wash away the stickiness. "Are we ready?" I gathered the reins. The whisper came again. Gandalf snorted and tossed his head up and down. I spoke to him in Cherokee.

"But Tullah, there isn't any wind," Ella remarked.

"Or maybe it's old Adolph Rasmussen trying to speak from the grave." Grandmother gathered her reins.

I asked Ella to hold Gandalf while I gave Grandmother a leg up into the saddle.

Sunny tried to mount Banjo. He walked her around in a circle, until I grabbed the side of his bridle and held him while she climbed into the saddle. She said, "I've heard about the curse. I can't say that I believe in such nonsense."

In my heart of hearts, I knew if Banjo was spooked, then the whispers were not our imaginations. I scanned the area, not sure what I was expecting to see. I made light of the situation. "It could be the coyotes. Either way, we have about eight hundred more acres to cover."

I touched Gandalf's flank and urged him into a trot. The yodels seemed to follow us. I unsnapped the safety strap from my rifle boot, even though I knew it wasn't coyotes that stirred. At the center point of the swamp, we came to a wide, water-filled chasm. I walked my horse down the line, looking for a place to go around or shallow enough to walk the horses through. No such luck. "Sunny, are you comfortable taking this jump?"

She bunched her brows together and caught her top lip between her teeth. Ella sidled next to her mother. "Mom, you can do this."

Sunny heaved a heavy breath. "I'm not the horsewoman you think I am, daughter." She looked at my grandmother and said, "Tanti, can Banjo take the jump?"

Grandmother assured her, "He's a great trail horse. You give him his head, and he'll clear the ditch like it was a puddle."

Sunny hesitated. "Tell me what to do."

I said, "Grandmother, you go first. Sunny, watch

what she does."

Grandmother walked Moon a distance away from the watery gap. She let out a whoop and gigged the gelding hard. He leapt forward, and like a feather in the wind, Tanti Crow lifted in the saddle, leaned forward, and woman and horse moved as one, landing neatly on the other side. My heart swelled, my eyes teared. If only my mother could have been with us on this day to see such a feat.

"I don't know if I can do that without falling off, Tullah."

I knew what I had to do. Otherwise, we'd be here debating the issue all day. The whispers grew louder. An urgency filled me. It was like this place wanted to swallow souls.

I grabbed the bridle's cheek strap and led Banjo to where Grandmother had started her run. I said, "Sunny, hold on to the saddle horn and grip your legs tight. Do not grab the reins." She did as I directed. I continued. "Lean forward, look between Banjo's ears like you are sighting down the barrel of a rifle, and plant your feet in the stirrups."

Without giving Sunny time to think, I brought my hand down with a hard smack on Banjo's rump. The startled animal bolted forward like his hooves were on fire. He cleared the ditch with room to spare. In a magical moment, Grandmother reached out and snagged his rein. Moon moved like a cowpony, which helped Grandmother keep her seat.

"Oh, my God, Tullah, I don't know whether to hate you or kiss you," Sunny screamed. She managed to catch her balance before she tumbled out of the saddle. "That was scary awesome!"

Ella glowered at me. "She could have been killed."

"You can be mad at me later." I nodded toward the ditch. "Go. I'll follow."

Once we were both on the other side, Sunny laughed. "I've never been so startled, so scared, or so exhilarated in my entire life. Honestly, I think that was better than sex."

"Mother!"

River and Rascal decided to swim across. They climbed up the bank and shook themselves, spraying us with water.

We all laughed, although I was sure Ella was still angry with me. We urged the horses into a gallop. The day was growing hotter, and soon we'd be fighting mosquitos and yellow flies. Another hour passed. I deliberately led us closer to the Lampson house.

We slowed the horses to a walk. The only sound was our breathing and the snap of brittle grass under the horses' hooves. Grandmother rode next to me. "Where exactly are we, Tullah?"

"We're at the corner section of Enigma County, where it meets Dixie County." I stood in the stirrups and pointed. "That house is where Edna Lampson and Junior live."

"Really? C'mon, I want to see."

There was a long silence as we trotted toward the dilapidated house. Window air conditioners sagged from rear windows on either side of the house. It was my guess that if Junior had any wits at all about him, he could have lifted out one of the units and raised the window higher to give himself a way to escape. We rode up to the rusted chain-link fence that acted as a barrier between us and the yard. I concentrated on the gate, hoping to see trodden grass leading to the swamp. This would prove my theory that Junior had planted the bodies. A part of me was disappointed.

Concern tinged Ella's voice. "Tullah, don't forget about the pit bulls."

I nodded and was about to turn my horse away when a loud banging caught our attention. "What the heck is that?" Grandmother asked.

I dismounted and walked close to the fence. "It seems to be coming from the storage shed." I handed the reins to Grandmother and lifted the latch on the gate.

"Tullah, don't," Ella's voice cautioned.

I started rethinking my reasons for being here. That I should leave well enough alone. I took two steps inside the yard, my hand still on the gate. The two brindle pit bulls crawled from beneath the house. I knew they meant to make mincemeat of me. I made haste getting through the opening and dropping the latch in place. I didn't bother with stirrups but catapulted into the saddle. Like before, the dogs snapped and slobbered as they reared against the gate.

A door slammed. Ella said, "We should leave."

A voice shouted, "Shut the hell up! Junior, get your ass out here and come get these damned dogs."

The back door slammed as Edna Lampson appeared, holding a broom. Her white hair stood on end, like she'd stuck her finger in an electrical socket. She wore a faded blue, snap-down housedress. She swatted the dogs with the straw end of the broom. "Shut up…shut the hell up!" She whacked each dog. They ignored Edna and continued with their attempts to attack.

Junior appeared from the shed. A towering giant, he was barefoot, bare chested, and clad in a pair of dingy briefs. He lifted both dogs, one under each arm, and held them like they were oversized puppies, kissing each one on the head. He looked directly at me. He stepped forward, then remembered he held the dogs, opened his arms, and dropped them. They yelped. He placed his hand on the gate. "Maw-maw, her's special. My special."

Edna slapped his muscled arm. "You ain't decently dressed. Get back in the shed."

She looked at Grandmother. "Mrs. Crow, Doctor Holliday, if you're spying on us, what goes on in my yard and my house is none of your damned high-and-mighty business." She shifted eyes filled with malice toward me.

I matched her hard stare. "We are simply out riding, Mrs. Lampson. Perhaps you've heard that the great-grandson of Adolph Rasmussen deeded the swamp and its surrounding land to Enigma County."

"Uh-huh. Then you're 'bout five miles off course." She lifted her hand and pointed. "This corner of the property is in Dixie County, which means the bunch of you are trespassing."

"We didn't mean to upset you, Mrs. Lampson. However, I have permission from the owners of the property to utilize it anytime."

She raked a pale, wrinkled hand with gnarled fingers through her hair, making it stand up on end even more. "So you say. Junior and me, we don't like people snooping around. Somebody is always trying to find a reason to take him away from me, to put him away in one of them awful institutions. They say he's a danger to society. Well, he ain't."

Her voice rose until she was screaming. She lifted the broom and swung it back like a weapon. "Get on out of here before I open the gate and let the dogs out."

I listened, certain I heard banging coming from the shed. "Just one question, Mrs. Lampson, and we'll go. Why is the shed air-conditioned?"

By this time, the old woman was visibly shaking. "None of your damned business." She squinted hard at me. "But if you must know, Junior is a man. He needs a man's privacy to…to…to satisfy himself without his mama being around to watch." She balled her fist and yelled, "I'm counting to five, and if you ain't gone, I'm telling Junior to sic the dogs on you."

We turned the horses. I motioned with my head. "Let's get out of here, fast."

Junior's voice followed us as he screamed, "Come back! My special… Maw-maw, I want my special!"

With me in the lead, we let the horses run until arriving at the gate that separates my property from the swamp. Ella dismounted and opened the barbed-wire gate wide to let us through. She climbed back in the saddle and led the way home.

Once we were in the yard, we walked the horses to the corral and unsaddled them. Grandmother sounded a little rattled. "Sunny and I'll make iced tea while you and Ella finish up outside."

I turned on the sprinkler. While the horses cooled off, Ella and I were in the barn filling their buckets with feed. By the time we finished tending the animals, I was ready to remove my boots and prop up my throbbing leg.

Once in the house and seated, Grandmother

brought me a glass of tea. She also smiled as she handed me a packet of crackers.

Ella was somber. "Tullah, did you hear him? He was saying that same thing he said to you when we were at the Pancake House. What do you suppose it means?"

Grandmother looked up worriedly. "What do you mean he was saying the same thing?"

Ella sounded a little rattled. "At the Pancake House, he looked at Tullah and said, 'My special…my special.' Lottie, the waitress, said Junior had caused a problem with a young girl, and he'd said the same thing to her."

I held my glass with one hand and massaged the calf of my leg with the other. "I have no idea what he means."

Grandmother tried to smile. "I'm telling Henry about this, and I'm serious when I say that I'm worried, Tullah. One thing is for sure, and two things are for certain—Junior Lampson is dangerous."

A listless moon had risen by the time Ella and I walked our company to the front porch. Ella hugged her mother and bid all of us goodnight. She walked around the corner of the house. I did likewise with my grandmother, promising I would lock the doors and keep my Glock handy. I stood watching the taillights of her little sports car disappear down the long drive.

I sighed and turned to walk up the steps. The barred owl sat on the porch rail, its tarnished gold eyes shimmering in the dark. For a moment, my heart hung in my throat. I didn't move. The bird studied me, and then lifted its body, ruffled its black-and-gray feathers, spread its wings, and flew away.

I stared into the dark, the moon casting shadows across the yard. Too many thoughts crowded my mind as I entered the house and locked the door. River and Rascal lay sleeping next to my recliner. I walked to the kitchen and closed down the doggie door. I didn't like the way my fingers trembled as I secured the deadbolt on the kitchen door.

Chapter Twenty-Five

Sunday afternoon was a contrast from the day before. Thunder rumbled in the background. It was dreary and overcast with the promise of rain, and humidity caused my shirt to cling like a second skin. After mucking out the stalls and feeding the horses, I showered and dressed. Charlie had invited us to sample a new sauce recipe he planned to enter in the annual BBQ cook-off contest.

Sprinkles of rain dotted my head as I stepped from my truck and ambled toward the Whitehorse Saloon. I looked at my watch—a few minutes past one. The 'Closed' sign greeted me. I lifted my fist, and Charlie opened the door before I could give my knock, knock, knockity-knock rap.

A gust of wind kicked up dirt and swirled it across the parking lot as Charlie studied the gray-blue sky. "Mother Nature teases us. It will not rain tonight." Giving me his usual bear hug, he walked me to the table where Dad, Patty, and Grandmother sat. As usual, it took my eyes a minute to adjust to the dim room. Flora usually doesn't join us on Sunday unless Charlie needs her for a big party. Today she was here to help us sample the new sauce and give our honest opinions.

Flora hasn't had an easy life. Grandmother and I feel a certain kinship to her. Like us, she knows what it's like to lose a loved one under tragic circumstances and the disappointment of never having the murder solved or the murderer found and brought to justice.

"What'll it be, Tullah, the usual or otherwise?" Flora knows me too well.

"The usual, cola with lemon."

"You got it, hon."

She returned with my drink and refills for the others. Charlie followed with a large round tray of food balanced in the palm of his beefy hand. He set plates in front of us along with bowls of red sauce. "Shrooms, and pulled pork sandwiches with my new secret sauce. Honest opinions, okay?"

Patty dipped a spoon in the bowl of sauce and brought it to her mouth. I watched Charlie. He stood like a statue. Only the faintest tic under his right eye revealed any expression. Patty took her time. She dipped her spoon again. I knew she was teasing him. Finally she said, "Joyce is so going to hate you, *again*, Charlie." She grinned and gave him two thumbs up.

We enjoyed the tasty new sauce on our sandwiches and talked about everything until we were nearly finished eating. That was when Grandmother related yesterday's incident. Her face was filled with concern. "And there he was. Junior standing naked except for dirty undershorts, and yelling, 'My special.' He was definitely leering at Tullah." She gave a little shiver.

All eyes turned to me a second longer than I felt comfortable with. I set my drink on the small square napkin and put my hand over hers. "I'm not a bit worried, Grandmother. I'm keeping the doors locked, plus I've got River and Rascal to protect me."

Dad took a sip of his beer, his expression sobering. "If I had grounds to bring Junior in, I would.

Unfortunately, leering and spouting nonsensical words isn't cause for an arrest. Until he actually makes an attempt to hurt Tullah—then I'll nail his ass."

"Not unless I get to him first," growled Charlie.

The conversation filtered around the table, with Patty recalling an incident in the bakery. "Edna's brought Junior to the café a few times to buy donuts. He gives me the creeps."

I gave an exasperated sigh and rubbed my forehead.

Charlie looked at me as if he had some mystical power to read my mind. "What is it you're not telling us, little sister?"

"It's the owl."

"The barred owl from the swamp?"

"I'm certain it's the same one."

"What about it?"

"It keeps showing up." I told how I'd walked Grandmother and Sunny to the car, and then when I turned, the owl was perched on the porch rail. "The strange thing is that always just before or just after it appears, I hear the same whispers coming from the swamp. I know it's not my imagination."

Charlie took his time speaking. "You are Cherokee on your mother's side and Irish on your father's side. Your ancestry is strongly attuned to the spirit world. It is not your imagination, little sister. Pay attention. The owl is warning you of danger."

"What about the whispers?"

Charlie's eyes remind me of ebony marbles. No one spoke. The only sound was the shuffling of shoes under the table. I somehow knew he was visiting another dimension. "Little sister," he said, his voice laced with unease, "It is not the wind that speaks to you, but a voice from the grave. She is one of us. Her spirit will not rest until her killer is punished."

Patty laughed nervously. Flora placed her hand over Patty's. Grandmother moved closer to me, and Dad drew a deep breath.

Calm settled over me. It was good to know that I was not borderline insane. "She is Savannah Deer. Her name struck a chord with me when I was looking through the photos of the murdered women, so I sent Vaneeta a text asking her to verify the woman's ethnicity. Vaneeta stated that she and her assistant had performed morphology on the skulls of each victim, and Savannah's is Native American. However, DNA alone cannot verify which tribal nation."

Charlie says, "Ah, that is too bad. Deer is a common name in many of the Native clans. Do you have a picture of her in your phone?"

I removed my cellphone from my pocket and opened the photo gallery. I held the picture for everyone to see. Charlie took the phone and then passed it to Grandmother for a closer look. "What?" I said.

Grandmother asked, "Do you know where Savannah Deer lived?"

"Only that she was from North Carolina."

Grandmother and Charlie remained quiet. I waited. "Well, don't keep us in suspense."

Grandmother's eyes glittered with tears. "*Ahawi* is Cherokee for Deer. I believe Savannah is one of the Cherokee people."

My throat closed up, and it was a moment before I could speak. "Then we should honor her, and the others, too."

Grandmother lifted her glass of wine. "To Savannah Deer and to the spirits of the women of Dolphy Preserve—may you soon be vindicated so your spirits will know freedom and happiness."

All glasses at the table were lifted in tribute to the memories of the women who were no longer forgotten.

Charlie excused himself from the table and headed toward the kitchen. Flora followed. They returned with coffee, mugs, and a large pink box filled with chocolate eclairs. Of course, we all knew who was responsible, because the box was from Sweet's 'n' Eats.

Eventually the conversation died as we enjoyed our dessert. Grandmother polished off her éclair and licked a glob of chocolate from her fingers. "Perhaps I should move back to the ranch for a little while."

"What on earth for, Grandmother?"

"Listen to Tanti, Tullah. All this talk of owls, and whispers on the wind—and that creep Junior is just plain spooky." Patty dabbed her lips with the corner of a napkin.

I looked across the table at Dad, his expression worn and tense. "Patty, as much as I agree with you and Tanti, I know my daughter. Along with her Cherokee and Irish bloodlines, from somewhere she inherited a large dose of stubbornness from the mule clan." The tone of his voice let us know he didn't mean it as a joke.

Charlie came to my rescue with one of his prophetic sayings. "If you capture a she-wolf pup and smother it with love, it is still a wild thing and will always yearn for its freedom."

Grandmother's cheeks flared pink. She stood. "Charlie Whitehorse, you are a wise man. Are you sure you weren't a shaman in another life?"

He shrugged his broad shoulders, then looked at me and winked. Grandmother's standing seemed to signal that the party was over. Patty gathered her purse. "Charlie, I'm glad I'm not one of the BBQ cook-off judges this year. If I were, I'd have to excuse myself because my taste buds will definitely remember your sauce."

Grandmother wrapped her arms around me. She whispered, "Even a she-wolf pup needs protecting. Don't fault Henry and me for loving you too much."

"Never—Grandmother—never."

Dad and Charlie walked us out into the late afternoon. In the distance, a streak of lightning rent the sky, followed by rumbling thunder. Dark clouds bunched and bumped together, temporarily shuttering the sun. Charlie said, "Mother Nature is a fickle woman. She changed her mind. It will storm tonight and for days after."

"Good. I hope it does storm. Ella and I need a slack day. Maybe all of tomorrow's clients will call and reschedule." I hugged Charlie goodbye. He left Dad and me standing in the parking lot. Dad opened the door to my truck. Before I climbed in, he kissed the top of my head.

"Dad, did you ever stop to think that because of your job I worry about you just as much as you and Grandmother worry about me? And because of her age, I worry about her. I guess we're all haunted by my mother's…" I couldn't finish.

He held my gaze before looking past me. "Her death has marked us, and we haven't yet fully dealt with it."

I turned the key in the ignition and rolled down the window. "We will, someday. Until then, I guess we have to deal with the way her death reverberates in our lives."

He slapped the side of the truck and turned to walk toward his 4Runner.

Chapter Twenty-Six

It was getting dark. On the drive home, I tried to hold bland and harmless thoughts about the round-table conversation at Charlie's. Ahead of me the evening skyline was laid out like dirty dishwater on a matte board—faded denim, gray, and black bleeding together in horizontal strips. Charcoal clouds plump with rain pushed against each other. The temperature outside had changed. I reached over and lowered the air conditioner setting and turned up the radio. The weatherman was reporting that due to a hurricane moving northeasterly from Texas, a tropical storm was sweeping toward us, and to expect high winds, clusters of torrential rain, and possible tornadoes over the next four days.

My mind clicked through an inventory to-do list for a potential tornado: take bottled water and ready-to-eat canned goods to the basement, place on the horses the halters that have my name and phone number, and if necessary, turn the horses loose. I knew Dad would make sure Grandmother and Patty got to the safety cellar in town.

By the time I drove under the carport, the air was rapidly cooling, and a damp breeze ruffled my hair. River and Rascal sat on the back steps, waiting. Ella's truck was parked in front of the trailer, and the lights were on. A misty rain fell. I decided to call her instead of walking to the trailer.

My cellphone was ringing by the time I let myself in the house. The pets followed me. "Hey Dad, I'm home. Just walking in the door."

"Good. I'm not checking on you. I thought you might like to know that I've spoken with Malachi about Junior. Interesting conversation."

"Yeah, how so?"

"He's been arrested sixteen times, with fourteen dismissals due to his mental condition and intellectual level. He's been placed in mandatory counseling and behavioral modification classes twice, but nothing seems to have affected the nature of his behavior, which appears nearly pathological in its thrust. His juvenile record has been expunged. Malachi even said that he once re-arrested Junior for urinating on the cot and on the jail cell walls, and that he took a fork and scratched dirty words on the cell wall—for which, of course, his mother footed the cost of the washing, cleaning, and repainting. Malachi said he tried to convince her to let Junior work off the debt, and she flatly refused."

"Hmm, Junior Lampson is a real champ, and I don't mean that in the nicest meaning of the term. In a way, I'm sorry for Edna, and then I'm not. Does that make me a bad person, Dad?"

"It makes you human. The way I see it, Edna is responsible for the decisions she's made concerning Junior. Apparently, she's satisfied with accepting the consequences of those decisions. I don't think we'll ever truly know why she doesn't want to institutionalize him."

"To change the subject, what have you heard about Lonnie Vickers as far as connecting him to the murders?"

"The dates he spent in jail and the dates of the women's disappearances don't line up. For now, he has a clear alibi."

"Where does that leave us? It has to be a person or persons who live either in Enigma or Dixie County and is familiar with the swamp."

"I'm following up on two solid leads. A semi-truck driver and a construction worker."

I knew the conversation was over and there was no need for me to probe for more information. "Dad, have you listened to the weather report?"

"I have. Don't worry about Tanti. I'll take care of her, and Patty, Joyce, and Dr. Ritter. What about you and Ella?"

"I'll make sure she's in the basement with me."

By now, I could hear the rain tapping against the roof. I ended my call with Dad, and while I waited for Ella to answer her phone, I filled a mug of water and put it in the microwave to heat.

"Hey, Tullah, have you heard the weather report?"

"That's why I'm calling. I have a basement. Once the sirens go off, don't wait."

"Okay. What do we do about tomorrow's appointments?"

"It depends on how bad it's raining. Most clients will call and cancel or reschedule. I'll keep you posted."

"What do we do about the horses?"

I explained to her about the halters with my name and phone number engraved on an attached nameplate in case my horses got out of the pasture. I let Ella know she could get one made at almost any pet supply store, but meanwhile there was an extra one in the barn for her horse.

"Ella, about the encounter with Junior and his mother, did you hear a noise, like banging or kicking against the walls of that rickety old metal shed?"

There was a moment of silence. "Honestly, I was too shocked by his appearance and scared he'd turn the dogs loose, so I didn't really notice. It was probably that clunky old air conditioner straining to keep working."

"Yeah, you're probably right. I'll touch base with you in the morning about opening the office."

The microwave dinged. I stuck a bag of Darjeeling tea into the mug of hot water, stretched out in my recliner with a mystery novel, and that's how I spent the rest of the evening until bedtime.

The rain had escalated, waking me twice during the night as it lashed against the bedroom windows. It sounded like someone throwing buckets of water against the house. At intervals, thunder rumbled in the distance and my windows flickered with blue light, instantly leaving the room dark again. I burrowed deeper under the blankets and delighted in the idea of sleeping late.

I woke at eight o'clock, showered, dressed, and went downstairs to unlock and lift the doggie door. Both dog and donkey were hesitant to venture out into the rain. I brewed my coffee, scrambled two eggs, and fixed toast and jelly. Ella called while I was washing my plate.

I stood at the sink and looked out the window. The barn and office were barely visible. "I doubt if we'll get any patients today. Enjoy your day off."

"Gotcha," she said and hung up.

Around noon the rain slacked enough for me to slip into my slicker and rubber boots. The sky was thick with clouds, and small branches littered the yard. Puddles were everywhere. I made a dash for the office, my head down against the wind. To keep from tracking mud on the office floor, I entered through the barn door. "Hey, you guys, warm and comfy? No one upset over the thunder?" The horses stuck their heads over the stall doors and greeted me. I walked down the aisle and slid back the double doors that led to the corral, and then I opened each stall to allow the horses to choose their own time to leave their warm, dry quarters.

I removed my rubber boots and padded around the office in my socks. I answered a few calls to reschedule appointments. I touched base with my answering service to let them know to forward all calls to my cellphone. I rocked back in the office chair with my hands cupped behind my head and wondered about Cindi Redfern. We had lost touch with each other, although I'd heard that she was considering buying Dr. Cooper's business and settling down in Dixie County. That would be good, I thought. She and I always worked well together.

I used the entire day to inventory the pharmacy, balance the checkbook, pay a few bills, and even vacuumed and dusted. As much as I've always desired days with nothing to do, I was feeling antsy.

It was now after five, and my stomach craved more than a pack of cheese crackers and a cola from the office refrigerator. I locked the door between the office and the barn, pulled on my rubber boots, and filled the horses' buckets with oats. After slipping on my raincoat, I braved the rain, leaping over puddles like a child playing hopscotch.

The light was fading fast, and the chill in the air was more pronounced. Rain made pocking sounds on my slicker. The interior of my house was dark. I stood under the carport and draped my wet raincoat over the hood of my truck. Woofs and brays greeted me from behind the closed back door. I opened it and was assailed with furry happiness.

Four hours later, the outer bands of the hurricane had fully impacted Enigma. The cloud cover completely obstructed the moon. A pounding at the door caused me to jump. River woofed his *it's okay* bark. I flipped on the porch light, and Ella called out, "It's me."

I opened the door. Water poured from her raincoat to puddle on the steps. She clutched a black plastic garbage bag. Her face was pale in the light. "Can I spend the night with you?"

I opened the door wide. She handed me the garbage bag as she shucked out of her raincoat and laid it next to mine on the hood of the truck. "It sounds like a full symphony of bass drums pounding on the trailer."

I filled the kettle and turned on the burner. "What's in the bag?"

Ella offered a sheepish grin. "Pillow, pjs, change of clothes, and my toothbrush."

"In truth, I'm happy you're here." I showed her to the upstairs spare bedroom and the shared bathroom.

"I'm glad you have the security light next to the office. It's really dark outside."

Our dinner was hot chocolate, canned chili, and buttered saltine crackers. We changed into our sleep clothes and hung out downstairs for a while, making small talk. Ella said, "In Texas, Mom and I weathered a few scary hurricanes. I never dreamed a storm could travel this far from the coast."

I assured her it was rare. "We get some rough winters. I hope you like snow." I suggested she take her truck to the tire shop and purchase a pair of snow chains. I also let her know about the potential of a tornado following this storm. "I have the weather alert on my phone. If the siren is sounded, we need to get to the basement as quickly as possible."

Her smile dimmed a few watts. "I'm calling it a night. Thanks for letting me stay over."

"Sure."

Still restless, I wandered to the living room to peer out the front window. Rain buffeted the front porch, and the swing swayed back and forth in the wind. I opened the door and walked out. There was no moon and no stars. Rain reached out and touched me with icy fingers. Thunder rumbled like colliding cymbals. I felt the vibrations under my bare feet. A surge of dread raced through my veins, sending trembles down my legs. The wind whispered, *He's coming.*

I returned to the living room, bolting the door. River and Rascal stayed with me. After a long moment, I climbed the stairs to my bedroom. It doesn't matter how many times I point to their oversized pet bed, my dog and donkey wait until they think I'm asleep and then quietly find their spots next to me. I smile and roll to my side.

It feels like I'm awake even though I know I'm asleep. I see myself bounding out the door, pigtails flying. Dad stands holding the reins of a pinto pony. I'm six today. Somewhere in the background I hear a loud boom. My subconscious tells me it's thunder. And then there is music. I'm standing on Daddy's boots. He's waltzing me around the room as my mother plays the piano. A cake with twelve candles sits on the dining table. Mama looks at us, smiling. Her smile turns to tears that resemble threads of blood. I can hear the rise and fall of her shrill voice calling for help. No, not Mama's voice…

The bed shifted. River lifted his big head. A growl hung in his throat. I forced my eyes open and rubbed my hand against the bristled hair along his back. I resisted the urge to turn on the lamp. I listened. No sound except the wind blowing swirls of rain against the house. I waited until my eyes were completely adjusted to the dark. I ran my hand under my pillow, gripped the butt of my Glock, and released the safety. I opened the bedroom door and listened. I was certain I heard a woman's voice. I looked at the bedroom where Ella was sleeping. No sound came through the closed door. I eased down the stairs, the animals behind me. At the bottom, I walked to the kitchen and did a quick scan. Nothing appeared out of place.

"Tullah?"

I mentally jumped. "Shazam, Ella! You scared me."

She loudly whispered, "Sorry. What's going on? I thought I heard a voice."

I gazed into her eyes, afraid and distressed, yet clear and concerned. "Good. At least I know I'm not losing my mind."

River trotted to the back door, a low growl rumbling in his chest. I shushed him. "Ella, my phone is upstairs beside the bed. Run up there and get it. As bad as the weather is, if we have an intruder I'll need to call Dad."

"Intruder—oh, I'm really scared. Is that why you're holding a gun?"

"Yes. Go!"

She disappeared in the dark, her bare feet barely making a sound as she raced up the stairs. In seconds she returned. Her voice huffing from the fast sprint, she said, "Shouldn't we call your dad now?"

I took the phone and tapped the screen to wake it up. Dad's image smiled from beneath his cowboy hat. I returned the phone to her and pointed. "This button is the emergency button. It goes straight to Dad. He'll answer almost immediately. If I have to use my weapon, make sure you press that button and tell him to get here asap!"

She nodded. I went to the door where the deadbolt was firmly in place. We stood in the dark. The only sound was our breathing. Lightning flashed, filling the kitchen with an almost blinding light.

A scream. A woman's scream.

River reared against the door. Warning barks erupted from his throat. I raced to the kitchen window and looked out. I saw her, naked, long hair hanging in her face as she struggled to climb over the metal gate. "Oh, my God! Ella, call Dad! Now!"

I unbolted the door, commanding River and Rascal to stay as I rushed out. Rain beating against my nightshirt chilled me. The screen door slammed, and I heard the bark—River chased after me.

The woman lost her balance and fell. Muddy water splashed up from the ground to cover her. I shouted, "I'm here. Over here. Run!"

She stumbled, righted herself, and looked around as if she'd lost her direction. She sobbed as she ran. She was close…getting closer.

I swallowed to keep the panic from rising in me. She hit me with a force that knocked me off my feet. The Glock flew out of my hand. I could see nothing in the dark.

Lightning splintered the sky. A human-shaped object catapulted over the fence. River lunged. Rascal waded in with high-pitched brays.

Clinging to me with both hands, she was pleading, "Please save me!" She was crying, her body shaking so badly she could barely speak.

My bare feet slipped in the mud, but I managed to regain my balance. Ella ran into the rain. Between the two of us, we succeeded in getting the woman to the house and up the steps. Behind us were screams of fury. River yelped, and I heard a thud. A myriad of emotions raced through me—rage that someone or something had hurt my dog and fear that we were all about to die. I needed a plan and challenged my brain to unfreeze. I grabbed the metal baseball bat. For one exuberant moment, I thought we were safe. Then the monster, naked as the day he was born, rammed against the wooden door, splintering it as it crashed to the floor.

Junior Lampson's head and face were wild with tangles of wet, black hair. The look in his eyes was wild and fierce. Those dark eyes bored into mine with a look that chilled me. My heart thumped, and I found it difficult to breathe. He stared at me as if going through some sort of mental debate. "My special." His erection was engorged like that of a stud horse. He laughed and again said, "My special."

The words and his manic leer filled me with unreasoned fear. I realized I was holding my breath. If I didn't breathe I would pass out. I concentrated—inhale…slowly…exhale… I thought I heard a faint, distant siren. No. It must be my imagination.

Junior stepped forward, his long hairy arms reaching, his fingers shaped like claws, and in some sick, furious glee, he howled as he lunged. I don't remember swinging the bat, putting as much force behind it as I could muster. He sagged, his strength withering. He moaned and gasped for air as he came up on one knee. He put a hand to his head. Blood oozed between his fingers. Sweat beaded on his upper lip. He reached out, grabbed my leg, and I swung again, this time connecting hard against his chin. I heard bone break. I'm sure his jaw shattered. He bellowed and leaped forward, glowering and slavering like the enraged beast he was. I skittered backward on my butt. Not fast enough. His hand went around my throat. Black dots floated in front of my eyes. I heard screaming and knew it wasn't me. *Ella and the woman… I have to save them… I have to…*

The night exploded and flashed. I was certain the storm had entered the house. I saw my mother. She smiled. *It's not your time.*

The gun roared again. I felt blood splatter against my face. Junior's body rolled off me. He reached, snarled his fingers in my hair, with a grin, and said, "My special." He lay still, his breathing tortured and shallow. Then it stopped.

Dad squatted next to me. I managed to gasp, "River?"

"Just had the wind knocked out him. He's okay."

Relief mingled with the pain and fear and came out in rattling sobs.

Dad lifted me into his arms and hugged me to his chest. "It's okay, Punkin. It's over. I'm here."

Chapter Twenty-Seven

Sheriff Malachi Dotson had contacted my dad with an all-alert emergency that a Mr. Bruce Young had reported his wife missing. As a home health care nurse, Wanda Young was scheduled to do a home visit on a new patient. When she didn't show, the patient notified the medical office in Somerset, who in turn called Mrs. Young's home to see if she was there. Bruce Young said that when his wife didn't respond to his phone calls, he was naturally concerned and immediately telephoned the sheriff's office.

Dad said something resonated with him that caused him to look at the map pinpointing the locales of the missing women. The town of Somerset is thirty-five minutes from Paducah, the home of Megan Hobart, JD #11. Somerset is less than twenty minutes from Dixie County. Putting two and two together and adding our recent encounter with Edna and Junior to the mix, Dad detailed his suspicions to Malachi, who instantly dispatched himself and a deputy to Edna's house.

Malachi reported that Edna was a blubbering mess and that she confessed to having been the kidnapper. Because she worked as a pharmacy tech, she found it quite easy to slip one ketamine tablet into her pocket whenever she needed. Because it was only once every couple of years, she said the pharmacist never noticed.

When asked why she began kidnapping the

women, Edna casually explained that when Junior could no longer control his sexual outbursts, she knew she'd lose him sooner or later to a bullet or an institution. Prior to his eighteenth birthday, she devised her plan and mapped out her route, then drove to Indianapolis and slipped a ketamine into a young exotic dancer's beer. "I was younger then," she said, "and it was easier to help the women to the car. I told Junior I had brought him a special present. I even fixed up that old metal shed so he'd have a place to play with the girls." She went on to say that she had no idea he'd end up killing them. That's when she led him to the swamp and they buried the first victim, Roxie Gilbert.

"After Roxie, it became easier," she admitted.

When asked if her conscience ever bothered her or if she ever felt guilty, she only shrugged and said, "Meh."

Edna even showed Malachi the journal she'd kept of all the women's names, their ages, occupations, and locations.

At Wanda Young's request, I was present during her interview with my dad and Malachi. She explained that her GPS sent her down a deeply rutted dirt road. "My gut sensed I had made a wrong turn. When I backed up to turn around to return to the way I'd come, the car slid into a ditch. It was raining so hard I could barely see, even with the headlights on. I tried telephoning my husband, but there was no signal."

She continued her story, saying that she walked to the only house with lights shining. Because of the two dogs, she was afraid to enter the yard. "I yelled and yelled until the door opened and an old woman walked to the porch. She called her son to get the dogs. She invited me into the house to use the telephone and to have a cup of hot tea. I was wet and cold and happy for the offer of a warm beverage."

She explained she drank about half of the tea before she noticed the unusual bitter aftertaste. "I'm not sure why I became suspicious. I thought maybe my imagination was working overtime. Either way, I didn't finish the tea."

She broke into tears and hugged herself. We waited until she controlled her emotions. "Sorry," she said. She drew a deep breath and continued. "Everything after the tea is a little fuzzy. I don't remember being carried outside, although I do remember feeling the rain on my face." She shuddered. "It was almost like an out-of-body experience. He grabbed my uniform top and ripped it. I-I think his mother yelled at him to mind his manners and to be a good boy."

She stopped talking. Her body trembled. "May I have a drink of water?"

Malachi said, "Would you rather have a cup of coffee?"

Her voice was soft. "That would be nice. Thank you."

Malachi lifted his hand. The door opened, and a young female deputy walked in with white cups and a metal carafe. She poured a cup for each of us. We waited for Wanda to continue. She toyed with the cup, staring into the rich, dark coffee. I wondered what she saw.

She said, "I asked what she'd given me, and she said, 'ketamine.' I knew I had consumed enough to make me loopy but not enough to put me completely out. I willed the fog from my brain, trying to think of a way to escape."

Wanda lifted the cup and sipped. "She pushed me down on a cot. I remember the walls of that shed were littered with pictures. You know, pictures of people doing—erotic things." She nearly choked on the next sip of coffee. It took a moment for her to get over the coughing spell.

"After they finished undressing me, the old woman left." Wanda's voice hitched. "Before she left, she said to her son, 'Don't kill this one.' While he undressed, I grabbed the end of the metal cot and shoved it against him. I guess my attack took him by surprise, at least long enough for me to push against the door. It practically fell off its hinges. A streak of lightning flashed, and I saw the gate. It had a chain looped and padlocked around it, so I climbed over, and I ran. I didn't care where I ran as long as it was away from that…that hideous monster."

Malachi's voice was gentle. "How did you manage to find Dr. Holliday's house?"

"I hope this doesn't sound trite, but when I was a child I was a Girl Scout, and then I attended summer camps where I earned my wilderness badge. When I spotted the barbed wire fence, I knew it had to lead someplace. I followed the fence, running as fast as I could. I heard him behind me." She covered her face with her hands. "Oh, God, I was so scared."

Mr. Young rubbed her back as if telling her not to be afraid. She shuddered a sigh and nodded. "I grabbed a strand of wire, not even feeling the barbs puncturing my palms, and I held it high enough to climb through."

"So that's how you got the gouges on your back?" Malachi asked.

"Yes."

"And then what?"

"He was screaming, 'My special...my special.' It seemed like I'd run forever. Sometimes I'd trip and fall. Once, when I fell, I was ready to give up—" She was quiet for longer than a minute.

We waited. I listened to the large round clock ticking away the seconds. She looked at me, the look on her face pleading. Pleading for what? I thought.

Her husband said, "Wanda?"

She nodded. "I know this is going to sound crazy, but I heard a voice...a woman's voice, telling me not to give up."

I offered a reassuring smile. She continued, "There was a frightening crash of thunder. I felt the ground under my feet vibrate. So many bolts of lightning streaked the sky. That's when I saw a light. It was raining so hard I thought maybe it was just the aftereffects of the lightning. I wiped my eyes, and I really did see it. It was like a hazy beacon. I started running toward it, praying the whole time that there was a house with people in it who would help me. That's when I came to the metal gate."

Her entire body trembled. She reached across the interview table and grabbed both my hands. "Oh, thank God, it was your house."

I shared her tears.

****

The day of the trial, I sat on the plaintiff's side of the courtroom. Judge Michael Duval presided. Thomas Amboy was the public defender representing Edna Lampson.

Edna looked small and shriveled sitting in the

witness chair. Her face was pale from too much powder and no lipstick. Her gray hair, snagged over her ears, was held by silver barrettes. She wore a black dress. I couldn't guess how old she might be. The court records placed her birth year as nineteen forty-eight. That would put her about age seventy-one, the same age as my grandmother. I shook my head. There was a significant contrast between the two women—one virtuous, the other filled with wickedness.

Edna looked at me, her smile fleeting and bitter. Her last words before she was handcuffed and led from the courtroom were, "Junior couldn't help that he was born with the devil in him. He was a shithead, but he was all I had."

Epilogue

Charlie never opens the saloon on Sunday. No exceptions. However, he'd explained to Flora that he'd pay her extra to work a small event for a special friend. We gathered along the scarred oakwood bar. Dad sat in the middle with Tiny, Joyce, and Charlie to his left and me seated next to him on the right, followed by Grandmother and Patty. In this sense, the seven of us were the small party, and without her suspecting it, Flora was the special guest.

I almost felt giddy when the back door slammed, indicating she had arrived. I think everyone seated at the bar felt the same excitement. We all looked at each other, trying to maintain a serious demeanor.

Flora walked into the bar, her hands behind her back tying a crisp, white apron around her waist. She wore her usual uniform—black slacks and a white golf-style shirt with Whitehorse Saloon embroidered in red letters above the pocket. Her salt-and-pepper hair was pulled back in a neat ponytail at the nape of her neck.

She stopped, looked up and down the bar, and then around at the empty room. It was difficult to read her emotions. Surprise? Irritation?

She glanced at her watch and then back at us. "Am I early?"

No one said a word.

She said, "Okay, what's going on? You're creeping

me out."

Charlie cleared his throat. "The party is for you. You are the guest of honor."

Her eyes widened and her hand flew to her mouth. "I don't understand. Why is the party for me?"

"Because you're retiring next week, and we wanted to let you know how much you've meant to us, and still mean to us."

We all pushed off the bar stools and stood aside. Charlie spread his arm toward a table decorated with a festive red tablecloth, gifts, and a cake as the centerpiece. He pulled out a chair and motioned for her to sit.

I've seen Flora when she's dealing with mouthy, disrespectful customers—a force to be reckoned with. I've never seen her on the verge of tears, except once, and that was when she'd mentioned her sister.

We gathered around the table. Charlie said, "The cake is from Patty." He grinned as he reached down and snagged a purple sugar rose and plopped it in his mouth.

Patty had shaped the cake in the form of an open book. On the pages, she had piped in purple icing, "Happy Retirement! Happy Reading! We love you!"

Flora gushed over the cake.

Tanti declared she was next and hefted a purple tote bag to the table. "You've been a faithful member of the Bookworm Biddies for years. We know how much you love to read." She patted the bag. "It's filled to the brim with all your favorite genres. Enough books to keep you from getting bored for a little while, at least."

Flora reached into the bag and lifted out a copy of *Lady Adel's Captain* and one of *Bitter Autumn.* She said, "You know me too well, Tanti. Thank you."

Joyce held out a large white box. "I made this for you. It's to keep you warm on those cold winter nights when you're reading."

Flora opened the box and lifted out a crocheted afghan in variegated shades of purple. "Oh, Joyce, it's perfect."

Charlie handed Flora a long envelope. She opened it, removed a check, and gave him a quizzical look. "I honestly don't know what to say, Charlie, except, why?"

He wrapped the elderly woman in a bear hug. I feared he might break her bones. He said, "I inherited you. You came with the bar. You've worked long hours, never called in sick, often worked on your days off without complaining, handled ruckuses, but most of all you taught me about the bar and restaurant business. The Whitehorse is what it is today because of you."

None of us knew the amount of the check. Knowing Charlie's generosity for the people he cares about, I surmised it was a substantial sum. This time a tear meandered down a wrinkled crevice in Flora's cheek. She barely managed to squeak out, "Thank you."

Tiny scooted his chair back and walked to a dark corner. He returned pushing a bright purple adult tricycle equipped with a large rear basket. "We all know you don't drive, and that old bicycle of yours has seen its better days. I hope this one will serve you for a long time."

Flora actually squealed. "Tiny! Oh, my, it's…oh, my…you big galoot! Don't make me cry…"

We all laughed.

It was my turn, and I wanted to make it quick

because Dad's gift was the ultimate icing on the cake. I offered a humble smile and hoped my gift would help ease the pain Dad's gift would bring. "Flora, I know how sad you were when your little Muffin crossed the rainbow bridge." I held up my hand and said, "Don't move."

I raced to the room that Charlie reserved for small private parties and opened the door. I returned leading a golden Labrador retriever and handed the leash to Flora. "This is Bella. Her owner recently passed away, and her last wish was for Bella to have a loving home. She's ten years old, spayed, completely housebroken, and—" I didn't get to finish. Apparently it was love at first sight. Bella laid a paw in Flora's lap. Flora bent over and kissed the large golden head. Her shoulders shook with silent tears. When she looked at me, her eyes spoke the words that wouldn't come out of her mouth.

Now I was really skeptical about the last gift. I looked at Dad. He apparently read my mind and shrugged. We had already anticipated that what was in the large brown folder in front of him would be emotionally painful.

Dad nodded at Charlie. Charlie eased out of his chair and walked to the bar. He returned with a pot of coffee and mugs for all of us. Except in front of Flora he set a glass filled with rum and cola. Charlie returned Dad's nod.

Dad cleared his throat. "Flora, a while back you mentioned your sister to Tullah. She was so touched by it that she asked if there was anything I could do."

Flora's eyes widened. She gasped and wrapped a skinny arm around Bella's neck.

Dad continued as he pushed the envelope forward. "Tiny, Joyce, Tullah, and I have spent many hours trying to solve the mystery of Carlene's disappearance. We can only guess how painful this is after sixty years. It's only because of our love and admiration for you that we hope what's in the envelope will give you a little peace of mind. We know this is personal and private. You don't need to look at it now."

Flora glanced up at Charlie and said, "Rum and cola?"

He nodded.

She placed the straw between her lips and drew a long sip. She lifted a napkin and wiped the moisture from her hands. She stared at the envelope. No one at the table spoke. This was Flora's moment. We waited.

She reached forward, then drew back her hand as if she'd changed her mind. She lifted her eyes to Dad's. "Henry, I'm not sure."

"No hurry. Only when you're ready."

She lifted the envelope and held it to her chest for a moment. "I've never been a coward in my entire life. I'm not about to start being one today." She pushed open the flap and drew out a manila file folder. Across the front was stamped in broad red letters "Case Solved. Closed." She opened the folder. Her eyes flitted back and forth as she read down the page.

Flora's shoulders shook. Tears flooded. "That bastard." She swiped the tears, drew another sip of the rum and cola, and spouted, "Pardon my French."

Whether it was the effects of the alcohol that calmed her or the knowing that after sixty years she could at last lay her sister's murder to rest, either way Flora quietly inserted the manila folder inside the envelope. She gazed around the table and said, "This is the best day of my life." Her voice faltered, and I saw that she still struggled with emotions. At last she said, "Well, what the hell are we waiting for? Let's cut the cake."

****

I had almost memorized the information that I'd read multiple times. Tiny and Joyce had taken unused vacation days to travel to Louisiana. With a little persuasion from the governor, the case was reopened, and they worked with the local law enforcement. I flew out and worked with the forensics team, which led us to Phillipe Boussard, now seventy-six years old and serving a life sentence without parole in the Louisiana State Penitentiary for another woman's murder. Boussard confessed to killing sixteen-year-old Carlene Landry. She had left school to walk to her part-time job sweeping up at the local hair salon in Bayou Lafourche. She had accepted a ride from Phillipe, the son of a local gas station owner. Boussard admitted to doping Carlene. He placed her in a boat and drove to a gator shack in the bayou, where he assaulted her, beat her unconscious, and assaulted her again. In his words, "I didn't mean to kill her. I guess I got a little crazy. I sorta passed out from all the, you know, the drugs I was doin'. When I come to and saw all the blood, I panicked. There's gators in that part of the bayou. Lots and lots of 'em. Well, I just stripped her clothes off'n 'er and rolled 'er in the water. It didn't take long, and well, there weren't nothin' much left. I skedaddled out'n there."

Deputy Tiny Goodbody then asked what Boussard had done with Carlene's clothes. Boussard answered in a voice void of any emotion. "What the hell. I ain't never gettin' outta here. They're in an old orange crate in my daddy's old gas station garage. That is if'n the place is still standin'."

With local law enforcement and a search warrant, the orange crate was discovered where Boussard had stated. Inside a brown grocery bag, crumbling from age, were the alleged articles of clothing belonging to Carlene Landry as Boussard had described them. DNA samples from blood residue on the skirt and blouse matched with Flora's blood type confirmed that the clothing did belong to Carlene. Further damning evidence was a fingerprint pulled from the top of a heart-shaped necklace that Carlene had worn on the evening of her abduction. The fingerprint was a perfect match to Boussard.

****

The pontoon boat trip to the location that Phillipe Boussard described was emotional. Dad, Tiny, Charlie, Joyce, and I sat with Flora. I held her hand. The captain sidled the boat next to a rotting post. He cut the motor. The gator shack and the dock were nothing more than weather-bleached skeletons of days past. The water beneath the boat was black and ominous. The air was still and the bayou completely quiet, almost as if it were holding its breath.

The boat captain warned, "Folks, it's not safe to leave the craft. This is a favorite spot for the gator hunters, and the swamp itself is dangerous. Those boards are so rotten they'll likely collapse if'n you step on 'em. We'll stay he'yah as long as you like, though."

Flora stood. She gripped a handrail to steady herself as she gazed out over the dark watery expanse.

She closed her eyes and breathed deep. "I know this place. Daddy used to bring us here to fish. He'd always warn Carlene and me to keep our hands in the boat because of the gators."

She turned and held out her hand to me. I gave her the silk sack filled with rose petals. We stood. Dad, Tiny, Charlie, and even the boat captain removed their hats. As Flora scattered the rose petals over the water, she said, "She's from down in the marshes, she's fishin' with her daddy and cookin' with her mama. A real Cajun girl. She's everythin' she seems."

Flora tossed out the last of the rose petals. We watched as pink and red and white corollas of color drifted with the current before sinking out of sight. She looked at me and nodded. I recited Revelations chapter twenty-one, verse four, the same scripture that I'd memorized for my mother. "He will wipe away every tear from their eyes and their death shall be no more, neither shall there be mourning, nor crying, nor pain anymore, for the former things have passed away."

Flora sat down. She drew a shuddering breath. She looked at the captain and said, "We can go now."

As the pontoon glided over the water, I noticed a flock of white herons perched high in a tree. The birds spread their massive wings and took flight as the boat passed. Angels, I thought, angels spreading their wings and flying home.

Today we had paid homage not only to Carlene, who died before her time, but to the eleven women who had waited for so many years to be returned to their families.

Dad put his arm around me and held me close. No words were needed.

Chilled Watermelon Soup

There is nothing more refreshing on a hot summer's day than a cup of chilled watermelon soup. You can serve this with a meal or as a delightful snack. Serves 3.

Ingredients:
    4 cups cubed & seeded watermelon
    2 tbsp fresh lemon juice
    1 tbsp chopped fresh mint
    1 tbsp honey

Directions:
    Blend watermelon, lemon juice, mint, and honey in a blender until smooth. Refrigerate 2 hours before serving.

Optional: although in *The Boneyard* Dr. Tullah Holliday and her friend Dr. Vaneeta Sanreet did not add alcohol to their soup, adding 1/4 cup of tequila and substituting the juice of two limes for the lemon juice will add a happy little zing to the dish.

Loretta C. Rogers
Presents:

Another Suspenseful Doc Holliday Mystery

Lights...Camera...Murder!

It's a monumental day for the small rural town of Enigma, Kentucky. Premier Entertainment Productions is holding auditions for locals to play extras in heartthrob hero Cody West's upcoming western. After the extras are selected, PEP plans to open the movie set for tourists and other visitors to be given guided tours to get a firsthand, behind-the-scenes look at how a movie is created, plus have the opportunity to meet with the movie stars, producers, directors, and staff responsible for making it happen.

Dr. Tullah Holliday's vet tech assistant, Ella Sanders, and Tullah's grandmother, Tanti Crow, hope they are some of the lucky ones chosen to play a cameo role in the movie. Tullah is the attending veterinarian. She must juggle the daily duties of running her veterinary animal clinic while also making sure no animals are injured during the making of the movie.

But the morning of the event, two strange things happen—the Enigma civic center catches fire, putting the town itself in danger of burning to the ground, and Hollywood superstar Cody West is discovered lying face down in the movie set's corral—dead. It is assumed from the hoof prints on Cody's body that the semi-wild palomino stallion recently purchased to stand in for the aging palomino gelding used for stunts is responsible for killing the actor. The Hermann brothers, owners of PEP, pressure Tullah to euthanize the stallion.

When strange accidents begin to happen on the movie set and a stunt man is shot to death, Tullah must connect the cases before the bodies pile up and she is forced to kidnap an innocent horse to keep from permanently putting it to sleep.

Don't miss any of the suspenseful installments in Loretta C. Rogers' bestselling series featuring Veterinarian Dr. Tullah Holliday, who uses her empathic abilities to solve crimes.

A word about the author…

A native Floridian and proud of her Scots-Irish heritage, Loretta C. Rogers is a bestselling author. Her books are in libraries throughout the USA and Europe. She lives in Florida with her husband and dog.

Thank You!
If you enjoyed *The Boneyard*, your review is highly appreciated.
www.lorettacrogersnovels.com

Thank you for purchasing
this publication of The Wild Rose Press, Inc.

For questions or more information
contact us at
info@thewildrosepress.com.

The Wild Rose Press, Inc.
www.thewildrosepress.com